More Extraordinary Praise for *Sister Noon*

"In *Sister Noon*, Karen Joy Fowler re-creates a lost world so thrillingly, with such intelligence, trickery, and art, that when you at last put the book down and look up from the page it all seems to linger, shimmering, around you, like the residue of a marvelous dream."

—Michael Chabon, Pulitzer Prize-winning author of *The Amazing Adventures of Kavalier and Clay*

"Fowler's prose is full of shimmering melancholy, and a ruminative irony that brings her characters and their world alive in the most unexpected ways—reading *Sister Noon* is like staring at early portrait photographs until the eyes begin to shine and your head is filled with voices that urge you to recall that these vanished lives, and your own, are stranger than you allow. A dazzling book."

—Jonathan Lethem, bestselling author of *Motherless Brooklyn*

"A playful, mysterious, highly imagined narrative set in San Francisco of the 1890s . . . Never ever boring."

—*The New York Times Book Review*

"A playful literary mystery." —*The Atlanta Journal-Constitution*

"The novel unfolds in mysterious and, at times, supernatural ways . . . A satisfying read." —*The Cleveland Plain Dealer*

"Fowler's lyrical prose and deft use of historical fact are a joy to read. She also exhibits a sly sense of humor . . . A strange and enchanting novel." —*The Oregonian*

"A secret-filled, sometimes deliciously macabre book."

—Salon.com

KAREN JOY FOWLER is the author of two novels, *Sarah Canary* and *The Sweetheart Season*, as well as the recent story collection *Black Glass*.

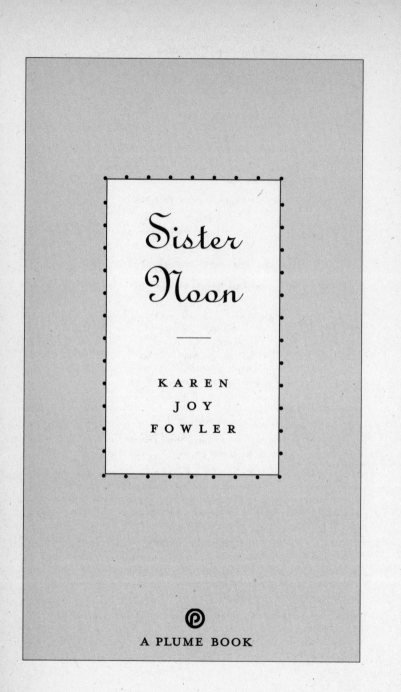

Sister Noon

KAREN
JOY
FOWLER

A PLUME BOOK

PLUME
Published by the Penguin Group
Penguin Putnam Inc., 375 Hudson Street,
New York, New York, 10014, U.S.A.
Penguin Books Ltd, 80 Strand, London WC2R 0RL, England
Penguin Books Australia Ltd, Ringwood, Victoria, Australia
Penguin Books Canada Ltd, 10 Alcorn Avenue,
Toronto, Ontario, Canada M4V 3B2
Penguin Books (N.Z.) Ltd, 182–190 Wairau Road, Auckland 10, New Zealand

Penguin Books Ltd, Registered Offices:
Harmondsworth, Middlesex, England

Published by Plume, a member of Penguin Putnam Inc.
Previously published in a Putnam edition.

First Plume Printing, June 2002

10 9 8 7 6 5 4

Ⓟ REGISTERED TRADEMARK—MARCA REGISTRADA

The Library of Congress has catalogued the Putnam edition as follows:

Fowler, Karen Joy.
Sister noon : a novel / Karen Joy Fowler.
p.   cm.
"A Marian Wood book"
ISBN 0-399-14750-0 (hc.)
ISBN 0-452-28328-0 (pbk.)
1. San Francisco (Calif.)—Fiction.
2. Women—Fiction.   I. Title.
PS3556.O844 S57   2001   00-046025
813'.54—dc21

Printed in the United States of America
Original hardcover design by Amanda Dewey

PUBLISHER'S NOTE

This is a work of fiction. Names, characters, places, and incidents either are the product of the author's imagination or are used fictitiously, and any resemblance to actual persons, living or dead, business establishments, events, or locales is entirely coincidental.

For Marian and Wendy,
East Coast angels

I had, as always, a lot of help. Thank you, Debbie and Darcy Smith, Clinton Lawrence, Alan Elms, Sara Streich, Carter Scholz, Angus MacDonald, Pat Murphy, Michael Blumlein, Laura Miller, Michael Berry, Richard Russo, Sean Stewart, Nancy Ogle, Jonathan Elkus, and Jeff Walker.

Most particular thanks to Kelly Link. I couldn't have finished without you, Kelly.

Thanks to Helen Holdridge for the Holdridge Collection at the San Francisco Public Library.

And to the MacDowell Colony for time and space.

Marian Wood and Wendy Weil.

Hugh, too.

Words were invented so that lies could be told.

MARY ELLEN PLEASANT

Sister
Noon

PRELUDE

In 1894, Mrs. Putnam took Lizzie Hayes to the Midwinter Exhibition in San Francisco's Golden Gate Park, where they both used a telephone for the very first time. They stood behind curtains at opposite ends of a great hall, with only their shoes showing from the outside. "Isn't this a wonder?" Mrs. Putnam asked. Her voice was high and tight, as if it had been stretched to reach. "And someday you'll be able to call the afterlife, just as easy. Now that we've taken this first step."

There was a droning in Lizzie's ear as if, indeed, a multitude of distant voices were also speaking to her. But that was merely the thought Mrs. Putnam had put in her mind. Lizzie might just as easily have heard the ocean or the ceaseless insectile buzz that underlies the material world.

It made little practical difference. The dead are terrible gossips. They don't remember, or they don't care to say, or, if they do talk, then they all talk at once. They can't be questioned. They won't change a word, no matter how preposterous. The truth might look like a story. A lie might outlast a fact. You must remember that, for everything that follows, we have only the word of someone long dead.

In 1852, while on his way from Valparaiso to San Francisco aboard the steamship *Oregon,* a clerk named Thomas Bell met a woman named Madame Christophe. Mr. Bell was an underling at Bolton, Barron, and Company, a firm specializing in cotton, mining, and double deals. Madame Christophe was the most beautiful woman he had ever seen, very tall, with clouds of dark hair and rosy, satiny skin. Her most remarkable feature was her eyes, for they didn't match. One was blue and one was brown, and yet the difference was subtle and likely to be noticed only on a close and careful inspection and only when she was looking right at you. She did this often.

One night they stood together at the rail. The stars were as thick and yellow as grapes. There was a silver road of moonlight on the black surface of the ocean. Thomas Bell was asking questions. Where had she come from? Madame Christophe told him she was a widow from New Orleans. Where was she going? Who was she? Whom did she know in San Francisco?

She turned her eyes on him, which made him catch his breath. "Why do you look at me like that?" he asked.

"Why do you ask so many questions?" Her voice was

full of slow vowels, soft stops. "Words were invented so that lies could be told. If you want to know someone, don't listen to what they say. Look at them. Look at me," she said. "Look closely." Her voice dropped to a whisper. "What does that tell you?"

Mr. Bell couldn't look closely. His vision was clouded by his ardor. But he saw her shiver. He rushed to his cabin for a wrap to lend her, a green and black tartan shawl.

They debarked in San Francisco. In the crush of people, she got into a carriage, and he lost sight of her.

She should have been easy to find. There were so few women in San Francisco. Fewer still were beautiful. He sent inquiries to all the hotels. None had a Madame Christophe registered. He asked everyone he knew, he spoke of her everywhere, but could say only that she was a widow from New Orleans, that her eyes didn't match, and that she had his shawl. He was forced to depart for Mexico, where he would conduct negotiations concerning the New Almadén mine, without seeing her again.

In the 1850s, most of the people who made up San Francisco's society had once been or still were distinctly disreputable. In 1855, when Belle Cora, a popular madame, inadvertently caused the murder of a United States marshal simply by assuming she could sit in that part of the theater occupied by respectably married women, it was not always so easy to explain why one person was top-hole and another was not.

But Mrs. Nora Radford's case was simple. Her husband had died owing everyone money. Her conversation, she overheard young Mrs. Putnam say, was interesting enough, only there was too much of it. This observation was as hurtful as it was inaccurate. She had always been considered rather witty. Mrs. Putnam and everybody else knew that she was more surprised than anyone by her husband's debts.

She refused to blame him for any of it. In fact, she was impressed. How clever he must have been to have fooled them all.

And she was touched. How hard he must have worked to give her such a sense of security. Much harder than if he'd actually had money. Forty years of marriage and he'd never once let it slip. She moved into rooms and missed her husband hourly.

Her new home was in the country, overlooking a graveyard. This was not as dismal as it might sound. She had a curtained bed and a carved dressing table. The cemetery was filled with flowers. On a warm day, the scent came in on the sunshine. The boardinghouse was called Geneva Cottage.

Her landlady was a tireless southern woman named Mrs. Ellen Smith. Mrs. Smith took in laundry and worked as housekeeper for Selim Woodworth, a wealthy San Francisco businessman. It was Mr. Woodworth who had suggested the arrangement to Mrs. Radford. Mr. Woodworth was a prominent philanthropist, a kind and thoughtful man whose marked attentions to her after her husband's death, in contrast to the disregard of others, vouched for his quality. "My Mrs. Smith," he said warmly. "She works hard and makes canny investments. I don't know why she continues on as my housekeeper. Perhaps her fortunes have been so vagarious, she can never be secure. But she is a wonderful woman, as devoted to helping the unfortunate as she is to making a living in the world. That's where her money goes." He tipped his hat, continued his way down the little muddy track that was Market Street. Mrs. Radford hoisted her heavy skirts, their hems weighted with bird shot as a precaution against the wind, and picked her way through the mud. She took his advice immediately.

Mrs. Radford's initial impression of her landlady was that she was about thirty years old. In fact, this fell somewhat short of the mark. But also that she was beautiful, which was accurate. The first time Mrs. Radford saw her, she was sitting in a sunlit pool on the faded brocade of the parlor sofa. In Mrs. Radford's mind she always retained that golden glow.

"You'll find me here when the sun is shining," Mrs. Smith told her. "I never will get used to the cold."

"It seems to get colder every year," Mrs. Radford agreed. The words came out too serious, too sad. There was an embarrassing element of self-pity she hadn't intended.

Mrs. Smith smiled. "I hope we can make you feel at home here." She looked straight at Mrs. Radford. Her eyes didn't match. There was a shawl of green and black plaid on the sofa.

Mrs. Radford thought of her friend Mr. Bell. She couldn't remember the name of his vanished shipmate, but she was sure it wasn't Ellen Smith. Something foreign, something Latin. Mrs. Smith's beauty was darkly Mediterranean.

She stood and was surprisingly tall, a whole head above Mrs. Radford. "Take a cup of tea with me."

The kitchen was an elegant place of astral lamps and oil chandeliers. There were golden cupids in the wallpaper, and a young Negro man who swept the floor and washed the dishes while they talked. Mrs. Smith filled her cup half with cream, heaped it with sugar. She stirred it and stirred it.

"I can't quite place your accent," Mrs. Radford said.

"Oh, it's a mix, all right. I've lived a great many places." Mrs. Smith stared into her clouded tea. She lifted the cup and blew on it.

"I lived on the hill," Mrs. Radford said, coaxing her into confidences by offering her own. "Until my husband died. I'm quite come down in the world."

"You'll rise again. I started with nothing."

Mrs. Radford had often been embarrassed at how much beauty meant to her. At the age when Mrs. Radford might have been beautiful herself, she suffered badly from acne. It pitted her skin, and her lovely hair was little compensation. At the time, she'd thought her life was over. But then she'd made such a happy marriage and it had hardly seemed to matter. God had granted her a great love. And yet she had never stopped wishing she were beautiful, had apparently learned nothing from her own life. She would have been the first to admit this. It would have hurt her to have had ugly children, and this was a painful thing to know about herself. As it turned out, she had no children at all. "You had beauty," she said.

Mrs. Smith raised her extraordinary eyes. "I suppose I did." The day was clouding. The sun went off and on again, like a blink. Mrs. Smith turned her head. "My mother was beautiful. It did her no particular good. I lost her early. She used to fret so over me—what would happen to me, who would take care of me. She told me to go out to the road and stand where I would be seen. That was the last thing she said to me."

It had been just a little back lane, without much traffic. The fence was falling into ruins; she stepped over it easily. She could see to the end of the road, shimmering in the distance like a dream. There was an apple tree over her head, blossoming into pink and filled with the sound of bees. She stood and waited all morning, crying from time to time about her mother, until she was sleepy from the sun and the buzzing and the crying, and no one came by.

Finally, in the early afternoon, when the sun had started to slant past her, she heard a horse in the distance. The sound grew louder. She raised her hand to shade her eyes. The horse was black. The man was as old as her grandfather, who was also her father, truth be told.

He almost went by her. He was half asleep on the slow-moving horse, but when she moved, a breath only, he stopped so suddenly that saliva dripped from the silver bit onto the road. He looked her over and removed his hat. "What's your name?" he asked. She said nothing. He reached out a hand. "Well, I'm not fussy," he told her. "How would you like to go to New Orleans?" And that was how she moved up in the world, by putting her foot in the stirrup.

"I was ten years old."

"Oh, my dear." Mrs. Radford was shocked and distressed.

Mrs. Smith put her hand on Mrs. Radford's arm. Mrs. Radford had rarely been touched by anyone since her husband died. Sometimes her skin ached for it, all over her body. Where did an old woman with no children go to be touched? Mrs. Smith's hand was warm. "It wasn't the way you're thinking. He turned out very kind," she said.

Mrs. Radford adjusted to country living as well as could be expected. The laundry was a busy place. The cemetery was not. She especially enjoyed her evenings. She would join Mrs. Smith. The parlor would be brightened by a lively fire. They would drink a soothing concoction Mrs. Smith called "balm tea." "Just a splash of rum," Mrs. Smith assured her, but it went straight to Mrs. Radford's head. In these convivial surroundings, she told Mrs. Smith how she had planned once to teach.

"I had a train ticket to Minneapolis. I had a job. I'd only known Alexander a week. But he came to the station and asked me to marry him. 'I want to see the world before I get married,' I told him. 'See it after,' he said. 'See it with me.'"

"And did you?"

His actual language had been much more passionate—things Mrs. Radford could hardly repeat, but would never forget. His voice remained with her more vividly than his face; over the years it had changed less. It pleased her to speak of him; she was grateful to Mrs. Smith for listening. "I saw my corner of it. It was a very happy corner."

In her turn, Mrs. Radford heard that Mrs. Smith's original benefactor, a Mr. Price, had taken her to a convent school in New Orleans. She spent a year there, learning to read and write. Then he sent her to Cincinnati. She lived with some friends of his named Williams. "I was to go to school for four more years and also to help Mrs. Williams with the children. She made quite a pet of me, at first.

"But then Mr. Price died. I know he'd already paid the Williamses for my schooling, but they pretended he hadn't. They sent me to Nantucket as a bonded servant."

The weathered wood and sand of Nantucket was a new landscape for her. Her mistress was the Quaker woman who owned the island's general store. She came from a line of whalers—very wealthy. She invited Ellen to the Friends meeting house, where they sat in the darkness on hard wooden benches and waited for the Spirit. "It didn't take with me, I'm afraid," said Mrs. Smith, fingering the locket she wore at her throat. "I'm too fond of nice things. But she was also very kind. I called her Grandma and worked for her until she died, quite suddenly, and then again there were no provisions made for me. By now I was sixteen or so. I sold off some of her stock and got to Boston. Her real granddaughter lived there and I thought she might take me in, but she didn't." It was there that Ellen met James Smith, a wealthy and prominent businessman. They were married. He died. "It's been my pattern," Mrs. Smith conceded. "Life is loss."

Mrs. Radford could see that Mrs. Smith had not loved her husband. It was nothing she said; it appeared on her face when she spoke of him.

Mrs. Radford had not decided what to do about Thomas Bell. He'd been back from Mexico for almost a year now. He was an old friend, so she owed him some loyalty, although he hadn't, in fact, been to see her since his return. Served him right, really; if he'd come to call, to express his condolences, he might have seen the woman. Virtue provided its rewards.

And what of her loyalty to her new friend? Mr. Bell was not the sort of man who married. There were rumors that he had been seen going into a house of assignation on Washington Street.

Before her husband's death, Mrs. Radford would only have had to write the invitations and San Francisco's most eligible men would have gathered. Sometimes she let herself imagine the dinner. Alexander pouring wine. The gold-rimmed china. The sensation of the beautiful Mrs. Smith.

But Mr. Bell had been so desperate. Mrs. Radford was a great believer in love. She longed to do her little bit to help it along. Marriage was the happy ending to Mrs. Smith's hard and blameless life. The right man had only to see her, and it still might be Thomas Bell, who already had.

The most enjoyable parts of a social occasion are often the solitary pleasures of anticipation and recollection. But it is sadly true that one cannot relish these without having had an invitation to the party itself.

The MacElroys, who were special friends of Thomas Bell's, had announced the engagement of their middle daughter. There was to be a fabulous ball. Although Mrs. Radford had, with her husband, been a guest at the party celebrating the engagement of their first daughter and also at the marriage of their youngest daughter, there was no certainty that she would be included now.

It was only a party. Only a fabulous ball. She did not

mind for herself, not so much, really, although she had always enjoyed a party. But it would be just the setting for Mrs. Smith. With this in mind, Mrs. Radford finally called on Thomas Bell. He was living in the bachelor club on Grove. He apologized for the cigar smoke, which did not bother her, but not for the fact that he had never come to see her, which did. His blond hair had receded over the years, giving him a high, wide forehead. He had always been a handsome man; now he'd attained a dignity he had lacked before. He looked marriageable. "Did you ever find your lovely shipmate?" she asked him, quite directly, with no cunning preamble.

"Madame Christophe?" he said immediately. "No. I looked everywhere."

"In the servants' quarters?"

He responded with some heat. "She was a queen."

"And if she was not?" Mrs. Radford watched his face closely. She was looking for true love. She thought she saw it.

And also rising comprehension. "You know where she is." Mr. Bell reached excitedly for her arm. "Take me to her at once."

"No. But if she were invited to the MacElroys' ball, I would deliver the invitation. Then you could take your turn with every other eligible man in San Francisco." She meant this quite literally, but she allowed a familiar, teasing tone to come into her voice to hide it.

"Dear Mrs. Radford," he said.

"She is a working woman," Mrs. Radford warned him. "With a different name."

"She is a queen," Mr. Bell repeated. "Whatever she does, whatever she calls herself. Blood will tell."

———

Mrs. Radford was in black. Mrs. Smith wore a gown of pink silk. It was fitted at the bodice, but blossomed at the hips with puffings and petals. The hem was larger still, and laced with ribbons. The MacElroys' drawing room had been cleared for dancing, and she entered it like a rose floating on water. Couples were just assembling for the grand march. Every head turned. Mr. Bell made a spectacle of himself in his effort to get to her first. He was slightly shorter than she was.

"Mrs. Radford," he said politely. "How lovely to see you here. And Madame Christophe. I mustn't imagine that you remember me, simply because I remember you."

"Though I do," she said. She glanced at Mrs. Radford and then looked back to Mr. Bell. "And my name is not Madame Christophe. I owe you an explanation." There was a pause. Mr. Bell rushed to fill it.

"All you owe me is a dance," he assured her. He was eager, nervous. He drew her away from Mrs. Radford, who went to sit with the older women and the married ones. The music began. She watched Mr. Bell bend in to Mrs. Smith to speak. She watched the pink skirt swinging over the polished floor, the occasional glimpse of the soft toes of Mrs. Smith's shoes. She attended to the music and the lovely, old sense of being involved in things.

Some of the men seemed to know Mrs. Smith already. Young Mr. Ralston engaged her for the redowa, and everyone knew he never danced. Mr. Sharon took the lancers, his head barely reaching her shoulder. Mr. Hayes chose her for the waltz, leaving his wife without a partner. And Mr. Bell danced with no one else, spent the time while she danced with others pacing and watching for the moment she came free.

In her own small way, Mrs. Radford also triumphed. People approached who hadn't spoken to her since her husband's death. Innocuous pleasantries, but she could no longer take such attentions for granted. Eventually every conversation arrived at Mrs. Smith.

"That lovely woman you came with?" said Mrs. Putnam. "I've not seen her before."

"She's an old friend," Mrs. Radford answered contentedly. "A widow from New Orleans." She said nothing else, although it was clearly insufficient. Let Mrs. Putnam remember how she had accused Mrs. Radford of talking too much!

At the end of the evening, Mr. Bell went to find their cloaks. "I so enjoyed that party," Mrs. Smith told Mrs. Radford.

"You'll have many nights like this now. Many invitations. You were such a success."

Mrs. Smith had a gray velvet cloak. Mr. Bell returned with it, settled it slowly over her shoulders. He was reluctant to release her. "About my name," she said. They were walking outside, Mrs. Smith in the middle, the women's skirts crushed one against the next, like blossoms in a bouquet. On the steps, they joined a crowd waiting for carriages. To the right were the Mills family and that peevish, gossipy attorney, Henry Halleck. "I had a need to change my name to get out of New Orleans. I was born into slavery in Georgia," Mrs. Smith said. Everyone could hear her. "I became a white woman to escape. Ellen Smith isn't my real name, either."

And then Mrs. Smith and Mrs. Radford were alone in their carriage. The ride to the country was a long one. Mrs. Radford's feelings were too tender to bear examination. It seemed as though Mrs. Smith had deliberately humiliated her. "Is it true?" Mrs. Radford asked.

"Everything I've told you is true."

"Why pick that moment to say it?"

"It was time. I've been a white woman for so many years. And I didn't want what that was bringing me. It wasn't aimed at you. Or your ideas about love and beauty."

The horse hooves clapped. The carriage rocked. "You don't want to be the same person your whole life, do you?" Mrs. Smith asked. The carriage wheel hit a stone. It threw Mrs. Radford against Mrs. Smith. Mrs. Smith caught her by the arm. She was wearing gloves, so they didn't actually touch.

This was the last party Mrs. Radford would attend in San Francisco. One month later she left on a boat filled with missionaries going to Hawaii. One year later she was one of only seven white women in Edo, Japan. From there she sailed to Russia; from there she made her way to Peking. She died somewhere near Chungking at the age of seventy-four.

In 1883, many years after her death, Selim Woodworth received a message from her. It was a bedraggled note, crumpled, carried in a pocket, trod upon, lost, left out in the rain. Even the stamps were indecipherable. "The mountains here!" was the only legible bit, and it wasn't even clear where, exactly, Mrs. Radford had been when she wrote those words. It didn't matter. Selim Woodworth had been dead himself for more than thirteen years.

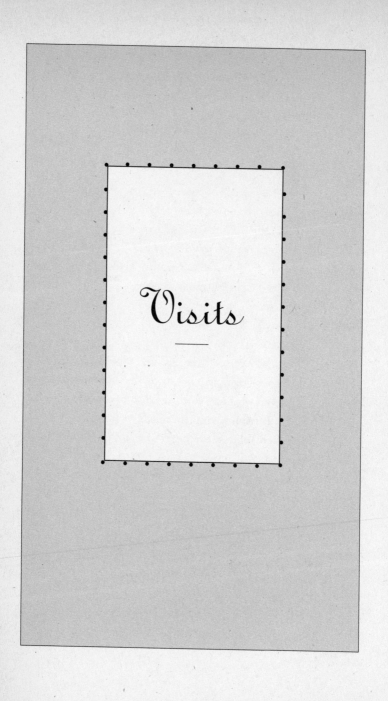

Visits

ONE

By the 1890s, San Francisco was an entirely different city from the one Mrs. Radford had left behind. The streets were paved. The sand was landscaped. Cable cars ran up and down Nob Hill. The Railroad Kings were old or dead, and also the Bonanza Kings, and also the Lawyer Kings. Society had arrived and settled, its standards strictly maintained by Ned "I would rather see my sister dead than waltzing" Greenway. Fashionable women belonged to the Conservative Set, the Fast Set, the Smart Set, the Serious Set, the Very Late at Night Set, or the highly respectable Dead Slow Set.

There were still many more men than women in the city. This imbalance resulted in a high percentage of unrequited passions. Afflicted men consoled themselves with horse racing, graft, and most frequently, liquor. Any woman whose nerves did not compel her to depend on Lydia Pinkham's Vegetable Compound (alcohol, dandelion, chamomile, and licorice) or Jayne's Carminative Balm (alcohol and opium) or Dover's Powder (opium and ipecac) could count on the advantage of sobriety in her dealings with men. The destabilizing effects of widespread heartache combined with widespread drunkenness were somewhat alleviated by the rigging of local elections.

The city was propelled in equal parts by drunken abuse and sober recompense. In those days every steamer that docked in San Francisco Bay was fitted with a large box. Each box was the same—pinewood, a sizable slot edged with brass, and the words "Give to the Ladies' Relief and Protection Society Home" burned in a circle about it. After the wreck of the SS *Rio de Janeiro,* one of these boxes was found floating past Alcatraz Island, and miraculously, the money was still inside. When levered open, the box contained rubles and yen, lire and pesos, all shuffled together like cards.

Successive treasurers for the Society counted out coins stamped with the profiles of queens they couldn't name and birds they'd never seen. Some of the coins were worn so thin there was no picture at all, just a polished disk with no clue remaining as to its history or origin. Occasionally during rough seas someone would donate a holy medallion, usually Saint Christopher. One box held a single amethyst earring with a small drop pearl.

It was still charity, it was still begging, but it bore the semblance of adventure.

Lizzie Hayes wore one of the more puzzling coins on a

chain around her neck, so whenever they looked at her, the people of San Francisco would be reminded that she needed their money. The coin was imprinted with a mermaid curled into a circle, her hair so wide and wild it netted the tip of her own tail. If anyone asked, Lizzie said it was the currency of Atlantis.

Lizzie Hayes had been a volunteer for the Ladies' Relief Home for almost ten years, its treasurer for three. She had few intimate friends, but attended two churches, Grace Church and St. Luke's Episcopal, which was good for her soul and also for fund-raising. In 1890 she was a spinster who had just seen her fortieth birthday.

She was working in the cupola one day in January, sorting through a box of donated books, when one of the older girls came to tell her Mrs. Mary E. Pleasant was at the door. "The front door," the girl said. "She'd like to speak to you."

Culling books was surprisingly dirty work, and Lizzie could feel a layer of grit on her hands and face. She wiped herself with her apron and went downstairs at once. She'd never spoken with Mrs. Pleasant, never been in the same room with her, although two years earlier she'd waited on an overloaded streetcar while the driver made an unscheduled stop so that Mrs. Pleasant could ride. Mrs. Pleasant walked the half-block to the car, and it seemed to Lizzie that she had walked as slowly as possible. She had given the driver an enormous, showy tip.

Lizzie had also seen Mrs. Pleasant on occasion in her opulent Brewster buggy with its matched horses from the Stanford stables. Mrs. Pleasant dressed like a servant, but she had her own driver in green livery and a top hat, and also her own footman to attend her.

If she hadn't ever seen her, Lizzie would still have recognized Mrs. Pleasant's face. It was one of the most famous in the city, appearing often in editorial cartoons, particularly in the *Wasp*. (Although actually the last drawing had not used her face. Instead, a black crow had peered out from underneath Mrs. Pleasant's habitual bonnet.)

"Now, I never cared a feather's weight for public opinion," Mrs. Pleasant had been once quoted as saying, "for it's the ghostliest thing I ever did see." It was fortunate she thought so. Here are just a few of the things people said about Mary Ellen Pleasant:

She'd buried three husbands before she turned forty, and in her sixties had still been the secret mistress of prominent and powerful men. At seventy years of age, she'd looked no older than fifty.

She had a small green snake tattooed in a curl around one breast.

She could restore the luster to pearls by wearing them.

Although she worked as Thomas Bell's housekeeper, she was as rich as a railroad magnate's widow. Some of the city's wealthiest men came to her for financial advice. Thomas Bell owed his entire fortune to her.

She was an angel of charity. She had donated five thousand dollars of her own money to aid the victims of yellow fever during the epidemic in New Orleans. When she got to heaven, she would soon have the blessed organized and sending cups of cool water to the sinners below.

She practiced voodoo and had once sunk a boat full of silver with a curse.

She was a voodoo queen and the colored in San Francisco both worshipped and feared her. She could start and stop pregnancies; she would, for a price, make a man die of love.

She trafficked in prostitution and had a number of special white protégées with whom her relationships were irregular, intimate, and possibly sapphic. She was responsible for all of poor Sarah Althea Hill Sharon Terry's mischiefs and misfortunes.

She ran a home for unwed mothers and secretly sold the infant girls to the Chinese tongs.

She was the best cook in San Francisco.

Here is what people said about Lizzie Hayes:

She would have married William Fletcher if she could have got him.

No one had asked Mrs. Pleasant into the parlor. Lizzie found her standing just inside the heavy oak door under the portrait of philanthropist Horace Hawes, with his brooding Lincolnesque looks. No one had offered to take her wrap, a bright purple shawl, which she nevertheless had removed and carried over one arm.

Lizzie Hayes had not kept Mrs. Pleasant waiting, but neither had she taken off her work apron. Mrs. Pleasant was better dressed. She wore a skirt of polished black alpaca, a shirtwaist with a white collar, gold gypsy hoops through her ears, and her usual outdated Quaker bonnet, purple with a wide brim. She noticed the apron at once; Lizzie saw her famous mismated eyes, one blue, one brown, flicker over it, but her facial expression did not change. Her skin was finely wrinkled, like crushed silk, and she smelled of lavender.

There were no courteous preliminaries. "I've brought you a girl," Mrs. Pleasant said. She'd come to California forty years earlier with the miners, but never lost the southern syrup of her vowels. "Named Jenny Ijub. She's just off a boat from Panama. Her mother took sick on the voyage and was buried at sea. When I ask how old she is, she holds up all five fingers. Quiet little thing. She doesn't seem to know her father."

One of her hands rested on the little girl's hair. Mrs. Pleasant dipped her head as she talked, so her face was hidden by the bonnet brim. "I have my friends at the docks. I'm known to care for such cases." As her face vanished, her voice grew softer, more confiding. She knew how to make white people comfortable.

She knew how to make them uncomfortable. Where had she really gotten the child? Lizzie felt the contrast between them. Mrs. Pleasant was tall, elegant, and spotless. Lizzie was short, dusty, fat as a toad. She was a person who rumpled, and not a person who rumpled attractively.

She cleared her throat. "We have a waiting list." Lizzie would have said this to anyone. It was the simple truth. So many in need. "And I'd have to be certain of her age. She's quite small. We don't take children under four years."

"I'll have to find somewhere else, then." Mrs. Pleasant smiled down at Lizzie. It was an understanding smile. Seventy-some years old and Mrs. Pleasant still had all her own splendid teeth. She stooped a little and aimed her smile farther down. "Don't you worry, Jenny. We'll find someone who wants you."

Lizzie looked for the first time at the girl. She was dark-haired and sallow-skinned. She had sand on her shoes and stockings, it was impossible to get to the Home without picking up sand, but was otherwise as clean as could be. Neatly and simply dressed. Hatless, though someone—Mrs. Pleasant?—had woven a bright bit of red ribbon into her hair. Her cheeks were flushed as if she were too warm, or embarrassed. She did not look up, but Lizzie imagined that if she could see the girl's eyes they would be large and tragic. She held her back stiffly; you could deduce the eyes from that.

Lizzie hated saying no to anyone about anything. Saying no, however you disguised it, was a confession of your own limitations. Not only was it unhelpful, it was galling. She reached out and touched Jenny's arm. "I have some discretion. Since she really has no one. We'll find a bed somehow. Would you like to stay with us, Jenny?"

Jenny made no response. Her eyes were still lowered; she had one knuckle firmly hooked behind her front teeth, and her spare hand wrapped around the cloth of Mrs. Pleasant's skirt. When Mrs. Pleasant was ready to leave, Jenny's fingers would have to be pried apart.

"That's lovely, then," said Mrs. Pleasant. "Now I know she'll have the best of care."

"We might even find a family to take her. Be better if she had a bit of sparkle. Don't put your fingers in your mouth, dear," Lizzie said. She reached into her apron pocket and pulled out a silver bell. "This is how we call Matron," she told Jenny. She rang the bell twice. "We have two Jennys already, but they are both much older than you. So we must call you Little Jenny. Shall we do that?"

The bell sounded very loud. Jenny's fingers twisted inside Mrs. Pleasant's skirt. Mrs. Pleasant knelt. She pulled a violet-hemmed handkerchief from her sleeve and wiped Jenny's mouth with it. She had the face of a grandmother. "Listen," she said. "You must be brave now. Remember that I'm your friend. I'll send you a present soon so you'll see I don't forget you, either." Mrs. Pleasant said these things quietly, intimately. It was not for the matron to hear, but she arrived just in time to do so.

"I hope your present is something that can be shared," the matron told Jenny as she took her away. "If you have things the others don't, you can't expect them not to mind."

The matron was a fifty-year-old woman named Nell Harris. She had come to the Home as a charity case; she had stayed on as an employee. She had soft-cooked features and a shifting seascape for a body. Her bosom lay on the swell of her stomach, rising and falling dramatically with her breath. Her most defining characteristic was that no one had ever made a good first impression on her.

She took Jenny down to the kitchen and offered her a large slice of wholesome bread. "Mrs. Pleasant gave me cake," Jenny told her. The kitchen counters were piled with dishes, half clean, half not. Two girls in aprons were washing; another was drying. That one smiled at Jenny and flicked her dishrag. The air was wet and warm and smelled of pork grease.

"And that's all it takes to make you think she's nice as pie. She gave you away pretty fast, didn't she?" Nell said.

T W O

Lizzie Hayes went back upstairs to the cupola. Out the window was an unbroken view of sand dunes, loosely strewn with scrub, chaparral, and bunches of beach grass. A storm was coming. Far to the west, the clouds were black and piled solidly against one another like rocks in a cairn.

Straight beneath Lizzie the prow of Mrs. Pleasant's bonnet cut through the wind toward her carriage. Her purple wrap was around her shoulders and the ends of her bonnet ribbons whipped about her head. Mrs. Pleasant walked away quickly, like someone who had someplace to go.

The foghorn blew in the distance. Gulls streamed inland, shrieking, and the wind spun the ghosts of sand castles into the air. Lizzie returned to her box of donated books. Suddenly, unjustly, she found herself resenting them. What did such donations do but make more work for the staff? Nothing arrived in good shape; everything needed to be sorted and cleaned and mended.

She blew the dust off *The Good Child's Picture Book.* The author had the improbable name of Mrs. Lovechild. Lizzie opened to a woodcut of two girls picnicking together in an English garden. One of them had dark hair, the other light. They wore sun hats, which circled their heads like the auras of medieval saints, but tied in bows on the side. The flowers were as large as the girls' faces.

Lizzie brought the picture closer. The book had an odd smell, like fermented fruit. The title page had been torn out, but a handwritten message on the flyleaf remained. "To my darlingest Mitzy," it read. "On the occasion of her fourth birthday. Hope you feel better soon! Your Uncle Beau." The book was probably filled with infectious germs.

Lizzie Hayes was an easy person to underestimate. Slow to act, she often appeared indecisive, but once she'd fixed on a course, it was fixed. She was hard to dissuade and hard to intimidate.

As a child she'd been passive and biddable. "So dependable. Quite beyond her years," her mother had said on those frequent occasions when Lizzie did as she'd been told. But just beneath this tractable surface lay romance and rebellion. She loved to read, engaging books with such intensity that her parents had allowed only the dullest of them, and then curtailed the time she spent with those. Her mother was quick to spot the symptoms of overstimulation, and Lizzie had spent many hours lying in bed, sentenced to absolute inactivity until she could be calm again.

It was an ill-conceived punishment. With everything but her imagination forbidden to her, Lizzie's reveries grew ever more fevered. She could lie without moving for hours in the semblance of obedience, and all the while an unacceptable cascade of pirates, prophets, and Indians pounded through her mind.

She was not trusted with fairy tales until she was sixteen years old; they were so full of murder and mayhem. She was not trusted with poetry at all, not since, at the age of six, she had wept bitterly while listening to Sir Walter Scott's "Proud Maisie." She had made it only as far as the second stanza.

> *"Tell me, thou bonny bird,*
> *When shall I marry me?"*
> *"When six braw gentlemen*
> *Kirkward shall carry ye."*

Sermons could have the same effect. When the Reverend Paul Clarkson came to luncheon, her mother was forced, over a nice lobster bisque, to suggest a little less exaltation on Sundays. "For a woman, religion should be a steadying thing," she'd suggested, and the reverend, who had just burned his mouth on his soup and was taking great gulps of cold water medicinally, had not disagreed.

In adolescence, Lizzie had been prone to the type of satisfying melancholia that expresses itself in diets and music. "I'm not raising any saints," her mother had said one morning when Lizzie was irritating her by fasting. She stood at the doorway to Lizzie's bedroom, carrying a breakfast of steak and peas, and then stayed to watch each

27

bite. In our modern age, she informed Lizzie, extravagant holiness is ill mannered as well as ill advised. "The world is as the world is," she was fond of saying. "And just as God made it. You're ungrateful to Him when you wish it otherwise."

Lizzie's mother knew that she hated peas. Lizzie ate them all silently, offered them to God, one by one, as a form of fleshly mortification.

As she'd aged Lizzie's inner and outer aspects grew increasingly ill matched. Her breathless, romantic imagination, charming in a young woman, and delightful in a beautiful young woman, was entirely ridiculous in someone short, fat, and well past her middle age. Lizzie was sharp enough to know this, and since there was no way to keep the outer woman private, she generally kept the inner woman so.

The outer woman: Often when she'd misbehaved, her mother would march her to the dressing room mirror to look at herself. "That's what a bad girl looks like!" her mother would say, her own sagging eyes floating behind the bad girl's head, as if the mere sight of Lizzie's face was a punishment. (As a consequence, Lizzie didn't like mirrors much. When she was finally allowed to read the story of Snow White, she'd instantly understood that the mirror was the real villain of the piece. "Why, I couldn't possibly choose between two such beautiful women," is what the mirror would have said if it hadn't been bent on blood.)

"You have only the beauty of youth," her father had told her when her refusal to marry his good friend, Dr. Beecher, had made him angry enough to be honest. "I'm not a fussy man," Paul Burbank had said on the occasion of her second proposal. "*You* won't be expecting romance," Christopher Ludlow had said on the occasion of her third.

Lizzie remembered these things partly because they'd hurt, but mainly because for most of her life her appearance had been so rarely commented on.

The inner woman: And yet, as far back as Lizzie could remember, she had suffered from a kind of self-importance that expressed itself as the conviction that every move she made was watched. This made a certain sense among ladies out in society, where the mere whisper of eccentricity could cost a reputation, and among the religious, since God was interested, exacting, and everywhere. Lizzie was both out and devout.

Even so, her conviction was pronounced. Add to society and God that special circumstance familiar to every passionate reader: An unseen narrator hovered somewhere behind Lizzie, marking her every move.

And *then* add the fact that for most of her life Lizzie had been haunted by a photograph of an angel in a christening gown. Her mother had made the picture frame herself, an intricate, heartbroken oval of ribbon roses and wax lilies encircling the likeness of Lizzie's brother, Edward. Lizzie was five years old when Edward was born. He'd lived less than three weeks and died, sinless, of inanition. Lizzie hardly remembered him alive.

Dead, he'd been inescapable. His picture hung first in the nursery and later in her bedroom. "To watch over you," Lizzie's mother had said. It was the sort of misunderstanding Lizzie and her mother were likely to have. Eventually Lizzie knew the difference between watching someone and watching over someone. Eventually she understood that her mother had intended this as a comfort. But by the time she'd made the distinction, Edward was a pale, palpable, disapproving presence who could be neither banished nor appeased.

Nell Harris appeared, startling Lizzie with her large pudding face rising over the top edge of the book. "She's in the kitchen, having a bite now," Nell said. "I'm afraid she looks to be a fussy eater. So I'm to squeeze a bed in for her somewhere?" Everything about her tone and posture expressed reproach. We have a waiting list, she might as well have said. We have no beds. We have no money. We have standards. Deciding who we take in is not your job.

"She's a friendless child," said Lizzie. "With a father somewhere. And unless I miss my guess, a wealthy father. Out of wedlock, of course. But quite, quite wealthy. Mrs. Pleasant wouldn't bother, otherwise."

"So you don't think that the child might be colored?" Nell asked.

The idea had been so far from Lizzie's thoughts as to shock her now. She responded slowly. "There's nothing of the colored in her face."

"You can't go by that. Mammy Pleasant herself fooled a lot of people for a long time, if the stories are true. Though I never credited them myself. You saw, she's black as a Mussulman. But if this child comes out of the Home, if she's adopted somewhere, no one is going to question her. They'll just take her as white. It will be as if we've said so."

Lizzie set the book down and wiped her hands on her apron while she thought this through. Lizzie Hayes believed it was better to be white than colored, believed it so absolutely that this was not the part she thought about. But within these confines, she was a well-intentioned woman. She genuinely didn't care what or who Jenny was. Lizzie wanted to be an influence for good in the world. If she could take in a motherless colored girl and turn her out white and adopted, she would count it a good day's work.

Still, many of their most generous donors would no doubt feel differently. The Ladies' Relief Home had no savings, no margin for error. Even a small drop in donations could mean ruin. Wasn't Lizzie's first obligation to protect the wards already there? Could she set them all at risk for the sake of one child?

The next book was a *Robinson Crusoe* someone had evidently dropped in the bathtub. Lizzie picked it up and tried to flatten the crusty cover with her hand. What she admired most about Crusoe was his calm sequentiality. He found himself in an overwhelming situation and survived simply by dealing with each task in its turn. The mere sight of the book was clarifying.

These are the things Lizzie thought, and in this order:

Today's task was to take care of Jenny. Possible repercussions were not today's task.

Besides, she had often noticed that charity made misers of donor and recipient both. She had always sworn that it wouldn't work this way on her.

Plus, she genuinely thought it likely Jenny had a wealthy father. What might such a man not do in gratitude for the preservation of his daughter? Lizzie was in charge of the Ladies' Relief Home finances, and in her professional opinion the financial risk was easily outweighed by the possible benefit.

And then Mrs. Pleasant was no one to trifle with.

Lizzie would do nothing wrong to please her, but if she did the right thing and it pleased Mrs. Pleasant as well, wasn't that a bit of luck?

And who would not be moved by little Jenny's situation?

"You're not to say this to anyone else," Lizzie told Nell. "Once you've said it, it won't be unsaid, no matter how untrue. And it is untrue. Mrs. Pleasant cares about money. She doesn't care about the colored. You mark me, she'll be back within the month with a wealthy father in tow." Her voice began friendly, but sharpened as she spoke.

"What kind of a name is Ijub?" Nell Harris asked, and since Lizzie didn't know the answer, she said nothing, but she said it to good effect. It shut Nell up entirely.

Two weeks later a box arrived for Jenny. Lizzie Hayes was there to open it. It contained a doll, wrapped in tissue, and a note. "I have noticed that many young girls are more interested in their needlework if they have a friend to sew for," Mrs. Pleasant wrote. "This is a doll that needs just such a friend." Her penmanship was as twisty as wrought iron. The note was signed "Mrs. Mary E. Pleasant."

Lizzie unwrapped the doll. Her head was made of china, her hair was paint. She had a sweet, pouting face. She wore a necklace with a tiny coin, and a work apron over her dress. She fell out of Lizzie's hand and her head broke into several curved pieces. On one piece Lizzie could see a little heart-shaped mouth.

Mary Ellen Pleasant was a voodoo queen and Lizzie

Hayes was an Episcopalian. They had had a very cordial exchange. There was no reason for Mrs. Pleasant to be angry. Except that Lizzie hadn't removed her work apron. Such a small thing, a careless thing, an oversight, honestly, when the big thing, Jenny's care, had all gone exactly as Mrs. Pleasant wished. Lizzie told herself that Mrs. Pleasant would not send a doll to curse her, and reminded herself that she couldn't be cursed by a doll even if Mrs. Pleasant had.

In fact, Lizzie had parts of this right. Mrs. Pleasant was angry about the apron, but the doll was just a bit of a joke, a bit of misdirection. There was no need to curse Lizzie with a doll. Not when she'd been given Jenny Ijub.

No one ever mentioned the doll to Jenny. It would have been pointlessly cruel, since she was already broken.

THREE

The Ladies' Relief and Protection Society Home occupied a lot on the corner of Geary and Franklin. There
wasn't a tree on the property, just scrub and sand, so
storms hit hard. The Home was familiarly called the Brown
Ark. Though blocks from the ocean, it had a shipwrecked,
random air, like something the tides had left. In this re-
spect, it matched the fortunes of most of its residents.
During the year of 1890, the Ark housed a total of two
hundred thirty-nine women and children, many only on a
temporary, emergency basis.

The motif of randomness was carried up from the
basement, with its kitchen, laundry, and schoolrooms, all
the way to the bell-tower cupola. The furnishings had been
donated, and represented the worst taste of several decades.

The parlor, into which Mrs. Pleasant had not been asked, contained a clock face painted with clouds and trapped under a bell jar, a handmade mantelpiece decoration of gangrenous velvet, pinned into tufts with brass studs, and an old set of stuffed chairs that crouched before the fireplace like large, balding cats. The effect was little offset by the posting of embroidered quotations intended to uplift and edify. "He who loves a friend is too rich to know what poverty and misery are." And "Some flowers give out no odor until crushed." And "The true perfection of mankind lies not in what man has, but in what man is."

The last had been gleaned from the deplorable Oscar Wilde. In 1882, Wilde made a visit to the city and was absolutely undone by the vulgarity of it. He said so in public lectures addressed to the badly dressed perpetrators themselves. "Too, too utter," he said, though they all felt this described him far better than them. His observation on the parlor wall of the Ladies' Relief and Protection Society Home was unattributed.

The Bell place was only a few blocks away, on the corner of Octavia and Bush. It was known throughout San Francisco as the House of Mystery, although there was a second House of Mystery, out on the beach at Land's End, owned by the Alexander Russells. Mrs. Russell, despite her increasingly vehement denials, was widely believed to be the center of an Oriental cult whose disciples all called her Mother. Soon there would be a third House of Mystery, the Winchester house, but that would be down by San Jose.

The Bell House of Mystery was the occasional home of Thomas Bell, his reclusive wife, Teresa, an indeterminate but large number of children, servants, and Mrs. Mary

Ellen Pleasant. Mrs. Pleasant was the housekeeper, although everyone knew she was too rich and too old and too famous to be a servant. This was part of the mystery. In the 1890 census she listed her occupation as "capitalist."

Mr. Bell had another house on Bush Street where he sometimes stayed. Mrs. Bell had a house in Oakland. Mrs. Pleasant had a house called Geneva Cottage on the San Jose Road, and properties on Washington Street and in Berkeley and Oakland. She was currently thinking of buying a large country ranch in the Valley of the Moon.

The Octavia place was a thirty-room mansion shadowed by blue gum trees. It had a red mansard roof, a southern mood. The interior was stuffed with hidden passageways, spiral staircases, statuary, and gold-veined mirrors. Rock-crystal chandeliers dripped from the ceilings. Every Saturday, even in winter, cut roses were arranged in vases with ferns and peacock feathers. The rooms smelled faintly of old bouquets. Mrs. Pleasant had chosen the decorations, many of which were imported from Italy. She had a fondness for vaulted ceilings and also for the gilt cupids that were so liked by everyone.

Lizzie Hayes was seriously considering walking from the Brown Ark to the House of Mystery. The distance between the two was not best measured in blocks; the Bell home was simply not a place one visited. Lizzie had never even passed by it. But she'd recently suffered a series of devastating headaches. Though she'd had headaches before, had them all her life, these were particularly rough going. The night after she dropped Jenny's doll, she'd had a vivid dream in which both her hands were encased in a block of ice. She tried to free herself by raising the ice and dashing it against a stone. Her hands broke off at the wrists instead. She could see them dimly through the scarred surface, floating, with the fingers widely separated and streaming off like jellyfish tentacles. She woke terrified, and although the feeling subsided, it did not disappear. The next day, the headaches began in earnest.

It occurred to her that nothing would be more natural than to go to Mrs. Pleasant and offer a report on Jenny's settling in. Dress with care and behave with the same. It would be a courteous attention and would show Mrs. Pleasant that Lizzie was a good-hearted, respectable woman.

Part of her recoiled from her own plan. She did not believe in voodoo and would not be governed by superstition. Good-hearted, respectable women did not visit Teresa Bell in the House of Mystery, much less Mrs. Pleasant. "How does Jenny like her doll?" Mrs. Pleasant was bound to ask, and then what would Lizzie say? Plus there was the matter of Lizzie's card. This wouldn't be a social call, but it would take place in Mrs. Pleasant's home. Would Mrs. Pleasant expect her to leave her card? If she did, would Mrs. Pleasant feel compelled to return the visit? If she didn't, mightn't this merely compound the original rudeness?

Besides, Lizzie didn't really know how Jenny was settling in. With sixty-two children now in residence, she could scarcely be expected to keep track of them all.

She rang the bell for Nell Harris. Nell took some time arriving and appeared impatient when she did so. "Yes?" she said.

"Little Jenny. Jenny Ijub. How does she get on?"

"Well enough."

"Has she settled? Does she eat heartily?"

"She's not much of an eater, I'm afraid. I believe I told you as much the first day."

"Does she get on with the other children?"

"She's not entirely truthful. The other children naturally resent it. And the dress she came in. It was turned. I don't think she's as wealthy as you hoped."

"Has she said anything about her home and family?"

"Not a whisper. She claims to remember nothing about it. But then, she's not a truthful child."

"But she seems content?"

"She thrashes at night. Her bedclothes are a rat's nest by morning. Miss Hayes, I'm dishing supper. If there's nothing further . . ."

Lizzie had a sudden memory of her own dining room table many years before. Her mother at one end. Her father at the other. And she between them, balanced unsteadily on two cushions, her legs dangling. No one was allowed to speak at meals, so she could hear her father swallowing his soup, her mother rustling a napkin under the table, out of sight.

It must have been a special occasion—she was never permitted to eat with her parents. It might have been her birthday. Lemon ices were to be served. But then Effie had been summoned to carry her off. "I simply cannot have you thrashing about," her mother told her. Lizzie could still feel the bewildered humiliation of it. She would have said she was sitting still as stone.

"Thank you," said Lizzie to Nell.

It was not the report she had wanted. But was it, after all, such a bad one? An imaginative little sprite, Lizzie could still say to Mrs. Pleasant. She so entertains the other children with her fanciful tales. An active, spirited girl.

FOUR

*B*efore she'd made up her mind about the visit, something occurred to necessitate it. Jenny was taken with
several of the other children to Layman's German castle on
Telegraph Hill, as a treat for learning her Bible verses. The
middle school children were reading *Ivanhoe,* and there was
to be a special exhibition of armor and swordfighting. Mrs.
Lake, a postman's widow who taught the middles, had been
assured that the thrusts and parries would be accurately
medieval. There were rumors of actual tilting, and she assumed this meant horses. Tilting afoot would be a sad
spectacle even for orphans.

The children were sorted into pairs, an older child
with each younger. Jenny Ijub was partnered with Minna
Graham, a pretty ten-year-old with fat black braids, and

front teeth that folded toward each other like an opened book. The two girls held hands on the cable car. Mrs. Lake was getting a cold, and she sneezed until her nose swelled.

A large crowd had gathered at the castle, whose Gothic turrets and parapets had been decked from top to bottom with banners. At noon the copper time-ball fell through its glass shaft. A group of strolling musicians sang madrigals. Minna Graham was not musical, but she was entranced by the women's costumes. She wished that she, too, wore dunce caps with feathers and veils, velvet bodices with brocade inserts, high waistlines and yards of skirt. She followed the singers a few steps only, fell behind the other children. When the first combat began, people pressed forward to see it.

Mrs. Lake complained to Lizzie later that little chivalry was shown to her and her pupils. There were several moments of confusion in the crush. But they all heard Jenny scream.

By the time Mrs. Lake got there, Jenny was being held and petted by a fat, handsome man in a yellow waistcoat. He said that Jenny had been frightened by the appearance of the black knight. The black knight wore a facemask that looked like the back of a shovel, with a row of stiff bristles over the top of his head. The bristles appeared to Mrs. Lake to be cut by machine and therefore not something that would have been available to Ivanhoe, although the metal part might well have been old enough.

In any case, Jenny denied being frightened of the knight. She said instead that a man had tried to snatch her, a man in green trousers. It was the only description they were able to get. He had clutched her by the neck, one hand over her mouth. She bit him and screamed as he dropped her. Then he'd disappeared into the crowd. Mrs. Lake could find no one who had seen any of this.

She lost control of the children. The older boys abandoned their partners and dashed off to look for green trousers. Mrs. Lake was unable to stop them. She used her energies to keep the little ones huddled together. This was not hard; many of them were frightened. Others, especially Minna Graham, were clearly envious. Minna was one of those children who liked to turn attention to herself whenever possible. She did so on this occasion by fainting.

Minna's head hit the pavement with a crack they could all hear. Blood seeped into her hair, and Mrs. Lake found a large lump on the scalp. The lump was as soft as a cooked carrot and gave slightly when poked. Minna was too dizzy to walk. Mrs. Lake, who was planning on confronting Minna with her failure to watch over Jenny, instead saw her carried from the castle to the cable car on the back of the black knight's horse, the crowd cheering as she passed. "She actually waved to everyone," Mrs. Lake told Lizzie and Nell, "as if she were Queen of the May."

All in all, the children were judged to be overexcited, and when Mrs. Lake collected them again, she brought them straight back. As a result, she couldn't know about the tilting.

She gave Lizzie and Nell an aggrieved report, blowing her nose into her handkerchief frequently but silently. She then went home to rest. Nell stayed with Lizzie a few moments more, to give her own version of events, events to which she was not a witness. Nell had no time for knights; it amazed her that anyone did. And she had three particular points to make. The first was that Mrs. Lake was the kind of woman who lived a life of high drama in which nothing ever actually happened. The second was that *Ivanhoe* was likely to overexcite, even when it wasn't combined with unnecessary outings. It was a swoony sort of book, and she wondered at Mrs. Lake for encouraging the children to read it. The third was that it was time to know more about Jenny Ijub. Where had she come from? Had they put themselves and the other children in danger by taking her in? Someone needed to go to Mammy Pleasant and ask some hard questions.

Lizzie guessed that Nell was right on all counts.

Ivanhoe: Swoony indeed—why, Lizzie had only to think in the most glancing way about the licentiousness of Norman nobles to feel a flush coming up her neck and into her cheeks. How many nights she'd drifted to sleep imagining herself struggling futilely, imprisoned for love by the swarthy, ardent Bois-Gilbert!

Mrs. Lake: Mrs. Lake was a neat, pretty, red-haired woman of thirty and could still carry on about knights and steeds and beheaded queens (how that woman loved the Stuarts!) without looking the fool, but her day was coming. Since Lizzie secretly shared all of Mrs. Lake's shortcomings, she was quick to find Mrs. Lake silly and sentimental. It was a form of protective coloration. Nell's veins ran with a heavier ore.

Questions about Jenny: The staff was busy and Lizzie was the only member of the board at hand, so these were bound to fall to her. She fixed her hair with combs, fixed her hat with pins, fixed her face in a smile, and walked to Octavia Street. By the time she reached the Bells' front porch, she had worked herself into such a state over occult rituals and blood sacrifices she could hardly knock on the door.

FIVE

Lizzie was not the sort to retreat, not when she'd made up her mind to call, and especially not with the elderly gardener watching her. He stood staring, scary in his very ordinariness, armed with a shining set of pruning shears and the thorny stems of a dozen dead roses. Lizzie picked up her skirts and climbed the steps to the front doors. These were of carved cherry wood, inset with a high pane of beveled glass. The knocker was a roaring lion with a ring in his mouth.

A white girl, very pretty and dressed in a green uniform, answered Lizzie's knock, took her hat and gloves, and showed her into a white-and-gold drawing room. She was told to sit, but went instead to examine a set of statues of women, white marble on black onyx bases. They held various poses of resignation and supplication. They were women who wanted something they would not get. And they were quite naked. There was a slight shadow of dust in the marble crevices. Lizzie could imagine a housemaid too embarrassed to clean more thoroughly. Lizzie herself did not much like them. She didn't mind the lack of clothing; she knew about art. She was no prig. But a lady shouldn't need to beg.

A gold-and-white woman entered the room. She wore pearls in her ears and gold on her wrists. Her hair was brown with a little meander of gold; her eyes were like trout ponds. A complicated fragile white dress gathered and spilled over her. She seemed about Lizzie's own age, though much more beautiful. "I'm Mrs. Bell," she said. Lizzie had expected Mrs. Bell to be younger.

"Miss Hayes. Of the Ladies' Relief and Protection Society Home."

"I suppose Mr. Bell has made contributions." Her tone was distant and uninterested.

Lizzie had no recollection of this, and since she kept the books, she should know. But it would be an awkward thing to contradict.

Mrs. Bell was already sweeping Lizzie back toward the door. "Perhaps we could do a mite more. I'm not the one to ask. I'm not the one to know when we have money and when we don't."

"I didn't come to ask for money. I'm here about a child."

"I love children," said Mrs. Bell. "Mr. Bell and me have our six. The oldest grown. I think Fred might be in San Jose. Or maybe Mexico. Somewhere south."

"This is a girl. She's only been with us a few weeks. Her mother passed away."

"I hardly knew my mother." Mrs. Bell's voice retained its formal-tea tone. "I had two older brothers who both died right after birth. When I was three months old my mother stripped me to the skin and set me on a windowsill in a thunderstorm. My father found me and he gave me to another family to raise."

"I'm very sorry," Lizzie responded uneasily.

"A three-month baby left soaking in the rain." Still, Mrs. Bell's composure was perfect; she might have been discussing the new fashion in women's sleeves or expressing hopes for a mild winter. "A pretty little thing, too, with a head of silky hair. Before it was even born, she hated it. Wouldn't nurse it. I refuse to think on her much. What might I do for your motherless girl?"

"Mrs. Pleasant brought her to us. Actually, it was Mrs. Pleasant I was hoping to see."

Mrs. Bell's poise proved as diaphanous as her dress. It slipped from her face like smoke. Lizzie watched this happen, and then looked away, since clearly it was something she shouldn't have seen. "Don't do that," said Mrs. Bell. "Just go. I won't say you been here. I won't say anything." There was the sound of brisk footsteps in the corridor. "See how fast she walks?" Mrs. Bell whispered. "She comes on you in a moment."

Mrs. Pleasant entered the room. "Teresa," she said. She spoke as quickly as she moved. "You've met Miss Hayes, then. I'm delighted. She's a woman of good works." She didn't look delighted. She didn't look surprised. Her face was gracious, but this could have been an illusion created by age, by the texture of her skin, like a crumpled hand-kerchief. Her hair was white about her face, but still, even now, when she was in her seventies, mostly black. She'd gathered it into a knot with bits curled tightly around her temples. Her eyes were sharp; they seemed to take much in while giving nothing away.

"Really?" said Mrs. Bell. "Now, she didn't say. I'm rather a creature of ideals, myself."

"Would you take a cup of tea?"

Lizzie did not want to stay long enough to drink a cup of tea. She didn't wish to make a social call. She didn't wish to conduct her business in front of the peculiar Mrs. Bell. She couldn't think of a courteous way to send Mrs. Bell from her own drawing room. "Tea would be lovely," she said. "Aren't you kind."

She took a seat on the couch. Mrs. Pleasant vanished. Mrs. Bell sat beside her, sliding her hand into Lizzie's, giving it the ghost of a squeeze. Her hand was cold, limp, corpselike. Lizzie could feel her own warmth draining out of her. Yet courtesy prevented her from withdrawing.

"Don't eat or drink nothing," Mrs. Bell warned Lizzie. Her tone suggested they were old friends now, co-conspirators. There was an odd footstep in the hall. "I'm not talking to you, Miss Viola." Mrs. Bell's voice grew louder. "You just run along," and a girl, dark-eyed and unnaturally pale, of perhaps sixteen or seventeen years, passed slowly by the doorway. She walked with some diffi-culty, her left foot twisted inward. "Not everything in this house is your business." Mrs. Bell turned back to Lizzie. "Viola is queen of the keyhole." She did not lower her voice, though Lizzie was sitting right there beside her.

Something exploded in Lizzie's peripheral vision. She turned to look out an arched window and saw a burst of silver light, as if a fairy were coming into the room. The fairy spun over the sill, darted into the corners and up to the vaulted ceiling, where it hung for a moment like a star. Then it dropped again, touched the roses, the statues, Teresa Bell's brown hair. Everything it touched remained under a silvery film, as if seen by moonshine and through ruffled water. The sight filled Lizzie with dread.

The first time Lizzie had seen such colors, she'd thought a Christmas angel was visiting. She'd cried, it was that beautiful. Later she imagined it was Baby Edward giving her the silver taste of his unhappiness, angry not to be the one alive when everybody would have preferred him.

She heard a noise deep in her own throat without understanding that she had made it. She hardly noticed Mrs. Bell's hand sliding away, Mrs. Bell herself leaving the room.

"Are you all right, Miss Hayes?" Mrs. Pleasant asked. Her voice moved at the wrong speed and was pitched in the wrong key.

"I must get home," Lizzie said. She took a great, unladylike gulp of air, pressed her hands into her temples to try to block the pain before it arrived. "Please. I don't believe I can walk so far. If I might have the loan of your buggy . . ."

"Your head aches?"

"Not yet." The blood was beginning to beat in her ears. She curled into her own lap, the corset cutting upward into the bottom of her breasts. "But I must go home."

There was no answer. She was alone in the room again, with the silent, pleading, naked silvery statues. She

47

tried to rise, but her legs shook beneath her. She heard a clock sounding the hour with a slow, sobering tune. She heard a tapping in the hall, footsteps entering the room, each louder than the previous and all of them too loud.

"I've made you something. Drink it up, but slow. You'll feel better."

Lizzie raised her head. Mrs. Pleasant stood before her, and behind Mrs. Pleasant, Mrs. Bell. Mrs. Bell's eyes flashed like silver coins.

Mrs. Pleasant guided her fingers around a china cup in which Lizzie smelled a foul sort of tea. Bay leaves, wet moss, blackberries, and rum. She allowed Mrs. Pleasant to lift her hand, tip the cup into her mouth. She was sluggish from apprehension, too limp to resist. The drink was bitter enough to sting, dribbling down her throat in a thin stream, leaving behind a runnel of heat. She drank more. With every sip, she felt the impending headache recede, the warmth spreading until it reached even her frozen fingers.

"There," said Mrs. Pleasant. "See how that helps." This might have been a question. It might have been a command. Followed by a command. "Keep drinking."

As she emptied the cup, Lizzie felt as if she were waking, finally, from a long dream. The dream was her whole life until now. The silver light leached from the room. The tables and flowers flattened into ordinariness and further, better even, to detachment.

Sometime after Lizzie finished her tea, Mrs. Pleasant asked if she was happy with her life. She should have said yes. She rarely felt unhappy. Daily association with the downtrodden kept her keenly aware of her advantages. She knew the pleasure of doing good. She knew moments of great joy, often in church during the high notes of particular hymns. She would open her mouth to sing them, and her heart would leap with her voice up to where the sunlight filtered through the colored glass, igniting the motes of dust above her head. So many pleasures. The sight of red tulips. The little buzz of life in the grass. A letter with her name and foreign stamps. The smell of rain. The taste of pomegranate jelly. Reading novels in the afternoon, with no corset and her shoes off and her feet on a chair.

And at the moment of the question, she was feeling nothing at all. It had seemed to Lizzie that as the room returned to normal around her, she herself shrank away like Alice in Wonderland in the "Drink Me" episode. Her concerns, her alarms, became tiny and laughable. She remembered how lovely it was to be small and cared for. She remembered a fever from many years before, not a high fever, just high enough to be exhilarating. She remembered Effie sitting on the edge of the bed and feeding her sips of a salty broth with one of her mother's special apostle spoons.

And yet she answered that she was not. In direct contradiction, she then went on at length about the gratifications of her work. She couldn't seem to stop herself. Somehow she mentioned that her mother had once said she played the piano as if she had hooves instead of hands. She felt no distress over this, and yet her eyes filled with tears. She pulled her handkerchief from her bodice and wiped her nose. The handkerchief was hot, and stiff with soap.

"My mother left me naked out in the pouring rain," Mrs. Bell said. Lizzie had already managed to forget this.

"My mother was sold off." Mrs. Pleasant sat with her arms crossed and her hands showing. Her fingernails were like white pearls against her dark skin. "The overseer was frightened of her eyes. He couldn't bear the way she looked at him. He sickened and died soon after."

Lizzie felt outdone. She was tempted to say something of her father—there were things she could say! But one look at Mrs. Pleasant made her see that she would not win this, either.

And she didn't really mind being bested. She was finding, to her surprise, that she was quite relaxed in the company of notorious women. Teresa Bell was said to have been a prostitute. Mary Ellen Pleasant was rumored to sell babies to Chinamen. Lizzie felt that she could say anything; how could mere words lower her here? "I've never been in love," someone said, and most likely it was Lizzie herself, although she very much hoped not. She put her handkerchief away, tucked it to the side of her breast and felt her heart beat as she did so. Her pulse was rapid and skimmed over the surface of her skin, delicate as a bird's. She could hear it, washing through her ears, loud and then soft and then loud again. She was so involved in these observations that she forgot the unseemly topic of love had been raised.

"Anyone who wants love can have it," Mrs. Pleasant said. "There are ways."

"Charms," explained Mrs. Bell.

"You can do anything you want. You don't have to be the same person your whole life. As to love, you're better off without. That's about all I know about that!"

"Mr. Bell and I are very much in love," said Mrs. Bell.

There was an odd pause. "With each other." She was seated by Lizzie again; she tapped on Lizzie's arm. "Mrs. Pleasant reads tea leaves," she said. "If you want to know your future. Not that it's always such a good idea."

"Miss Hayes doesn't believe in that sort of thing," Mrs. Pleasant observed, and rightly so, but Mrs. Bell's warning aside, who wouldn't want her tea leaves read?

"Please," said Lizzie.

She watched as Mrs. Pleasant peered into her cup, dumped the dregs onto a saucer, let them settle, looked again, and finally smashed them with the back of her spoon in a gesture that could only disturb. The clock struck and still Mrs. Pleasant contemplated the ruins of Lizzie's tea. She looked for so long that Lizzie suspected she was seeing something bad.

But when Mrs. Pleasant spoke it was all bland bits of other fortunes. "You've come to a magical juncture," she said, which was nice, since Lizzie had been feeling old and used up. Nice to think she was at the beginning of something. "A critical turning. You could lose your way." This was less nice.

"You must watch out for three signs. This is the order of them: a blue-eyed man, a white dog, and the number twelve. When you've seen them all, you'll have a choice to make." She looked straight at Lizzie's face and didn't look away. Lizzie hated being looked at.

"Your impulses are good," Mrs. Pleasant said finally, "but you don't trust them. You fret overly about appearances and say things you don't really think. Put all that away when you make this choice, or you'll blunder."

And that was it. "I see," Lizzie replied. "That's helpful,

then," which was not what she really thought. And nothing at all about falling in love, which she'd thought was the whole point. She would have liked to ask, but having already introduced the matter once, she felt it would be nagging.

At just that moment a large Negro in a black top hat entered the room. He whispered something to Mrs. Pleasant, who rose. "The carriage is hitched," she said. "I'll get you to it."

She took Lizzie's arm, which was quite unnecessary. Lizzie felt a small piece of paper pressed into her hand, a wave of lavender perfume. "Here's where to buy that tea. You just tell the druggist I sent you, he'll take special care. Sam, please see Miss Hayes safely back."

Lizzie's arm was transferred to Sam. "I'm perfectly well able to walk," she said crossly, and then looked up to see the crippled girl, Viola, who wasn't. "So sorry," she offered, vaguely aware that an apology would only make matters worse.

SIX

*I*n later years the *San Francisco Chronicle* would refer to the residents of the House of Mystery as the strangest bunch ever to live in the city. The Bell household had a predilection for assumed names and fanciful histories. The 1890 census showed several of them lying about their ages as well.

To have seen the inside, as Lizzie had just done, to have your tea leaves read by Mrs. Pleasant herself, was rare enough to be worth the telling of it. Yet Lizzie found she was reluctant to do so. Her own role was an ambiguous one; she had made herself too much at home.

In fact, Nell Harris told Mrs. Lake that Lizzie had returned to the Brown Ark in a disgraceful state of intoxication. The children all witnessed it, Nell said—Lizzie, with her hair tipped off the side of her head like a melting pudding, setting her feet down with such deliberation and laughing like a crazy woman about it. She had asked Nell if Nell thought she was happy. As if a person could think she was happy, but really not be. As if Nell had time to worry about such things!

And then, when pressed, Lizzie admitted to having learnt absolutely nothing further about Jenny Ijub. Oh, Nell could see poor Lizzie had been as clay in the hands of the cunning Mrs. Pleasant.

While Lizzie had been off tippling, a sparrow had flown into the basement of the Brown Ark. Before Nell could sweep it out the door with the broom, the orange cat had gotten it. This information reduced Lizzie to shockingly voluble sobs—"Poor bright little spirit!" she said in a trembly voice—and then she went upstairs to the tower room and fell asleep at once on the scratchy settee.

If Nell and Lizzie had been a generation older, if they'd read the *Pacific Appeal,* the paper that came from the Negro community, instead of the *Wasp*, the things they thought they knew about Mrs. Pleasant might have been quite different. As it was, their familiarity with her was based almost entirely on the coverage of a sensational and long-running court case commonly called the Sharon business.

A lady's name, Lizzie's mother had always told her, appears in the paper only twice, once when she's married and once when she's buried. Yet there Mrs. Pleasant was, often as not, on page six, or page twelve, a few paragraphs down, or in the very headline itself. On one side of the Sharon case was a red-haired beauty from Missouri named

Sarah Althea (Allie) Hill. On the other was William Sharon, ex–U.S. senator and executive of the Bank of California. Sharon was *a San Francisco millionaire,* a title reserved for those whose fortunes exceeded thirty million.

Sharon and Hill were either married or they weren't when she sued him for divorce on grounds of adultery. She had a letter from him attesting to the marriage, a letter Sharon claimed was a forgery.

In 1885, with the trial ongoing, William Sharon had died, leaving Allie widowed or not, disgraced or unimaginably wealthy, or some combination of the above. It took four years for the courts to rule finally against her.

Mrs. Pleasant was rumored to have paid all Allie's legal costs. She spent many days in court at Allie's side for no reason anyone could see, except to fix the judge with the evil eye.

The witnesses for William Sharon included an endless succession of star, palm, and tea-leaf readers, spirit mediums and charm workers, all of whom claimed that, under Mrs. Pleasant's guidance, Allie had fed the ex-senator love potions, placed items of power in fresh graves, pierced the dried heart of a pigeon with nine pins and worn it in a red silk bag about her neck. These were not seen to be the actions of a wife, and Allie had denied them.

The testimony that followed concerned previous lovers, suicide attempts, even the details of carnal intimacies, right there in the press, where any innocent child might read them. It was the sort of case that exposed no end of human frailties and, Lizzie thought sadly, no one's more than her own. It was so like a good novel, except for the being-real part. Real embarrassments, real heartbreak, real death.

She was ashamed of how avidly she'd followed it. Her mother would have canceled the paper first.

So there Lizzie was, only three signs shy of a magical juncture and too ashamed to tell anyone. She spoke only to Nell about the visit and was as brief as could be. In this way she hoped to conceal her intense interest.

It was an interest widely shared. How did a colored woman, an ex-slave, come to have so much money and influence, San Francisco asked itself, and gave itself three possible answers.

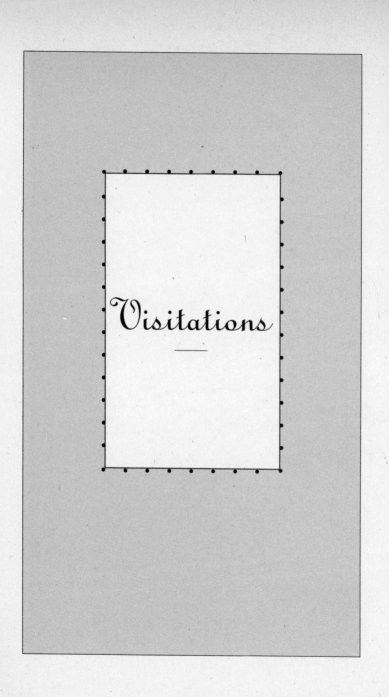

Visitations

ONE

Proposition One: Mary E. Pleasant rose to power and prominence in San Francisco through her cooking.

A better case can be made for this than one might imagine. When Mrs. Pleasant arrived in 1852, San Francisco was little more than a mining camp. Streets were made by sinking emptied whiskey bottles into the mud; shacks were made by dismantling boats and wagons. The food was revolting.

Mrs. Pleasant was already in possession of a sizable inheritance from her first husband when she went to work as housekeeper at an elegant bachelor club on Washington Street.

Among those who sat at her table in the early years were: The Woodworth brothers—Fred, part owner of the fabulous Ophir mine, and Selim, acting consul for China and a commodore in the U.S. Navy.

Newton Booth, who would go on to be governor and a U.S. senator.

Those kings of the Comstock, William Ralston, who ran the Bank of California and built the Palace Hotel, and William Sharon, senator from Nevada, who inherited the Palace after Ralston drowned.

Senator David S. Broderick and California Supreme Court justice David S. Terry, before the latter killed the former in a dubiously conducted duel and had to flee the state.

And Representative Milton Latham, a lawyer, financier, and railroad engineer.

Here were some of the wealthiest men in San Francisco, most of them quite fond of her. Stock tips, management concerns, and investment strategies were passed about the table as readily as salt and pepper.

Mrs. Pleasant was sharp, well funded, and well informed. By 1880 she owned a stable, a saloon, a dairy farm, a brothel, two boardinghouses, several residences, and considerable amounts of undeveloped land in Oakland and Berkeley. She'd invested in railroads, mining, and ranching, and managed to dodge the crash of 1873 and the crookedness of 1879.

No other explanation of her wealth is necessary. No explanation of power besides wealth is needed.

Many of her recipes survive. Some call for ingredients in proportions large enough to serve more than a hundred diners.

———

Proposition Two: Mary E. Pleasant rose to power and prominence in San Francisco through a system of carefully managed secrets.

At that same table, Mrs. Pleasant must have heard a great many things besides stock tips. She was widely known as a superior cook, but equally widely as someone who would keep a secret.

She was a woman for women to turn to in a scrape. She found hospitals for girls in trouble, homes for unwanted children; Teresa Bell's diaries connect her to one Dr. Monser, who ran a foundling hospital (and later died in San Quentin while serving sentence for a botched abortion). Both black women and white women depended on her; she made no distinctions.

Before the war, Mary Ellen Pleasant had taken enormous personal risks on behalf of slaves. She carried money to John Brown and participated in the Franchise League. She went to court to oppose those laws that penalized free blacks.

After the war, people began to refer to her as the Black City Hall. She loaned money to new businesses. She donated to black churches. She found domestic positions for new arrivals in the hotels and in the households of her wealthy white friends.

Any servant sees things, and some of these servants had been trained by slavery to be observant on penalty of death. If an unmarried daughter seemed tired in the mornings, if a married man had unusual appetites or an extra wife back East, if there were gambling debts or domestic violence or alcoholic madness, this information was likely to reach Mrs. Pleasant.

A favor can be freely extended out of gratitude for a

secret kept. A favor can be extorted in return for the promise of secrecy. From the outside it may be hard to distinguish the former from the latter. But Teresa Bell was not the only one to call it blackmail.

Proposition Three: Mary E. Pleasant rose to a position of power and prominence in San Francisco through Vodoun.

Mrs. Pleasant sometimes said that her mother had been a Vodoun priestess killed by slave owners frightened of her power. (Sometimes she said other things.) Sometimes she said that she herself had used her Vodoun power to escape slavery.

She was related through her second marriage to the famous Marie LaVeau and had been a guest of that house before sailing to California. In New Orleans, LaVeau created a political base through domestic spies, blackmail, and matchmaking. Mrs. Pleasant appears to have adapted these same methods to San Francisco.

She enjoyed close friendships with several white women for whom she'd found, if not husbands, then near-equivalents to husbands. She introduced Selim Woodworth to his wife, and Governor Booth to a woman whom he felt unable to marry for political reasons, but with whom he had a long relationship as well as a child. She introduced Thomas and Teresa Bell.

A few years before her death, the *Chronicle* ran an article on Mrs. Pleasant entitled "Queen of the Voodoos." It was a very unpleasant article, and one of the things it accused her of was genuine belief.

From an item in the *Examiner,*
October 13, 1895:

Safely locked in her loyal breast are the secret histories of many of the prominent families of the
coast. She has supplied the ladder upon which
more than one proud woman and ambitious man
have climbed to wealth and social position. Her
purse—for she has been for years a wealthy
woman—has ever been open to aid the needy and
unfortunate. . . . Neither creed, color, sex nor
condition in life ever had meaning for her when
her interest had been once awakened. Her deeds
of charity are as numerous as the gray hairs in her
proud old head.

An acquaintance, as quoted
in the *Call,* May 7, 1899:

"She has not a spark of affection, nor an atom of
conscience. She is the smoothest talker and the
shrewdest woman in San Francisco. She is child-
ish in her vanities, diabolical in her schemings, a
woman to whom the feeling of power is the
breath of life, and one who realizes that it is
money that gives power. An intellectual giant,
but a moral idiot."

TWO

On the night following her visit to the House of Mystery, Lizzie awoke sometime after dark. It took her a moment to know where she was, since she was not in her bed, where she ought to be. She couldn't imagine why she hadn't told Sam to take her home. A fat moon floated just outside the tower window, one small, dark cloud patting its face like a powder puff. There was a tatted antimacassar under her cheek; when she raised her head, she could feel its web indented into her skin.

She was still dressed, even to her shoes. She still had Mrs. Pleasant's slip of paper balled in her hand. The gaslights had been long ago put out. She took the paper to the window. She could see the halo of lights over the downtown, too far away to be useful. There was also Mrs. Pleasant's elaborate script to contend with. Plus the ink had smeared from the heat of Lizzie's fingers. But she thought the address was in Chinatown.

She'd not eaten since breakfast. She made her way, partly by sight, partly by touch, partly by memory to the basement and the kitchen. The Brown Ark groaned from her weight on the stairs. The parlor clock chimed a quarter-hour. She groped through the dark pantry for an apple. When she bit down, it became a potato instead. After her initial disappointment, she thought it tasty enough. She was very hungry!

What might Mrs. Pleasant and Mrs. Bell have eaten for dinner? Lizzie wondered whether Mr. Bell would have joined them; somehow she thought not. Lizzie pictured the two women at the table together, Teresa and Mary Ellen, both of them elegantly gowned, necklaces flickering in the candlelight, the murmur of their voices. Laughter. She herself might have been spoken of, though she couldn't imagine what would be said. It was strangely exciting to think of being talked of by two women so often talked of. Ordinarily Lizzie hated the idea of being a topic for conversation.

She took another bite of potato, less pleased with the taste this time. Then she heard someone who shouldn't have been there coming soft and halting down the stairs.

During this period, an eleven-year-old girl named Maud Curry also lived as a ward at the Brown Ark. Maud was a thin child, with white-blond hair that coiled down her neck so thickly it was kept cut short, to prevent the abundance from sapping her strength. Maud's mother was consumptive and had been separated from her daughter for the child's own health. Her father had owned a small dry-goods store, but it had been embezzled away by his bookkeeper. Unable to bear presenting his darling, ailing wife with bankruptcy and failure, he brought Maud one morning to the Ark, kissed her, told her he would return for her in a day or so, and disappeared. He was by nature a cheerful, hearty man, and he had never given any outward sign of distress.

It might have been easier on Maud if he hadn't dissembled so persuasively. As she saw the days pass and his promises turn to lies, she began to suspect his every emotion: Had he ever been happy with her and her mother? Had he ever intended to stay? Had he ever loved them?

Her mother's health was not improved by her father's desertion. She sent Maud many tender letters, but often they were not even in her own hand and she did not pretend that Maud was coming home soon.

After the initial shock, Maud's unhappiness settled so deep inside her she was rarely aware of it. She was her father's daughter. She made a place for herself among the other wards as someone who was ready for anything. "Maud is a sport," the boys said admiringly. "Maud will stop at nothing."

At least she had a mother and a father. At the Brown Ark, that counted for something. It was the first question they asked when a new child arrived. They'd asked it of Jenny Ijub. Did she have a mother? A father? Anybody?

Jenny Ijub was not settling in. She was small, but without the ingratiating manner that might have turned this to her advantage. She refused to be dressed and carried about like a doll, though this would have vastly improved her popularity. Lizzie believed her to be four years old, but she was, in fact, five. She had told the other children that her friend, Mrs. Pleasant, was sending her a special gift, loved her dearly, would be coming to take her away soon. This was what she had made of Mrs. Pleasant's promises.

Maud had once said something too much like this herself, had even believed it. She'd been made to look a fool. By the time of Jenny's arrival, Maud had lived at the Ark for almost a year. Jenny's assertions were preposterous. Jenny was trying to make fools of them all. Maud held Jenny's nose and mouth closed until she confessed as much. She pinched Jenny's nose hard enough to leave fingerprints.

"She sleepwalks," Maud told the matron when questioned about the bruising. "And she's such a liar! If there's one thing I can't bear, it's a liar."

She'd heard the matron say this herself often enough to know it would find its mark. "So a friend is coming to fetch you?" Nell asked Jenny. "And what friend would that be? You'll find no friends here, missy, if you can't learn to be truthful."

The warning had no apparent effect. Maud told the other children that Jenny boasted she'd owned a pony, a parrot, a silver cup with her initials, dresses, and dolls.

Her mother had allowed her lemon sticks whenever she liked, had kept a vase full of them on a low table within Jenny's reach. Her lies grew more and more fanciful. Her father had been as rich as a sultan. She believed in fairies, because she had actually seen them. She'd seen ghosts and angels, too. She didn't believe in God. Before a week had passed, everyone at the Brown Ark knew you couldn't trust a thing Jenny said.

Even Jenny was persuaded. Her memories tangled into the things Maud reported. Jenny thought there had been a pony, dresses, and candies, but apparently these were lies. And more confusing, she didn't remember telling Maud anything. She vowed to say nothing about herself to anyone—she already hated them all—but in the midst of her rigorous silence, her lies carried on without her.

Once her untruthfulness was known, she became an easy target for pranks. Cups of sand were poured into her shoes at night, followed by cups of water. Imogene Reed caught a fat black spider and saved it in a glass, to be dropped onto Jenny's face as she slept. The cores of several apples were stuffed into her pillowcase.

The food at the Brown Ark was not what Jenny was used to. The discipline was also a hardship. She'd never before been expected to stay voluntarily in her chair, with its terrible spindled back, for hours at a time. She had never been asked to envision God's disappointment in her. She had not been told to keep so clean. She reacted against confinement like a wild animal. She paced in her cage.

It was Jenny, then, whom Lizzie heard on the stairs. When Lizzie turned around, there she was, her eyes brooding, her hair wild as a nest of sticks. She had been unable to do up the laces at the back of her dress, but was otherwise fully clothed.

"Jenny Ijub," Lizzie said. "Little Jenny. You frightened me. You should be in bed."

"I know." Jenny began to back upstairs, her legs so short each step was a difficulty. Lizzie caught her by the arm. What a twig it was! Lizzie's fingers wrapped about it and squeezed, and she could feel right down to the bone.

"Where were you going?"

"Nowhere."

"All dressed up to go nowhere? It won't do, miss. I know you're fond of deceits. I'll have the truth from you now."

"I wanted the cat," Jenny said. "The stripe cat."

"The cats don't come inside."

"I didn't know."

Jenny's voice was unconvincing, but she met Lizzie's eyes steadily. The look on her face surprised Lizzie. It was an altogether adult look. It was anger.

"You know this very well, Jenny. Someone let the orange cat in today and it killed a lovely little bird. Jesus hates to hear a child lie."

"I can't sleep," Jenny said, her chin coming up and her mouth setting. "I want to go out."

Lizzie turned Jenny away, intending to march her smartly upstairs. Instead she fastened up the back of Jenny's dress. She smoothed her own hair with one hand. "Get your coat. I won't have you catching a chill. Matron has enough to do without nursing you."

She fetched her own coat, too. Complying with Jenny's wishes made no sense, but this seemed to be exactly the part that appealed to Lizzie. You don't have to be the same person your whole life, she told herself. She was excited to see that she could be impulsive, unpredictable. They don't expect that from me, she thought. She would show them. She had no idea at all who they were.

THREE

Nothing could have been more familiar than the walk in and out of the Brown Ark, but Lizzie had seldom done it at night. She was disoriented, exhilarated by the darkness and her own strange behavior. Everything common, the garbage and ash barrels, the cellar door, the dunes, was transformed into something she'd never seen before. She could be underwater, or in another century.

It was a clear, dry winter night. No streetlights lit this part of the city yet, and the moon had receded higher and smaller and dimmer in the sky. There were a preposterous number of stars. Who could ever need so many? Lizzie raised her chin to look at them all, strung like beads along the telegraph wires, scattered in handfuls across the netted void.

KAREN JOY FOWLER

The cold air made a mist of her breath. A scratchy wind came over the dunes and into the sleeves of her coat. The orange cat was lurking by the door. It took off into the scrub, then turned to watch them. "You're a bad one," she told it, softly, but she knew it heard. Lizzie could see the unearthly jewels of its eyes.

What now? It was too late to get the buggy. Jenny was too small to walk more than a few blocks. Lizzie had gotten this far on momentum, but now she had to invent something. Now she had to have a plan.

"Where are we going?" Jenny asked.

"Where would you like to go?"

"The ducks."

Lizzie had no idea where that might be, but since they weren't going there, it hardly mattered. "The ducks are asleep."

"Wake them," suggested Jenny.

There was really only one destination that Lizzie could think of within walking distance. She took Jenny's hand and started off. She wasn't sure exactly how late it was. There were still lights far away in the city, but no one else seemed to be abroad.

The streets were unpaved and full of obstacles, stones and dips and horse droppings. Lizzie was not used to walking with a child. People credited her with maternal instincts simply because she volunteered at the Brown Ark, but as treasurer, she worked solely with adults and accounts. She was actually quite awkward around the young wards. Jenny's steps were so small. She labored on the uphill slope to Sutter Street. Lizzie recalculated how long the few blocks would take, and then leaned over and hoisted Jenny.

"You're a bigger girl than I thought," she said, trying to keep the disapproval out of her voice. She could smell Jenny's hair, a stale-molasses smell, not entirely pleasant. If she were mine, Lizzie thought, I would keep her as clean as a kitten.

Jenny refused to put her arms around Lizzie, which would have helped balance her. "Where are we going?" she asked again.

"Do you want to go back?"

"No."

Lizzie turned left at the thorny rose garden of Trinity Church. The wind picked up considerably. A man walked ahead of them, going their same direction on Bush Street. She put Jenny down, glad for a reason to fall farther behind him.

"Will we ever go back?" asked Jenny.

"Yes, of course. Soon. We're just taking the air."

The man had heard them. He turned, but only briefly. Lizzie wondered who he imagined they were, what he imagined they were doing. A woman evinced her class in a variety of ways; Lizzie was good at reading the clues herself and assumed that she was also good at sending them. An unescorted woman could always be misunderstood, but surely the presence of a child conferred respectability. In any case, the man appeared uninterested.

It was very cold. Lizzie began to wish she'd sent Jenny straight back to bed. Why in the world hadn't she? She wished for a different place to go. She wished for lights and more people, or absolute dark and fewer.

"When I was just a little girl like you, you'd hear coyotes out here at night," Lizzie said. "The city hadn't come this far yet. I saw a horse race near this very spot with those big golden horses the Spanish had. It was Diego Estenegas's sixteenth birthday. We had *cascarones*. Do you know what *cascarones* are?"

"No."

"Eggshells filled with perfume and tinsel and flour. You break them over people's heads. Even my father came home streaked with flour."

"Why?"

"My father did business with the Estenegas family. He brokered their beef to local hotels. They were kind enough to include me in the invitation. It was a party."

Jenny sat down in the dirt. "Something's in my shoe," she said. She removed it.

Lizzie was forced to squat beside her. She took Jenny's shoe, shook out a thin stream of sand, like the drift in an hourglass. Lizzie had been to few enough parties as a child. Perhaps that was why this one remained so vivid. How could it be so long ago? She could see her mother, her hair falling from its pins, brandishing an eggshell, but that couldn't have happened, it must have been someone else's mother.

The Spanish women had been beautiful, with their bright dresses and diamond haircombs. Though some had married American husbands, few of the men had taken American wives. Were there really so many fewer Spanish families now, which was the way it seemed, or had the city simply filled in around them with Italians and Irish and Chinese? Diego Estenegas was like a prince and smiled once at Lizzie so she always remembered it.

Her father would have been furious with her if he'd

known she was waiting for a Spanish prince. Her mother would have sent her to bed until she got over the idea. Because she'd managed to keep it a secret, she never had gotten over it.

"You might be Spanish, Jenny," Lizzie said, "what with your dark eyes and hair. *¿Hablas español?*"

Jenny didn't answer. Lizzie replaced her shoe and picked her up. The man was gone. The ground was level again.

The sidewalk began on Octavia Street and ran beneath the blue-gum eucalyptus trees. Mary Ellen Pleasant had planted these herself, only a few years before, but they had grown quickly and were already tall by San Francisco standards. Mrs. Pleasant was rumored to use the bark and the seeds in her brews. Lizzie looked up the trunk to where the leaves hung, clustered and limp as Japanese wind chimes. The trees gave off the smell of unripened lemons.

Lizzie set Jenny down. The House of Mystery was dark, except for one window on the second floor. Its curtains were drawn, and glowed faintly with a backlight of gold. A dog barked in the distance; Lizzie couldn't tell whether it was inside the house or out. "Have you ever been here?" Lizzie asked.

"No."

"I've been to tea here. You can't imagine how beautiful it is. You can't tell from the outside."

"Like a palace?" Jenny asked.

Lizzie had never been to a palace. "Inside, yes. Exactly like."

Suddenly, all around the quiet mansion with its homey golden window was the illusion of tumult. Clouds flew across the sky like enormous birds, making the moonlight blink on and off so the whole landscape flickered. The shadows of the trees scudded over the ground; the wind rattled the leaves.

In all that movement there was no person. Lizzie wouldn't have been surprised if there had been. Reporters sometimes flocked outside the House of Mystery, pigeons pecking for crumbs. Occasionally someone sneaked into the yard to dig for the diamond necklaces Mrs. Pleasant was rumored to have buried there.

Quite inexplicably, everything combined to unnerve Lizzie—the lack of people, the flying clouds, the witches'- brew smell, the single lit window, the Wilkie Collins book at home that she was halfway through. The string of women who'd been murdered on the streets of Whitechapel a year or so ago.

There was a thought Lizzie wished she hadn't had! She tried desperately to unthink it. Diego Estenegas smiling at her.

No good! The women were fed with poisoned grapes. Golden horses! Diamond haircombs! Diamond neck- laces! Their hearts cut out as if they were voodoo chickens! Lizzie's breath was shallow and fast.

Jenny yawned and shivered. Lizzie picked her up and started back to the Ark, moving now as quickly as she could. On Bush Street they passed a pair of young men walking arm in arm. Lizzie heard their footsteps first and was re- lieved to see that there were two of them, and both appar- ently sober.

The men had almost passed before one of them spoke. "Are you an idiot?" he asked, in a tone no one had used with her since her father died. She turned to make sure he was addressing her and not his companion, and this allowed him to come too close. "Out here after dark with a child?" He was shaking his head. "What kind of a mother are you?"

The other man spoke next. "What kind of woman walks the streets at night? Is that what you want men to think?"

They were at least twenty years younger than she, and not so nicely dressed. She would not be chastised by boys. "How does it concern you?"

"We're compelled to see you safely home. It wasn't our plan for the evening."

"Nor is it my plan now."

"We don't want you," said Jenny.

"Go away," said Lizzie. She used her public-speaking voice and she expected to be obeyed. "You must see I wouldn't be here without a compelling reason. You must see that I wouldn't have brought this child out into the cold and dark, in the dead of winter, on a whim." There was an uneven place in the road. Lizzie stumbled.

One man offered his arm. One man offered to take Jenny.

Lizzie refused both offers. She carried Jenny without stopping, all the way to the edge of the Brown Ark's sandy yard, though her arms and back ached as a result. The men strolled beside her, smoking cigars and continuing a private conversation about a friend named Darby who'd recently fallen down a flight of stairs and yet was planning a balloon ascension. Lizzie tried twice more to send them off, but they were enjoying her embarrassment too much.

It was highly likely that one, at least, had blue eyes, but Lizzie refused to permit either of them the dignity of being portentous. There'd be plenty more blue-eyed men to choose from, men she liked better. When she turned in at the Ark, they finally left her, tipping their hats and congratulating themselves, no doubt, on their fine manners.

Lizzie was so angry her jaw hurt. She paused outside to remove Jenny's shoes and brush the sand from her stockings. "Let's not tell," she suggested. "Can you keep a secret?"

"Yes," said Jenny. Lizzie suspected she excelled at it.

"Of course, if they ask us right out, did you walk to Mrs. Pleasant's last night, we won't lie," Lizzie added. "You must never tell a lie, Jenny."

She led Jenny up the stairs to her cot, helped her undress and get into her nightgown. There was no movement or sound; the abandoned girls slept like princesses, each with a scuffed pair of shoes waiting by the bed.

Lizzie returned to the cupola, wishing for her bed at home. She could not get comfortable; she was not tired enough. Cold, anger, and the itchy settee kept her awake. Her first escapade, and nothing had come of it but her own ridiculous panic and the insults of chivalrous men. She had been laughed at in the public streets.

But by the morning she saw things quite differently. She had gotten away with it completely. Surely her impulsiveness could only improve. It just wanted practice.

FOUR

By morning Lizzie was finally tired. She went home for a restorative nap. On the breakfast table, she found an invitation from the Putnams. "I'll watch over Lizzie until the day she weds," Mrs. Putnam had once promised Lizzie's mother, and she'd been as good as her word. Lizzie's mother was on her deathbed at the time, so the promise was a binding one. So many people watching over Lizzie! Of course, no one had imagined Lizzie's wedding day to be quite so far off as it was proving.

She slit the Putnams' invitation open with her father's marble-handled letter knife and read that she was to be included in an evening of inquiry, in Suite 540 at the Palace. Dr. Ellinwood, a medium visiting from Philadelphia, would host an informal discussion of spiritism and its compatibility with the tenets of Christianity. If the aspects were favorable, if the guests then desired it, Dr. Ellinwood was prepared to contact the dead. "Such an obliging man," Mrs. Putnam wrote, "for you can't imagine how exhausting Contact is."

And yet Lizzie could imagine this perfectly well. Lizzie didn't really want to talk to the dead. It was a difficult thing to say to the Putnams. It was a difficult thing to acknowledge even to herself. Her parents had loved her. They were entitled to be deeply missed. Lizzie didn't want to be present when they came back and discovered they were not.

Besides, she had gone to séances before, heard many a table rapped, been a link in many a magnetic chain. In her experience, the dead had surprisingly little of interest to say. It seemed to be all me, me, me, after you died.

And on the other hand, the Palace! Eight hundred rooms, seven floors, and an enormous amber skylight topping the whole. The opulent hotel had been built with the profits of the Comstock Lode supplemented by the embezzlement of the Bank of California. Leland Stanford was the first name on its guestbook, Charles Crocker the first to enter its dining room.

Only recently the gaslamps in the restaurant had been replaced with three hundred twenty electric lights. In the suites themselves, major improvements were rumored to have been made in the bathrooms. If a ladylike opportunity presented itself, Lizzie would like to see one of those bathrooms.

Plus, the Putnams were rich and charitable and would invite more of the same. Contact with the dead would put all present in mind of their immortal souls. It was the best possible setting in which to ask for money. The Brown Ark needed more beds, the children coats and shoes. In point of fact, Lizzie had a clear duty to attend.

The evening of inquiry took place on the very next Saturday. Outside, a chilly rain fell, and the Putnams had kindly offered their carriage. Lizzie paused to remove her gloves and pet Roscoe, the closest of the horses. She had driven Roscoe herself as a girl. Blind in one eye, so you had to use a single rein or he wandered to the wrong side of the road, but utterly unprovocable, with a gait like cream. The rain left shiny streaks on his coat. His neck was warm and wet on Lizzie's hand, and he steamed like a teakettle in the cold.

She climbed into the carriage and the comfortable heat of Mrs. Putnam. Mrs. Putnam was an ample woman, dressed against the cold in a fashionable sealskin sacque and a new black straw hat. "Erma's had her fourth. A little boy," Mrs. Putnam told Lizzie straight off, hugging her so tightly she left the scent of almond soap on her sleeves. Erma was the Putnams' only child, and everyone imagined Lizzie was fond of her. Certainly they'd played together often as children. But since Erma had married and moved to Sacramento more than fifteen years before, Lizzie had hardly seen her.

"Six and a half pounds. Little Charlie John. The mother blooming. Father bursting with pride."

"Never you mind, now, Lizzie," Mr. Putnam said, when Lizzie didn't mind in the least. Any marriage that necessitated a move to Sacramento was nothing to envy.

Mrs. Mullin was seated opposite Lizzie. She was a gaunt woman with dark, deep-set eyes; it was hard to look at her face without imagining her skull. Her hat was more opulent but less smart than Mrs. Putnam's. Emerald wings spread over the crown as if her hair were a nest on which a headless bird brooded. "We'll see you with your own babies yet," she told Lizzie.

"I have sixty-two babies at present." Lizzie kept her tone light.

"That's the way to look at it," Mr. Putnam said. He turned to his wife. "Our Lizzie has sixty-two babies!"

Lizzie didn't often mind not being married. She'd had offers. Few women in San Francisco went entirely un-courted, and none of those had yellow hair and financial prospects. Dr. Beecher, a friend of her father's, had taken a fancy to her when she was just a girl. Strange how people would think better of her now if she'd only accepted him then, and him a man with a coarse manner, who smelled of brine, but dirty, and who stared at her as though she were something to be killed and eaten. Cats fled when Dr. Beecher entered a room.

Even now, her father's fury over her refusal was an aw-ful thing to remember. She'd spent five whole weeks con-fined to her bedroom under Baby Edward's reproachful eyes, and she suspected her mother had sent her there for protection as much as punishment. In the ten years be-tween her mother's death and her father's, Lizzie learnt what a shield her mother had been.

But even in the midst of his rage, Lizzie had never re-considered. And she hadn't known about copulation then; she'd merely wished to avoid dining at one end of a table with Dr. Beecher at the other. He was still alive, and some girl even younger than Lizzie had married him. She couldn't bear to think of it.

When she was in her thirties, Lizzie's body had developed a pronounced restlessness, a physical ache that was bone-deep and could manifest at any moment, from any cause. This was unsettling, but it wasn't her, of course, only her body. She didn't even know what was wanted; it might have nothing at all to do with men. When the feeling hit too hard, she dosed herself with baths and novels. She was in love with the men in books and particularly with the men in books written by women. She liked to describe herself as a passionate reader, knowing no one would take her full meaning.

The only thing she minded about not being married was how everyone knew. If she could have passed as widowed, there would have been little else to regret. She was not pitied by her friends so much as criticized. In San Francisco, demographics being what they were, an unmarried woman was looked upon as the most selfish of creatures.

Lizzie disliked being thought selfish, mainly because it was so likely true. She lacked the gift for intimacy. "The real woman regards all men, be they older or younger than herself, not as possible lovers, but as sort of stepsons toward whom her heart goes out in motherly tenderness," Lizzie had recently read. Where in the world was her own motherly tenderness? All spent on the characters in books.

"What if none of us married!" her mother had said in a voice like scratched glass at the time of Lizzie's second refusal. The new suitor was Paul Burbank, a quiet, clean law clerk whose main demerits were that saliva puddled whitely at the corners of his mouth when he talked and that he didn't seem actually to like Lizzie. She'd found him at the other end of her tangled string during the cobweb ball marking Erma Putnam's debut. She'd seen his face as she wound her way toward him, seen the moment he realized she was his partner for the evening, and he hadn't been pleased. Even when he'd proposed, he'd acted as though he had no choice in the matter. "What if we all thought only of ourselves and our own pleasures?" her mother asked.

This sentiment was echoed often enough in the daily press. A generation before, America's sons had perished in inconceivable numbers, in inconceivable agony, on the battlefields of the Civil War. Such a contrast to America's spoiled, selfish daughters. And them wanting the vote, some of them, likely the very ones with no children wanting it the loudest of all!

"I wash my hands of you," her father said at the time of her third refusal—Christopher Ludlow, an irritable flautist—but it turned out he'd washed more than that.

After her father's death, Mr. Griswold, the family solicitor, was too embarrassed to read his will aloud to Lizzie. They sat in her father's office with the smell of bourbon and cigars still hanging in the air. "There's a monthly allowance," Mr. Griswold said merely. "With stipulations. I want you to know I strongly advised against them." He passed the pages to her.

"I fear my estate," her father had written, "will make my daughter the target of fortune hunters. Elizabeth wouldn't marry while I was alive and wished it. I won't have her marrying on her own authority after my death.

"Old women are even more foolish than young ones. Let her live to be a hundred, these conditions will not change. On her wedding day all monies to her instantly cease."

"I'm willing to contest the terms," Mr. Griswold offered, "should an attractive offer of marriage ever be

made." Lizzie was at this time already thirty-seven years
old, and his tone suggested the unlikeliness of further pro-
posals. She agreed that no legal redress was necessary.
Contesting the will might suggest she wished to be married;
it would make her publicly ridiculous. She'd told herself
that she didn't even want money given so grudgingly, which
made her feel very high-minded, like the heroine of a romance, but now she often thought it would have also been
romantic to be wealthy. She would have made her own donations to the running of the Ark instead of having con-
stantly to beg them from others.

The carriage rocked. The sounds of the horses' hooves
and the rain were wonderfully steadying. Lizzie's necklace
danced in the space between her breasts; she caught it in her
hand. No one raised money for charity by sulking, she reminded herself. She contrived to brighten her voice. "Sixty-
two babies is more beds than the Home can offer. The
need always grows so much faster than the treasury. . . ."

No one was listening. "Little Charlie John"—Mrs.
Mullin threaded her knobby fingers together—"I long to see
him!" while Mr. Putnam fussed aloud that the weather
might worsen during the evening. "I mind for the sake of
the horses," he said. "I fear for poor old Roscoe's footing."

Lizzie did not press. She sat quietly, biding her time,
bouncing when the carriage bounced and listening to talk
of late rains in earlier years and how the roses and helio-
trope had not been pruned as they should be in the fall, so
there would be the very devil to pay for it soon, and that six
and a half pounds was neither so very large for a baby nor
so very small, but was, in fact, just right, until the driver
turned into the circular driveway of the Palace.

The courtyard was heated by enormous bronze braziers and covered with the dome of the amber skylight seven floors above them. Every balcony was lit; the hotel glowed like a birthday cake.

A huge hydraulic elevator took them to the fifth floor. From there they looked down on the Grand Court, with its splendor of Persian rugs, purple tablecloths, the flickering rose and gold of women's fans, the sharp black of men's evening coats, the bronze of the spittoons.

"San Francisco will not be civilized until the men stop spitting indoors," someone famous had said, but Lizzie didn't remember who. In any case, he was surely mistaken, because tonight the spittoons were dazzling in the hot civilized glare of electricity.

Lizzie had only the vaguest notion what electricity was. Lightning, she thought, collected and tamed somehow, broken to harness and spread throughout the room as evenly as melted butter. But there was something about the view that was not quite right tonight; something besides the lighting was different, only Lizzie couldn't determine what it was. She gave up trying and followed the Putnams down the corridor.

Suite 540 had high ceilings, bay windows, and Louis XV chairs. On one wall was a landscape of Yosemite, Half Dome at sunrise, with a tiny party of mules at its base. Dr. Ellinwood stood at the door to greet them.

He was a small man, smooth-faced, pink-skinned. His hair was the color of goose feathers, and something of the same consistency. His ears were large and round. His eyes, Lizzie noted, were brown. "I'm so glad you could join us in our little adventure," he said. "Mrs. Mullin, what a stunning hat!"

Lizzie was sorry to see Myrtle Rolphe across the room. Miss Rolphe ran a Christian school in Chinatown and was universally admired for it. Undoubtedly she also was there for money.

Sure enough, Miss Rolphe addressed the Putnam party first thing. "May I talk to you about one of my boys?" Her hands clasped and unclasped with charming earnestness as she spoke, and her voice had a throaty sweetness. Such an unfair advantage! If Lizzie could have duplicated it, she would have. "Eleven years old," said Miss Rolphe. "The brightest, sweetest child you'll ever see. And so eager to come to Jesus. His name is Ti Wong."

"He's lucky to have you," Mr. Putnam said encouragingly. "This young Mr. Ti. Whatever you're up against, you'll win through." Mr. Putnam was the sort of gentleman who felt obliged to flirt with any woman, but Myrtle Rolphe was especially flirtable—young, given to blushes, with a neck as white as a meringue.

"The forces arrayed against me are all of China!" she answered, her throat quivering like a wren's. "Wong is an orphan who lives with his aunt and uncle. He first came to us four years ago. I never saw a child so young so determined to belong to Jesus. His eyes when he sings! Then all of a sudden his uncle withdrew him. He told me he wanted no Jesus boy in the house."

Dr. Ellinwood was requesting their attention. Miss Rolphe acknowledged this by lowering her voice. "Last week I happened to see Ti Wong again. He's very troubled. His uncle demands that he participate in ancestor worship. If we don't find a way to remove him from the company of other Chinese, Jesus will lose him forever."

"Please!" said Dr. Ellinwood. His voice was loud and firm, though he was smiling good-naturedly. "Please come and sit."

"Do you think he might work at the Brown Ark?" Miss Rolphe asked Lizzie. "He so needs to be with other Christians."

"I'd have to ask," said Lizzie, fully aware that Nell would say no.

"Eleven years old, but he works like an adult."

"Let's not keep the dead waiting, ladies!" Dr. Ellinwood said pleadingly, when surely, of all people, the dead had time.

The chairs were arranged in a semicircle, at whose mouth stood a large cabinet with a glass door. This cabinet was open at the top and bottom, like a sentry box on wheels. A curtain of black velvet fell behind the glass. Dr. Ellinwood draped a cloak, also black velvet, over his shoulders. The cloak was lined with purple silk and had the signs of the zodiac embroidered in gold. The effect of this on Dr. Ellinwood was comical, a Christmas elf on All Hallows' Eve.

He then led a discussion on the compatibility of religion and science. Lizzie had no qualms herself on this score. She had a great interest in the Higher Criticism, through which the sources of biblical narratives were scientifically examined. She felt that such activities could only strengthen one's faith, by demonstrating the reliability of its origins; to object, as many in the church did, seemed to Lizzie to suggest a troubling doubt as to the findings. The God that Lizzie believed in was not the sort to set such traps for the faithful.

This evening's discussion came quickly to the same conclusion—although spiritism had had early, unfortunate associations with free love, it had long before outgrown and discarded them. A scientifically conducted dialogue with the dead could only, ultimately, reflect the Glory of God. Dr. Ellinwood invoked the name of Eilley Orrum several times during the discussion; apparently he was personally acquainted with the celebrated Washoe seeress. He contrived to give the impression that she wholeheartedly endorsed him as a fellow traveler in the realm of the occult. The whole thing took less than an hour, and then they were free to proceed.

Mrs. Putnam read aloud from Elizabeth Stuart Phelps's *Songs of the Silent World:*

> *"Death is a mood of life. It is no whim*
> *By which life's Giver mocks a broken heart.*
> *Death is life's reticence. Still audible to Him*
> *the hushed voice, happy, speaketh on apart . . ."*

while Dr. Ellinwood invited Myrtle Rolphe to tie his hands. He took a seat in the cabinet and allowed Mrs. Putnam to tie his ankles. "If everyone will please take the hand of the person next," the fettered Dr. Ellinwood then said, "right hands on left wrists, all around the circle."

He sent one of his agents to draw the curtains and put out the lights. The room vanished into utter black.

Miss Rolphe held Lizzie's wrist, and Lizzie held Mrs. Mullin's. Miss Rolphe's fingers were soft. Mrs. Mullin's wrist was cold and dry as wood, but pulsed forcefully. "I need everyone's absolute concentration now," Dr. Ellinwood told them. "Please shut out everything else." Lizzie heard the cabinet door open and close.

She expected an artful period of prolonged tension, but Dr. Ellinwood sacrificed drama for efficiency. The knocking began almost at once. Then an unfamiliar voice whispered into the silence. "Who has come here tonight? Who wishes something from someone on the other side?" Miss Rolphe's fingers fluttered over Lizzie's wrist.

The voice did not sound like Dr. Ellinwood, but Lizzie had no doubt that was who it was. Why else put the lights out? She couldn't even see the shapes of the women on either side of her, although she could hear each time Mrs. Mullin exhaled. The wind sent the rain against the window with a sound like the tapping of fingernails. Ordinarily such a sound would have made Lizzie feel warm, cozy, sheltered. Tonight it made her skin inch up the back of her neck. Mrs. Mullin's pulse throbbed against her fingertips as if trapped there.

"Please," said the voice. "I've come such a long way. Someone must need to communicate."

"Is my Aunt Rose there?" Miss Rolphe asked quietly. "I'd love to speak to Rose Schubert."

Rose was indeed present. She told them how peaceful it was to be dead. "Like sleeping in your mother's arms again." She and Miss Rolphe exchanged some family gossip; she told Miss Rolphe to be especially careful on the night of the nineteenth. More departed relatives were called. There were mysterious footsteps. A strong scent of roses. The usual rappings. The sleep-inducing darkness and the whispers of the dead.

Lizzie's attention began to stray. She suddenly realized what was wrong with the view of the Grand Court. All the waiters in the restaurant were white. The Palace was famous for its Negro waiters. She heard her parents' names.

"Harriet?" Mrs. Putnam was asking. "Harriet or Wellington Hayes? Are you there, my dears?"

Lizzie supposed Dr. Ellinwood had spent the afternoon cadging information about the Hayes family from the unsuspecting Putnams. The idea annoyed her. She dropped Mrs. Mullin's hand, deliberately breaking the magnetic chain, but Mrs. Mullin's sharp fingers closed over hers like a cat's paw on a bird's wing.

"We have your Lizzie here," said Mrs. Mullin. Her words resounded loudly in the absolute darkness. "Harriet?"

"Lizzie?" A tiny, sleepy, faraway voice came from behind. "Is it Lizzie?"

"Speak up, dear." Mrs. Mullin squeezed Lizzie's hand. "Your mother is asking for you."

"Yes, Mother," said Lizzie. Mrs. Mullin's nails dug into her skin. "I'm sitting right here."

"Oh, Lizzie. Your father says to tell you we miss you. And our darling Edward. He loves you very much."

"I love you, too."

"We're all watching over you now!"

Lizzie had never doubted it. "Thank you, Mother." She thought to provide a distraction. "Mrs. Mullin is here."

"But Lizzie, you have us so anxious."

"And the Putnams. Your dear, dear friends."

"Why do you put us through this worry? You were always so dependable. What's come over you?" The voice was beginning to sound like her mother's, after all. It had her mother's disappointed, unsurprised tone. It came closer, spoke in her ear. Lizzie thought she could have touched it, if Mrs. Mullin and Miss Rolphe weren't holding her hands so resolutely. Everything Miss Rolphe did was resolutely done. There was no reason for Lizzie to find this irritating. Miss Rolphe was a thoroughly admirable young woman.

Lizzie's corset was cutting off her air. Mrs. Mullin's grip was cutting off her circulation. Lizzie's fingertips began to throb. "Mother, I'm the treasurer for a charitable home. I'm quite good at it. I have sixty-two wards at present." The wind whined outside. Something scraped against the window.

"You're our only living child. We should be at peace. You never used to behave this way."

"What way? What have I done?" This was rash, and Lizzie immediately wished she could retract it. She was letting the mere semblance of her mother get to her, and in front of everyone, too. But even as she told herself to calm down, she felt her agitation growing.

"Stay away from Mammy Pleasant."

Lizzie shook abruptly free of Myrtle. "Don't tell me what to do, Mother!" she said. Her voice was loud and angry and unlike her voice.

Never before had she spoken that way to her mother in public. There was a stunned pause and then a shaft of light, as if someone had opened the door into the corridor. A gust hit the window like an explosion. The glass of the cabinet shivered and cracked into a spider web of fissures. Through the glass, a multitude of green hands and staring faces could be seen. They seemed to slide through the cracks, evaporating immediately, flattened and bleached, into the material world.

FIVE

*I*t took an entire glass of sour wine to calm Lizzie down. Everyone was looking at her, and she hated this above all things. Her corset was sawing her in half. She had the ghosts of ghosts burning in orange afterimages under her eyelids, which could easily bring on a headache, and she would blame Dr. Ellinwood if she got one, for all the good that would do.

Dr. Ellinwood hovered, rubbing his wrists where the bonds had been, to emphasize their tightness. "Obviously I unleashed something I couldn't control," he told the group. "I blame myself. Calling the dead is not a party game." He apologized to them all, just as if he hadn't orchestrated the entire catastrophe.

Which, of course, he had. From the other side of the

wine, Lizzie could see that her mother had not come back, certainly not. Was Lizzie the only one who'd read that Margaret Fox, the most famous of the American table-rappers, had admitted to fraud? Lizzie didn't know how Dr. Ellinwood performed his illusions, but that was no reason to credit them. Surely the dead led lives of more dignity than this feeble, grasping, greenish manifesting.

Mrs. Mullin raised her voice. "Dr. Ellinwood? Do you think the dead can still tell lies?"

"They can indeed," he assured her. "But they have no reason to." Which was, Lizzie thought, practically an admission of guilt.

She herself regretted nothing. She wished only that she'd been louder and ruder. In the category of small mercies, at least there'd been no ectoplasm.

Half an hour later Lizzie was safely back in the carriage and clattering out of the Palace courtyard. The rain was falling harder and colder. The streetlamps shone in the damp, soft and rainbowed like bubbles. On Mrs. Putnam's instructions, the driver was urging the horses to hurry—at Roscoe's age! with the road so wet!—and Lizzie couldn't help feeling guilty about this. Roscoe himself could scarcely believe it. He would take a quick pace or two, then slow until whipped, then take another quick pace, then slow again. His obstinacy was affecting the other horse. The carriage rocked like a train, bumped like a boat.

Rain was too ordinary in San Francisco to spoil a Saturday night. The streets were brightly lit. Sheltered under canopies and alcoves, bands played bravely along their route—ecstatic polkas and somber Salvation Army hymns. The carriage passed phrenologists and shooting galleries and the Snake Drugstore, with rattlers coiled in its windows. Revolutionaries shouted from the steps of jewelry stores, salesmen offered the afflicted the revivifying powers of aconite, tiger fat, and belts stuffed with cayenne pepper. The *nymphes du pavé* beckoned from beneath umbrellas, their smiles wet, scarlet, and practiced.

Mrs. Putnam was not speaking to her. Lizzie was clearly meant to feel guilty about this as well, but the impact was lessened by Mr. Putnam's need to fill any silence with labored gallantries. He was a naturally garrulous man; now he also appeared to be drunk. Mr. Putnam noted that Mrs. Mullin's shawl was as good as Italian, that Lizzie's color was attractively up. He observed his own good fortune in being the only man among three such elegant ladies. He informed them that the king of Hawaii, Kalakaua, was staying at the Palace. The livery boy had said so when he brought the carriage around. "They say he is very ill." Mr. Putnam's voice was serious and subdued. "Might die." Rain plonked on the fabric roof of the carriage, slid down the glass windows.

"Surely not," Lizzie answered politely, although how did she know? She imagined the stretched green dead people dispersing throughout the Palace, inhaled out of one room and exhaled into another through the pneumatic tubes. She couldn't imagine this would improve the king's chances.

"Death comes to king and commoner alike," Mr. Putnam intoned. He shook his head sadly.

And what if it didn't? People always said things like

that as if it were such a shame, but how much more of a shame would it be if death were selective? A brougham crossed them on the left. The driver sat, hunched in a thick wool coat, rain dripping from the brim of his hat onto his hands. A gray horse shook rainwater from its mane. The brougham's windows were draped, but twitched briefly as they passed. Lizzie had a quick glimpse of a woman's eyes in a veiled face.

"In Hawaii, they admire a dark skin," Mrs. Mullin said. "They see it as a mark of royal blood. The king is very dark."

"In Hawaii they admire a stout figure," Mr. Putnam said. "Not merely stout. Actually fat." Mr. Putnam was himself a remarkably thin man.

"I just this moment remembered." Mrs. Mullin was seated next to Lizzie, opposite Mrs. Putnam. She leaned forward as the carriage wheel hit a hole, and the broody, headless wings on her hat jumped in an unpleasant parody of flight. "You were there at the ball the night Mammy Pleasant turned colored."

Mrs. Putnam nodded once, a sharp, brief nod. Her face was turned away toward the street. The hair around her ears bobbed gently; the feather in her hat shook. In fact, she was atremble from head to toe. It was the carriage making her so. That, and the angry stiffness of her spine, a forced rigidity adding much to her bouncing.

The real cause, of course, was Lizzie's insulting behavior. Mrs. Putnam believed that mothers and the dead should be treated with the utmost deference. Rudeness to one's mother when she was also dead was beyond the beyond.

"Oh, yes," said Mr. Putnam. "Yes, indeed. Everyone was there. Mr. Ralston. Senator Sharon. Mr. Bell. Of course, they were young men, they were no one important yet. They were just like us. And all of them lining up to dance with her. She was a looker. No one called her Mammy that night."

"And her not nearly as young as everyone thought, neither," Mrs. Mullin noted.

Mrs. Putnam directed herself strictly to Mrs. Mullin; Lizzie was still only getting the profile. "And out of the blue, she just says it. I'm a colored woman, she says. I thought it was a joke, when I first heard about it. More and more people from the South were arriving then, with the war coming, so she must have known she'd be exposed. People from the South, they know what to look for."

"Once you were told, it was obvious," said Mr. Putnam. "She was dark. We all knew she was Spanish or something. But Ralston, Sharon, Bell, and her, they were great friends even after. They all got rich together."

"Nothing more needs be said on the subject." Mrs. Putnam shook her head, then continued. "There were so few respectable women in the city back then. No one maintaining standards. Vigilantes and hoodlums roaming the streets, vying with each other to see who could make the most misery for the most people. But those days are past and in the past may stay."

Roscoe had settled back into his usual pace with his usual roll. The ride had smoothed accordingly. The sounds of the rain on the fabric roof, of hooves and wheels on pavement, the warmth of the Putnams' lap robes, the smell of perfume and horsehair, and the wine she had taken medicinally combined to make Lizzie sleepy. She closed her eyes and let the conversation float over her. She'd heard about rough San Francisco all her life; she even remembered a bit of it. This and the sleepiness made her feel young as a girl.

"And then there was that business with Mrs. Bell," said Mrs. Putnam. Lizzie opened her eyes. "People have all but forgot about that. He's living on Bush Street, like a bachelor. She's over on Sutter with two of his children and calling herself Mrs. Percy. One minute the papers say they're married, the next, not. She vanishes for months, and Mrs. Pleasant hires the Pinks to track her down. And then Mrs. Pleasant up and invites everyone to a wedding party as if all is right as rain. With Thomas Bell still denying he's a married man."

"Were you invited to that as well?" asked Mrs. Mullin.

"I wouldn't have gone," said Mrs. Putnam, and no doubt she wouldn't have, though this clearly meant no.

The carriage swung slightly, following the curve of Mission Street. They were leaving the lamps of the downtown, heading into darkness. Lizzie covered a yawn with her hand. "What happened to the Palace's Negro waiters?" she asked.

"Fired," Mrs. Mullin told her. "Just this week. One of them was caught filching food from the kitchen, so Morgan fired the lot of them. You see how old and toothless Mrs. Pleasant has become since the Sharon business. No one would have dared do that to the colored when she was younger. She's always been a great one for the courts."

"Oh, Lizzie." Mrs. Putnam turned and seized Lizzie's hands, shaking her fully awake. Her face shone in the carriage, dim and yellowed by the black hat and deeply creased, pocked as the moon. She was a decade younger than Mrs. Pleasant, but she looked a decade older. "I have nothing against the hardworking colored. You know I believe in judging people by their hearts. But you don't know how treacherous she can be. Will you promise me not to see her? For your dear, dear mother's sake?"

When Lizzie was fifty instead of forty, she would still be a child to the Putnams. She didn't mind; it was one of the things she loved about them. Nobody else could make her feel young now that she so definitely wasn't.

One afternoon when Lizzie was twelve, and Erma seven, they'd begged to eat their supper on the Putnams' back lawn. They were playing castaways, they were playing Robinson Crusoe—Lizzie's idea, of course; this was a book she'd been allowed to read early, all except for the chapter with the pirates. "You'll break a dish," Mrs. Putnam protested, and they promised to be ever so careful.

"We'll make maps," Lizzie said, getting overexcited as usual, and then, racing into the house for pencils, she stepped on the pink rosebuds of her dirty plate, heard it crack, and ran home without another word to anyone, before Erma even knew. An hour or so later, Mrs. Putnam appeared in her room. "I hope the day never comes when I care more for a dish than for a little girl," Mrs. Putnam said. She didn't even tell Lizzie's mother. How could Lizzie ever bear to refuse her anything?

She opened her mouth to accede. In that moment she saw, through her left eye, the tiny disturbance in the air, the silver flash that presaged a headache. The emerald wings on Mrs. Mullin's hat hung like a hawk. There was a gummy silence within the carriage; without it, the mounting drumbeat of rain and hooves. She closed her mouth in a panic. Her vision improved immediately.

"Do you know what voodoo is?" Mrs. Mullin swayed in the carriage and her voice became a whisper. "What it *really* is? Black arts aimed at the destruction of the white race."

"You don't believe in magic, do you, Mrs. Mullin? Hocus-pocus? Habeas corpus?" Mr. Putnam shifted in his seat so as to engage Lizzie's eyes, involve her in the joke.

"I believe in malice. As if you or I or poor, fanciful, inconsequential little Lizzie could ever do Mammy Pleasant a speck of harm."

Lizzie's eyesight had normalized, but her breathing had not. Her voice was oddly tilted. "She came to the Brown Ark on business," she told Mrs. Putnam. "I don't expect her back, but I can't promise not to see her on business. I have to do whatever's best for the children." She touched her hands together to reassure herself that they were both warm. She pressed her fingers to her forehead.

"Her business is just what I want you kept out of," Mrs. Putnam said.

Lizzie lowered her hands and saw Mrs. Mullin patting Mrs. Putnam's knee. "Lizzie's not her usual type," Mrs. Mullin said. Mrs. Pleasant's usual type was a fragile beauty like Mrs. Bell.

"Lizzie is being very obstinate," Mrs. Putnam complained.

"Lizzie looks very handsome this evening," Mr. Putnam observed without looking at her. "I have spent the evening with three very handsome ladies."

"Are you getting one of your headaches, dear?" Mrs. Putnam asked.

"No," Lizzie said cautiously. It appeared not. She began to feel the charged, sweet heat of relief rising inside her.

"She was the most wonderful cook," Mr. Putnam said. All three women turned to look at him. He raised his hands in protest. "I was never at her table, myself. But everyone says. Cajun crab cakes and candied figs. Wine jellies. Caraway cheese. Dishes from the South."

And then Roscoe stopped, because Lizzie was home. She looked through the rain to her dark, cold house. A woman who had just released a quantity of dead people, including her own angry mother, into the city should probably not sleep alone. E.D.E.N. Southworth's *The Hidden Hand* lay on her bedstead, a popular, feverish book, and she was just up to the chapter where robbers hid themselves under little Capitola's bed.

Mr. Putnam prepared to help her down. Outside the carriage she heard Roscoe shake himself. She did the mental equivalent. Nonsense, she told herself firmly.

There was no room under her bed for a pack of robbers.

The green people were a fraud and an illusion.

And anyway, her mother's spirit, if it was loose at all, was at the Palace Hotel and surely happy. The Palace would be her mother's idea of heaven, especially if there was also a king dying there.

Teresa
Bell

———

ONE

Whatever complaints Lizzie may have had concerning her mother were slight compared with Teresa Bell's complaints regarding hers. Teresa Bell was obsessed. She referred to her mother often in conversation and, late in her life, wrote two similar accounts of their relationship. One of these she sent to the physician who attended her in her final years. The other formed the heart of her Last Will and Testament. Teresa Bell died in 1923.

Her maternal grandfather was one Colonel Nathaniel Tibbals. Colonel Tibbals distinguished himself during the Revolutionary War and was given, for his services, a parcel of land in Auburn, New York. He married Sarah Lydia Ward, one of a family of celebrated Kentucky beauties, and together they raised four healthy children.

The youngest was the youngest by far, and her father, rather an elderly man by the time she was born, doted most upon her. She had her own harp, her own pony, and she knew her own mind. Her name was Elmina Caroline, and her father would hear nothing against her. He died when she was only eleven.

Some years later Elmina married Wessel Harris. She brought six hundred acres of farmland to the marriage, as well as her own considerable beauty; he thought himself the luckiest man in the world. He kissed his bride and commenced his living happily ever after.

But in the next years he faced the inexplicable loss of his first two children. Both of them boys, they were full-weight, pink-cheeked, active babies. Labor and births unremarkable. Yet neither lived to see four months. When a third child was born, a pretty girl who favored her mother, with eyes like cornflowers and hair like cornsilk, Elmina refused even to hold her. Before the child was three months old, her father came home to find her stripped to the skin and set outside on a windowsill, sobbing her heart out in the soaking rain.

Wessel wrapped the baby warmly in an old, soft undershirt, tucked her inside his coat, and walked off in the storm. Five miles away lived the family of a bricklayer named John Clingan. The Clingans had recently lost their middle daughter, Matilda. Wessel Harris gave his baby to the Clingan family, and she remained with them for many years.

She was visited often by her grandmother Tibbals, her father, and even occasionally by her mother. One day her mother arrived alone. She took the child to play in a creek that ran through the Clingans' lot. The girl made a pile of wet silvery rocks. Elmina removed her own shoes and stockings and tucked up her skirt. She knelt and splashed her face with water while her hair tumbled down. She looked like a wild creature, a doe, a naiad.

"Come here," she told her daughter. "Come see the crawdad hiding in this pool here."

"I hear voices in the wind," the little girl confessed. She went to meet her mother's outstretched hand.

"What do the voices tell you?" Elmina asked.

The little girl didn't like to say, since the voices were telling her to run away. She felt her mother's damp fingers moving down her cheek to her shoulder. "Just my name," the little girl said. She really did hear her name.

"Kneel down here so you can look." Her mother's hand moved from her shoulder to the back of her neck. "Lean forward."

The little girl knelt with her face nearly touching the water. She saw how the surface twitched with waterbugs, how big and shivery the rocks looked. She thought she saw the crawdad's claws under one of those rocks. "Run while you can," the wind whispered. "Run away, Teresa. Teresa."

"Teresa! There you are!" her grandmother Tibbals said. She was out of breath and gulping like a fish. She came down the bank, sliding in her haste, losing her footing. "You're wanted back at the house." She pulled the child from Elmina's hands.

"Yes," Elmina said. She gathered her dripping hair together, twisted it so the water streamed down her arms. "You run along now, dear, since Mrs. Clingan needs you so immediately."

The Clingans may have been a hasty choice. Mrs. Clingan was a drunken, abusive mother. Mr. Clingan was a cardplayer who lost more than he won. There were two daughters in the family already—Mary Jane, who was six years older than Teresa, and Kate, who was four years older. "I know why you live with us," Kate said one day when Teresa was seven years old. Kate had light brown hair and a fat face.

"She's not to say." Mary Jane shook her head. "You're not to say," she told Kate.

"I didn't say I'd tell. I just said I know." Kate leaned toward Teresa, her lips pinched together so the words wouldn't pop out inadvertently.

Mary Jane dropped a hint. "It's the same reason your mother can't visit you alone."

"It's because she wants to kill you," Kate said. "Just like she killed your brothers."

This was instantly plausible. Wasn't Mrs. Clingan always saying, I'll kill you if you can't be quiet? I'll kill you if those dishes aren't washed when I get home? "Just like *your* mother," Teresa said, understanding, and the two girls looked at her with suddenly angry mouths and waspish little eyes.

"No," they told her.

"It's not anything at all like," said Kate.

In Teresa's will she refers to the Clingans as a bogus crew who may try to claim a blood relationship to her. She singles out Kate in particular as one of the vilest characters on earth, who once "even tried to claim that my father Wessel Harris begot me with the aid of her mother. Wessel was my father and her mother was my mother, so she said."

"Well, someone needs to tell you," Kate finished. "Because now your mother's run off and no one knows where she is or what she's up to. I'd be plenty scared if I was you."

The wind told Teresa to leave the horrible Clingans, to run away to the creek, but now she could hear that it spoke in her mother's voice, and she was too frightened to obey it ever again. She didn't leave the house for several days, and she didn't see Elmina for many years.

Mr. Clingan died. A neighbor turned the family in to the county and they were all shipped off to the county farm. Teresa went, too, her father and grandmother apparently unable or unwilling to intervene. From the farm the children were fostered out to separate homes. Teresa was now twelve.

"That I live is a wonder," Teresa wrote later in a letter to her doctor. "But that my soul lives is a still greater wonder." Describing herself at age twelve, she says she was "proud, sensitive, and refined clear beyond her years," with a delicacy of perception and a purity of soul. These things she attributed entirely to her father, Wessel Harris. Blood will tell, she often liked to say. We cannot know which of these qualities—the delicacy or the purity—first attracted the attention of a young man like James Percy.

Mr. Percy came calling when she was seventeen. He sat with Teresa in the parlor of a shabby boardinghouse that catered mostly to immigrants. The most intimate business could be conducted in that parlor, and if the conversation was in English, one's privacy was complete. James Percy's business with Teresa was of the most intimate sort. "I want to tell you everything I see in your eyes," he was saying. "I can read your fortune in them if you'll only look at me."

And then he suddenly stood. Teresa turned to see why, and there was Elmina, faintly reflected in the cracked glass of the parlor doors, in an expensive lilac dress. She didn't seem to have aged a minute, but then the parlor was a dim room, no good for sewing or reading whatever the time of day. Elmina entered and sat on a dirty chair, her skirt billowing in a lilac froth about her legs. "Aren't you pretty?" she said to Teresa. "Could I have just a moment alone with you, dear? If the gentleman will kindly excuse us?"

Teresa caught James's hand. "Don't go," she said, and he sat again.

"Which of us is the prettier, do you think?" Elmina asked him. She was flirting, in her costly dress, with her hair coiled about her head like a snake. Teresa might have been in rags by comparison.

"I couldn't possibly choose," James said, "when faced with two such beautiful women."

"Now you're teasing me. Though there are those think I've held up rather well for such an old lady, I won't deny it. But beauty can't last forever. That's why a woman wants children. So her beauty will survive her. It pleases a beautiful woman to have a beautiful daughter."

"You must be very pleased."

"Teresa is my only living child," Elmina said. "Naturally I'm proud of her."

It wasn't until Elmina left that Teresa realized she was still allowing James to hold her hand. He tried to kiss her then, because that was the idea her fingers had given him. That night Teresa blocked her door with a chair and kept her window closed.

The next day Kate Clingan drove by. She was a swollen tick of a woman but, even so, already married, and really her name now was Kate Gray. "Your father has died," she said. She didn't even get out of the wagon to say this. "He left six hundred acres of land and he left it to you instead of your mother. It only goes to Elmina if you die before she does. I thought you should know. I thought you should know she was there when they read the will and she said it was her land from her father, not your land from yours."

Teresa left New York hastily at the age of seventeen and in the company of James Percy. She arrived in San Francisco when she was twenty-three. She was calling herself Mrs. Percy in 1870 when Mary Ellen Pleasant first met her, although James was by then in San Quentin. He'd been caught robbing drunken farmboys in the bars of the Barbary Coast.

Teresa had asked the Bank of California for a loan to see her past this drop in income. On the application was a space for her maiden name, in which she wrote "Clingan," and a space for her mother's name, in which she wrote simply the word "mother."

Mary Ellen Pleasant thought her very lovely and very sad. "I own six hundred acres in New York," Teresa told her coolly. She was wearing a patched dress, a glass brooch, and shoes that didn't quite fit.

It must be noted that extensive rebuttal for all the above was supplied over the years in which Teresa Bell's estate was contested. Both Mary Jane and Kate testified that Teresa was their sister, the youngest daughter of John and Bridget Clingan. Their contention was supported by baptismal records.

Their mother was a drunk, but had never tried to kill anyone, they said. Teresa went to live with Wessel Harris and

his wife, Elmina, when she was fostered off the county farm.
He was no blood relation and he never did adopt her. Any
land he might have owned was certainly not left to her.

> Perhaps in some one great heroic act
> The soul its own redemption may attract
> And thus from sin and shame swift fly
> Made fit and ready to meet the Eternal eye
> Ah, to live until all is dead within us
> But ambition and that live to mock us!*

*Opening to Teresa Bell's Last Will and Testament.

T W O

According to official policy, abandoned girls could remain as wards at the Ladies' Relief and Protection Society Home until they were sixteen or, in special cases, even older, but boys weren't kept much past their twelfth birthdays. After this age, the danger of hoodlumism was seen to increase sharply.

In the winter of 1890, truancy was all the fashion; the boys had to be continually hunted down and punished. Lizzie had never seen such a season for starvation and isolation and paddlings, but no penalty proved a deterrent. The draw was the Presidio and the sight of soldiers marching back and forth on Van Ness.

"It's worth the licking any lady can hand out," twelve-year-old Tom Branan told Lizzie confidentially, just before he left the Home to work on a farm south of San Jose. "You all don't hit hard enough to stop us." He was standing in Lizzie's entryway on the Monday after the séance, with a red runny nose and a thickly inked note from Nell.

"Your friend Mammy Pleasant has just sent over a basket of food," Nell had written, pressing hard enough to tear the paper. "Including several chickens it will take a whole morning to pluck. Please join us for lunch." And to make the prospect as uninviting as possible—"Boxty will also be served."

Lizzie ate only rarely at the Ark, and only when invited. She would have liked to dine there more often, as food tasted so much better when taken with conversation. She fully enjoyed the company of the teachers—warm, impassioned Mrs. Lake, who taught the middles, and tiny, practical Miss Stevens, who taught the littles.

Miss Stevens had red hair, freckled skin thin as paper, and eyes the same green as Chinese tea. Her particular enthusiasm was nature studies. She was a woman who took the world as she found it, and did so with great interest if not actual approval. She had no problem showing small children a praying mantis devouring its mate, a rabbit eating its young, a large crab ripping the leg off another, smaller crab. She delighted in pulling the petals from flowers and, in this context, could talk about pistils and stamens, could even say the word "ovary" to an entire class with a great loud "O" to begin it and no sign of hesitation. In her spare time, for dissipation, she dissected.

She ran the littles with an organizational genius that bordered on military, but was actually, she told Lizzie, adapted from the habits of migratory geese. When she took the children out, they walked behind her in a V formation, only somewhat narrowed so they all stayed out of the street.

She'd recently joined a ladies' debating society. Mrs. Lake had complained to Lizzie that the discourse at table was increasingly competitive as a result. Lizzie sometimes wondered about the educational progression that sent children from the strict empiricism of Miss Stevens into the classroom of the sentimental Mrs. Lake. Fortunately, educational policy was not her concern.

But Lizzie liked picking over issues: the morality of hunting as sport, voting rights for women, the Hawaii question, separate schools for the city's Chinese children. She guessed she would enjoy those dinner-table debates.

Yet she could not impose. The staff would suspect her of suspecting them; they would think her a spy. "We take the same meals as the wards," Nell told Lizzie often when they were discussing expenditures, and of course, Lizzie had never thought otherwise. Nell periodically asked board members to lunch just to show there was nothing to hide, and she was already plenty offended to be doing so.

Apparently it was Lizzie's turn to enjoy this hospitality again. She arrived early at the Ark and found the children huddled in the yard. The cause was a stray dog—some sort of terrier, with coarse gray fur and a white belly, ludicrous white tufts like fishing lures at its cheeks, and a lively, intelligent face. The children told her the dog had belonged to a little boy who'd lived on Nob Hill until he died of influenza.

Lizzie couldn't imagine how they could know this unless the dog himself had talked, but before she could say so,

Mrs. Lake supplied even more details. The dog collapsed on the boy's grave, she reported to Lizzie tremulously, refusing all food and consolation and howling until the neighbors threatened to shoot it as a mercy to everyone involved. By the time it arrived at the Home it was half starved, and covered with fleas. Mrs. Lake's eyes ran with sympathetic tears. She went to give it another pat.

"Essence of Lake," Nell said sniffily to Lizzie. "Don't look half starved to me. Don't look one-quarter starved. But I'll grant you the fleas."

Lizzie nodded, as she was too distraught now to speak. She averted her eyes so Nell wouldn't see them. Dogs were just too good for this wicked world!

But she had to concede she saw no signs of noble grief. She watched the dog provoking the orange cat into stiff, furious poses, tangling among the children's legs as they played in the cold, nosing in their pockets for scraps from breakfast. Lizzie didn't want some stray eating the bread that the Swain bakery donated for the children. Yet as treasurer she made no objection to its remaining, even said it could come inside, sandy and germy as it was, whenever the pound man was sighted in the neighborhood. How could she do otherwise? Weren't the children all strays themselves?

She noted the coincidence of a dog's showing up when Mrs. Pleasant had predicted a dog. She didn't really believe in omens, but she couldn't help looking for them. This dog struck her as mostly gray, but there were those bits of white. "What color do you think it is?" she asked Nell, who answered that it was so grimy even the white was gray.

Lizzie saw little Jenny standing alone in the sand, but

they didn't speak and Lizzie was relieved to see Jenny ignore her. The secret of their nighttime excursion seemed to be safe. Lizzie was also the tiniest bit hurt. This was a preposterous feeling, and she disregarded it.

She was not currently inclined to credit the medieval festival kidnapping attempt. It was too overheated, too much like something Lizzie herself would make up, springing into her head from the pages of a book. Such things didn't happen, not in modern-day San Francisco.

She was also less and less sure of the wealthy father. No secretly wealthy child had sheltered with them yet. How could sullen little Jenny be the first? In short, there was really no reason to think much more upon her, and Lizzie didn't plan to do so. "Come with me," Nell said, and Lizzie followed her inside.

On the way downstairs Lizzie raised the question of hiring a devout, hardworking Christian boy from Chinatown. Nell said it was not to be thought of, Lizzie knew their budget as well as Nell did. Better! Did he even speak English? Nell asked, and was annoyed when Lizzie did not know. Nell did not have the time to be forever pointing and gesturing when she needed a thing done.

THREE

On the kitchen counter, surrounded by baskets of onions, lemons, jars of jelly, and an extravagant amount of spilt flour, a note had been caught under a teacup. Nell stood with her round fists on her round hips while Lizzie read it. "For Miss Hayes, to distribute as she sees fit," Mrs. Pleasant had written in her twisty hand, and also a recipe for the chicken.

Lizzie was both pleased and discomfited to have been so singled out. Mostly she was surprised. "How kind," she said uncertainly. Don't eat or drink anything, Mrs. Bell had told her.

Nell's eyes were sharp as pins. "The two of you are such chums now," she said. "Had such a gay time together.

She's also sent you rose-hip wine. Now there's all we need, to see poor blind Mrs. Wright in her cups."

The unspoken point here, the message in Nell's careless tone and rigid mouth and pinprick eyes, was Lizzie's drunken return from the House of Mystery. Lizzie refused to defend herself. Instead, as demonstration of her own clear conscience, she took the wine and two glasses and went immediately up to Mrs. Wright's first-floor apartment. I can be anyone I like, she thought to herself. I care nothing for appearances. If it all results in generous donations of food to orphans, where's the harm?

Mrs. Wright was more than eighty years old, a lonely soul who had survived most of her friends and the whole of her family. She'd lost her money in the rigged market of 1879, was one of those women who'd clustered each morning on Leidesdorff Street, hoping to see her shares of Sierra Nevada Mining turn to silver again. Such women were known in San Francisco as mud hens. On each new day, as the stock market opened, they were a little muddier, mothier, and more insane.

The Ladies' Relief and Protection Society Home had gathered Mrs. Wright in when she went blind as well as broke. Although she now kept herself clean as could be, the room smelled of camphor and the insides of old shoes. There was another smell, too, which Lizzie identified simply as age.

"We have Mrs. Mary E. Pleasant to thank for the wine," Lizzie told her. She turned her glass and watched the liquid in it spin. "It's a lovely color, a pale gold. Did you ever meet Mrs. Pleasant?"

"I recollect her calling on the Barclays once when I was there." Mrs. Wright's dentures were too large; they filled her *s*'s with spit. She'd chosen them deliberately, since the larger were the same price as the smaller. Value for money. "Their girl had just married and they must have invited her, people always used to, never expecting her to come, you understand. But she did, and she knew her mistake right away. So she just took a tray from one of the servants and began to pass it. I remember thinking that was clever. She was quick as they make 'em. Avoided the awkwardness, and half the guests didn't even guess. Nobody looks at the servants, don't you know."

This didn't match up with the woman who was so proud Lizzie's apron had insulted her. Lizzie couldn't imagine *that* woman passing a tray. "Did you ever see her as a white woman?"

"I know some people say so, but I don't recollect it," said Mrs. Wright. "I don't see how it could be true. She was a famous cook before she even arrived. Men met her at the docks to bid for her services. 'No washing up!' she said. She drove a bargain.

"And she was always proud of how far she'd come. She fought the Fugitive Slave Act, and she sued the trolleys for refusing her a ride. You wouldn't do that if you were passing."

"Did she win?"

"My word, it was so long ago. I don't remember, dear. But she was all for the colored in those early days. When they took John Brown, he had a letter from our Mrs. Pleasant right in his pocket. She was a big part of all that."

Mrs. Wright was giddy with wine and conversation.

Lizzie poured her a second glass, because she could see Mrs. Wright wanted one but wouldn't ask. Lizzie reproached herself for not visiting more often. She then suffered through a long story, which floated in and out of the past, a story in which many people Mrs. Wright had once known came to no good. There were mine cave-ins and ships lost at sea and deaths attributed to disease but so unexpected they might easily have been poisonings, and there were people who profited from these deaths. Even Lizzie, who could fill in the blanks in someone's story like nobody's business, was having trouble following.

She was rescued by Minna Graham. Come to fetch them to lunch, Lizzie assumed, but no, Minna said, the chickens weren't cooked yet, still running blood from the joints, but there was a man in the parlor Matron wanted her to deal with.

Only, Matron wanted specifically to see Lizzie first; she had something most urgent to say. "She does think he's here to adopt," Minna added, and Lizzie thought that, whatever his business, Minna should not have been informed of it. So when Lizzie returned to the kitchen, she also had things to say to Nell.

FOUR

Although Nell had taken an instant dislike to the man—
"A Mr. Finney, or so it suits him to have us believe. I
couldn't see one of our girls going home with him," she
had said—Lizzie's own first impression was most approv-
ing. He rose eagerly at her entrance. He should have been
relieved of his coat and hat, yet like Mrs. Pleasant, he still
had them. Lizzie wished Mrs. Pleasant could see this. It was
nothing personal. The wards were just ill mannered. Abet-
ted by Nell, who never wanted company anyway.

The coat was stained and the hat needed blocking. Mr.
Finney's shirt was worn clear through at the cuffs. But his
hair, face, and hands were clean. Lizzie appreciated the effort he had made. He was a young man, fine-looking, with
a trim moustache and gold-edged spectacles. One of his

teeth, the right incisor, was thin as a nail. His eyes were blue, but gray enough for argument.

He stood beneath the embroidery that read, "Never too late to mend." "Miss Hayes," he said. "It's good of you to see me." His accent was Irish, his voice melodious. "Isn't it a grand morning? Auspicious." There was a nervousness about him that appealed to Lizzie. She liked the way he met her gaze, as if this was difficult but he was determined to do it. She imagined him as naturally shy. He'd spread a handkerchief over the old, bald chair before seating himself, and she thought it was gracious of him to pretend the furniture was worth such care. He set his hat on his knee.

With some prompting, he told Lizzie that he owned his own hack and drove it for hire, though his real job was speculations. Investments. Futures. "I'm a man who takes the long view," he said, which Lizzie supposed meant he'd no ready cash in the here and now. "I'm a man who thinks several steps ahead."

His wife had recently given birth. "A boy," he said, "a delight to all," which made her think of the new Putnam grandchild. But his wife was "as little as a fairy," and the demands of the baby were wearing on her. She wished for a girl to help with the housework.

Then Mr. Finney said he feared he was giving Lizzie the wrong idea. They were not looking for a maid so much as a daughter. "What's wanted is a girl young enough to come to feel part of the family. Mrs. Finney thought of a miss about the age of five or so."

Lizzie had noted that parents often had preposterous expectations of children only a bit older than their own. A mother would excuse the behavior of her neighbor's three-year-old, having a three-year-old herself and knowing him quite a baby still. But she would expect her neighbor's seven-year-old to behave with adult patience and charity. What might the parents of a new infant expect of a little girl of five? "I'm afraid a child that young would only make more work for your wife," she informed Mr. Finney. "I'd recommend a girl of at least ten, perhaps even older."

"It's not help Mrs. Finney is after so much as company. She's an affectionate woman, a little girl would suit her down to the ground. I don't know how to explain it to you," Mr. Finney said. He turned his hat in his hands; his head was bent watching this.

The sun had just reached the parlor window. A pale wand of light turned Mr. Finney's hair the red of an autumn leaf. He looked up, smiling at her nervously, and tiny clouds reflected through the window onto his glasses. "She's always wanted a child. She was so happy during her confinement. But she seems surprised that the baby can't be played with, read to. 'He doesn't even have eyebrows!' she says to me. I tell her it only needs a little time and baby grows up and she's got the child she wants. But she won't wait."

"I see," said Lizzie. In fact she didn't see, and Mr. Finney knew she didn't. It all sounded a bit whimsical. New mothers were often prey to disappointments and frivolities. You didn't adopt a child in a mood.

"Perhaps her heart was set on a girl," Mr. Finney offered. "Not that she'd ever said."

Lizzie decided to let the point pass. "Still, you would want someone dependable," she said. "Sturdy."

"Ah, you can't go by that. Mrs. Finney is the littlest bit of a thing herself, but placid as a cow." Mr. Finney sat back.

"If you could just let me have a look at what you've got. I'll know what I want when I see it."

As if they were a kennel. And quick as that, Lizzie stopped liking him. It was unfair of her, unfair that good manners, which everyone understood to contain an element of artifice, should cease to be good manners the moment the artifice showed. But there it is.

The older children were taking exercise in the yard between the Brown Ark and the barn. Their voices flowed into the parlor on the sunshine, and Lizzie could distinguish no words, but the emotions carried clearly. She had no illusions about the sort of people they would grow into. She never told herself she might be helping to harbor a future president, or even a poet, much as she would have loved to think so.

But it didn't matter, because they were children. Lizzie didn't even like children particularly, but they went to her heart, just the idea of them. "I can't release a child to you without references," she said, which was only the truth and had nothing to do with her change of feelings. "And members of the board would want to meet with Mrs. Finney. I'm only the treasurer. Adoptions aren't really my concern."

"Look, now." Mr. Finney's charming voice took on an edge. The sun brightened suddenly, revealing all the disreputable aspects of the parlor, the tufts of velvet over the mantelpiece, the thready chairs. "I should think you'd want one of your orphans set up in a loving home."

"That's exactly what we do want," Lizzie said.

They stared at each other. "Perhaps I could just have a look at the little ones." His voice smoothed out. "If you've not got a miss to suit, then there's no need to trouble either of us further."

His insistence on seeing their littlest girls was beginning to disturb Lizzie. She had an irrational conviction that he had come for Jenny Ijub. His trousers were old and faded, but in the sunlight now, she might have called them green. If he had come for Jenny, if he was the same man who had tried to grab her at Layman's German castle, sending him away would not suffice. He must be made to believe that Jenny was no longer with them. "Very well," she said. "Currently we have only a few girls so young. Several have left us for loving homes only quite recently."

There followed a number of hasty and awkward arrangements. Lizzie contrived to remove Jenny from her class and settle her in the sewing room with a picture book. The nice thing about Jenny was that she asked for no explanations. Less nice was the sullenness of her submission.

Lizzie then asked Nell to take Mr. Finney to the sheltered yard where the babies took the air. She knew that Nell would discourage him in any way possible. Nell told Lizzie later that he expressed disappointment in their "selection." Nell's own opinion was that he wanted a child on whom he and his wife could practice being parents, a child to serve as a buffer between their inexperienced blunders and their own dear baby. "And then discard like a worn sock," she said. "Having served her purpose."

The gray mongrel had barked at him. Nell saw this as evidence of a canine shrewdness quite uncanny. She did not expect to see Mr. Finney again. "And a good riddance to the bad," she concluded.

Lizzie stood at the sewing room window until she saw

him drive off. She called Jenny over. "Have you ever seen that man?" she asked, but already he was too far away, a very commonplace figure, and Jenny said she couldn't know.

Lizzie lacked Nell's conviction. Now that the interview was over, it seemed more than possible that she had given in to an unwarranted suspicion. The feeling nagged at her. She wondered whether it was worth trying to track Mr. Finney down, to visit him in his home, interview his little fairy wife. She pictured Mrs. Finney's disappointment; she saw the two of them holding hands over the kitchen table, tears on Mrs. Finney's tiny radish-red cheeks.

Perhaps his eyes *had been* blue. But San Francisco was full of blue-eyed men. How was Lizzie supposed to determine the right one? Why was she even looking? She was too distracted to enjoy the lunch. Miss Stevens proposed the Chicago anarchists as a topic, and Lizzie had strong opinions regarding them—the mere thought of handsome August Spies, the hood over his face, his own death only moments away, saying without tremor, "The time will come when our silence will be more powerful than the voices you strangle today," was enough to send her heart straight up to her throat—but she found she didn't like the rules of debate. They transformed a disagreement between two or more people into an etiquette designed to obstruct rather than reveal the truth. The key was to misrepresent your opponent's position and then attack your own misrepresentation. It was all about strategies and generally invoked just as Lizzie was making her main point.

She went home in a pet and managed not to think

about Mr. Finney again until the next morning, when she was awakened at six by Jack, a stable boy at the Brown Ark, who told her Matron wanted her at once, as Jenny Ijub had vanished in the night. The new dog, the dog who was definitely gray and not white, was also missing.

FIVE

At that hour, the city lay drowning in a cold, dense fog that tasted faintly of salt. It sat like a tongue against Lizzie's cheeks, licked the hair at her temples into waves. Jack drove Lizzie to the Brown Ark, and she was glad not to be the one driving, she couldn't see the street at all. She couldn't even see the mule clearly, only its long ears sticking up, flicking to the left and to the right when other buggies passed. A dozen kidnapped girls could have been bundled by and she wouldn't have known. The harness broke and delayed them many minutes. The sounds of wheels and hooves continued about them, phantom carriages, audible but invisible. By the time she arrived at the Home, she was rigid from the damp cold and from fear.

It was something of a relief to hear that, among the

staff, Jenny was assumed to have run away. There had been an incident in the night. Nell was not immediately forthcoming, but apparently there had been an upset. Apparently it was not the first, though possibly the loudest.

According to Nell, Jenny was a troubled sleeper, making frequent complaints about the girls in her room. Last night had been once too often. Since Jenny couldn't manage to sleep nicely with other girls, Nell had told her, she must sleep alone. She was removed to the settee in the cupola room.

As Jenny was taken up the stairs, however, she grew more agitated. She begged to be allowed to return to her bed; she begged not to be left alone in the dark. This was distressing for Nell. She'd not intended the punishment to be a severe one, but there was no going back; it would not do for discipline in general if she was seen to retreat. She had to carry Jenny the final steps.

By now Jenny was hysterical, ungovernable, like an animal, Nell said. She was forced to stand at the door, holding it shut, while Jenny screamed and pulled at the handle and threw herself against it. Fully an hour passed in this manner, an hour at least; Nell had heard the clock. Finally Jenny quieted. Nell had waited, assuring herself the girl was asleep before tiptoeing down the stairs and back to her own bed. She had then spent a sleepless night herself, yet heard nothing more. "It didn't occur to me she might leave," she told Lizzie. "I never even thought. Seeing as she's got nowhere to go."

Nell was apologetic, but she had given Lizzie her first hopeful moment. Lizzie was afraid to share it, afraid someone would take it away again, show her that such a little girl could not walk so far alone in the dark. She put her coat and gloves back on, commandeered the mule, and told the staff only that she was going out to look for Jenny. She dismissed Jack; she wanted no witnesses. She drove herself to Octavia Street, stopped at the trees, which she could barely see, in front of the house, which she could not. Fog ran down the eucalyptus leaves and onto her straw hat with the gentle popping sound of rain. She secured the mule and made her way through the gate and up the brick walk. Sure enough, the dog came off the porch to meet her, the white tufts of its whiskers dripping with fog, its gums showing pink, its tongue limp with the pleasure of seeing her. This was a pleasure she fully returned.

Teresa Bell answered the door herself, in a silver dressing gown. She nodded politely and for a moment too long. It was clear she didn't remember Lizzie's name. "I'm looking for a little girl," Lizzie told her. "I'm Miss Hayes?"

"She's yours? I couldn't think what to do with her. Another hour I'd have sent for the police."

Lizzie began to cry. This was the final result of her mother's impatience with tears, that after a dry-eyed childhood, she was likely to cry at almost anything, and especially at the wrong times, her weeping matched forever to the wrong emotions—joy, relief, exultation. Mrs. Bell pretended not to notice.

"You'll come in, then." She gestured vaguely, brilliantly; in Lizzie's liquid gaze Mrs. Bell's rings flickered like tiny darting fish. "I thought she was one of Mrs. Pleasant's. So she said. Butter wouldn't melt."

Lizzie wiped her nose, leaving a wet smear on the back of one gloved hand, removed her hat, and let Mrs. Bell lead her into a dark paneled library. A chandelier of rock

crystal dripped from the ceiling, though the light was poor.
On the floor by the sofa was a metal bird, a canary with
painted feathers and a green hinged beak. It was a music
box, turned with a key, and Lizzie guessed the beak would
open and shut when it played. The bird's eyes were inset
rather than painted. Obsidian beads, they had the dead,
dull depth of taxidermy.

She looked about for Jenny, but there was no one else
in the room. She remembered how beautiful she'd thought
the house before. Now it seemed cavernous, poorly lit, a
place of whispers and echoes. She had never seen a library
with so few books.

"Join me in a cordial," Mrs. Bell suggested. There was
a decanter on a table by the door. "To settle your nerves."

"Where is the little girl?" Lizzie asked.

"Sleeping."

"Will you take me to her?"

"I had such a time getting her to sleep, I couldn't bear
to wake her just yet. Let's uncurl here with a glass."

"Is Mrs. Pleasant at home?"

"The whole house has fled to the country." She nodded in a reassuring way. "We're *quite* alone." She gave the
word a disquieting emphasis. Lizzie was not at all sure she
wished to be quite alone in the House of Mystery with
Teresa Bell, and certainly not *quite* alone.

Teresa Bell was rarely seen outside. She belonged to
no church, held no at-homes. Some thought she was
frightened of something. Some said Mary Ellen Pleasant
allowed her no friends. Some said it was Thomas Bell.
Some of the latter said Thomas Bell valued his wife's inno-
cence so highly that he kept her shut away from the con-

tamination of society. Others said he could never trust her, she being no better than a whore when they met. Still others thought she had tricked him into marriage and he'd retaliated by going into society without her, as if she didn't exist, for more than a decade.

Lizzie hoped that Mrs. Bell was merely shy. She wished to demand to be taken to Jenny at once, but saw how rude this would be. She removed her gloves, accepted a cordial. It was far too early for one, really—and wine just yesterday!—but she'd had such a fright. She took a seat on the sofa. Mrs. Bell sat next to her.

There was a long and uncomfortable silence. The cordial was in a tulip glass and tasted of fermented raspberries. The fog pressed against the windows to Lizzie's right, where she could see, dimly, the reflection of her own face. She watched a drop of water fatten until it was too heavy and then stretch thin as it fell. Just for fun, she repositioned her face until a teary trail ran down her reflected cheek. She glanced at a clock on the wall. It had stopped at three forty-three. There was no evidence of a servant anywhere. But surely Mrs. Bell's hair was too elaborate for her to have done it herself.

"Such a quiet house," Lizzie said, trying to make it sound a compliment. She set down her glass. "Your servants . . ."

"All of them drunk," Mrs. Bell said. "Or I miss my guess." Lizzie made a noise she intended as sympathetic but feared came out startled. She reminded herself that it was a scandalous household and Mrs. Bell a scandalous woman. Lizzie had not minded the last time she was here. She'd rather enjoyed it. She tried to find the mood of her last visit, the sense of waking up, the hope of her life taking a magical turn. What was missing now was the tea, the sun, and Mary Ellen Pleasant. "I'm sorry not to see Mrs. Pleasant," she offered. "She's in the country, you said?"

"Well, one never knows." Mrs. Bell's voice dropped confidingly. "But I've searched the house."

She put her cordial aside, the red liquid shivering in the glass, and reached for Lizzie's hands. Her own were as cold and soft as Lizzie recollected; the fingernails so icy they made the back of Lizzie's neck twitch, tightened the skin over her skull. Mrs. Bell continued to stroke Lizzie's hands, and Lizzie forced herself not to withdraw. She touched Lizzie's wrists, rubbed them with her thumbs. She seemed to be warming her hands on Lizzie like a cat. It occurred to Lizzie that Mrs. Bell might be drunk herself. Or drugged. Hadn't Mrs. Pleasant's tea come from Chinatown?

Lizzie wondered exactly how old Mrs. Bell was. Her skin was so translucent the shadows under her eyes were blue. Her gold-brown hair caught the lamplight and glowed like amber. When she smiled, tiny wrinkles opened like fans at the edges of her mouth and eyes. If she didn't smile, there were no lines in her face at all. Her shoulder touched Lizzie's, and Lizzie smelled milkweed powder.

"You should stay away from Mrs. Pleasant," Mrs. Bell whispered. "She don't like fine white women." She nodded for emphasis, then straightened. "She wasn't always that way. She was good to me at first, she introduced me to Mr. Bell. We married in this very house."

"Weddings are such lovely occasions," Lizzie said. Actually she thought they lacked spontaneity, but as an unmarried woman she could hardly say so. In books they were interrupted, protested, prevented. They were the scenes of great drama. Jane Eyre's wedding, for example, the one that had not taken place—you couldn't call it a lovely occasion, but so much passion! As a young lady, whenever Lizzie had imagined her own wedding, she'd imagined it not taking place the way Jane Eyre's had not taken place. (And not ever the way it had actually not taken place.)

"Ours was private. I left next day on my wedding trip. Mr. Bell stayed back."

This was interesting, and Lizzie would have liked to know more about it. "How sad for you both," she said encouragingly.

But Mrs. Bell waved the point past. "He's a businessman. Business prevented him."

SIX

On her return from her wedding trip, Mrs. Bell told Lizzie, Mrs. Pleasant felt there had been insufficient ceremony to mark the occasion. She insisted on a party. It was winter. Mrs. Bell wore a gown of green *crêpe de Chine* shot with silver thread, and her wedding gift from Mrs. Pleasant, a diamond choker. The mansion was strung with lamps, filled with flowers, and the food was extraordinary. Seven courses were served, smoked and fresh meats, out-of-season vegetables, pâtés and wines from France, fruits glazed with liqueurs; there were jewelry boxes containing teas from China for the guests to take home. "Mrs. Pleasant puffs herself a bit on her table," said Mrs. Bell. "She used to cook for Governor Booth when he came to town."

Mrs. Bell was not a good storyteller. Her affect was too

even, her chronology unusual, her vocabulary common. But Lizzie loved stories with *crêpe de Chine* and strings of lamps and out-of-season vegetables. She was a passionate reader. She was more than able to supply whatever details Mrs. Bell omitted.

Only the men had attended. One by one they arrived, without their wives. They made unconvincing, embarrassed excuses, agues and toothaches and unexpected family obligations; a few of one, a few of the other, as if it had been orchestrated. That's what angered Mrs. Pleasant most, the sense of collusion. She insisted on seating the men at the tables as set, with every other chair left empty. The men began to drink and, when drunk, to make discourteous comments. Teresa Bell was admired, but in an intimate, insulting way, not befitting a married woman. Ribald toasts were made to Mrs. Pleasant as well. Eventually Mrs. Pleasant told Mrs. Bell to leave, and she did so, fleeing up the stairs.

"Wasn't the insult to me?" Mrs. Bell asked Lizzie. Her voice was plaintive. "I was the bride." But Mrs. Pleasant insisted on appropriating it. Years before Mrs. Bell had even arrived in San Francisco, Mrs. Pleasant had tried to host a dinner for society's finest. The result had been the same. The result would always be the same.

Although at the time of their marriage she lived with Mr. and Mrs. Bell, Mrs. Pleasant still owned Geneva Cottage on the San Jose Road. She began to redecorate it. She put in oriel windows, reddened the wood floors with stains, bought gold-veined mirrors, marble basins, and fountains. She hung curtains of lace patterned with orchids. The gardens were replanted to make a large, lush greensward surrounded by groves and private trysting grottoes. There were cool shaded places where ferns and violets could grow, patches of sunny grass perfumed by hidden herbs. When she was finished, she sent out invitations again.

This time she invited only men, some of the most powerful in the city and all of them married to the women who had snubbed her. The invitations were delivered in secret by Negro messengers. Two of the men were bankers; there were a railroad millionaire, three mine owners, and a newspaper baron. There were a blind ward boss and a judge from the state supreme court.

"She never told me the guest list," said Mrs. Bell. "She does keep her secrets. But anyone could guess that much."

Mrs. Pleasant promised the men a special evening in the country without their wives. The invitations were written on heavy red paper; the ink was silver. Only one man declined.

The story moved briefly south. When Mrs. Pleasant had left New Orleans, under the name of Madame Christophe, she was only a step ahead of the hangman. She had been stealing slaves, connecting them with the Underground Railroad, and the plantation owners were closing in. She escaped through the help and intervention of Marie LaVeau.

"You've heard of LaVeau?" Mrs. Bell asked.

Lizzie hadn't, but Mrs. Bell did not elaborate further except to say that Mrs. LaVeau had taught Mrs. Pleasant many things and that one of them was how to give a party.

There was little to eat and much to drink. They called the drink champagne, but it was really something far more lethal. Mrs. Pleasant had put it down herself from strawberries she'd grown in special barrels. "The entertainment

tonight is voodoo," she told the men. There were ten beautiful young women, dressed like princesses, but with the skin
of slaves, to sit with the men while they smoked and to dance
the calinda with them after. There were drums. There were
ritual incantations. The ballroom grew hot from the dancing
and the liquor; the drumming quickened.

One of the women was a sixteen-year-old named Malina Paillet. She wore yellow roses on her wrist and yellow
silk on her shoulders. She caught the attention of one of
the men, perhaps a banker, perhaps a mine owner. What
appealed to him most was her shyness. She couldn't answer
his questions, couldn't smile at his jokes. Her movements
during the dance were slight, but this, he thought, made
them even more suggestive. He drank and she didn't.
When he put his hand on her skirt, groped through the
petticoat to squeeze the leg beneath, she froze suddenly,
awkwardly, and asked another of the women to change
places with her. There was a silence in the room. When the
dancing began again, the man had a different partner.

Mrs. Pleasant could see that he was angry and very
drunk. She took Malina aside and told her she was a fool to
be rude to a rich man. Mrs. Pleasant wanted the men en-
tangled, wanted the women installed as mistresses, draining
whatever time and money they could from the men's wives.

But this was not New Orleans. Malina refused to listen. "I hate him," she said, and it was loud enough to be
heard throughout the room. She was sobbing, salty tears
that would ruin the yellow silk, an expensive dress that belonged, Mrs. Bell noted, to Mrs. Pleasant and not to Malina.

Lizzie had begun to wonder whether this was a story
she should be hearing. Mrs. Bell's manner was so tranquil

there was no anticipating the things that came from her mouth. And yet Lizzie was far too engrossed to stop her. It was like a story by Conan Doyle, but with voodoo instead of Mormons. The Palace Hotel hired pretty young mulatto girls as maids. Lizzie could easily picture one of them in a floating silk, tears falling like diamonds from her eyes.

Malina ran from the room and the man went after her. She ran through the pink-and-white parlor, into the courtyard, and into the trees. The man followed. There was silence, and then a single scream. It might have been the peacocks Mrs. Pleasant had purchased to patrol the grounds.

When Mrs. Pleasant and the others reached the yard, Malina was returning. Her hair was loose about her face and she was not wearing her roses or her shoes. She stumbled between the two fountains with their statues—"statues of women," said Mrs. Bell, in a tone that Lizzie understood immediately to mean they had no clothes on—her head at a strange angle. She fell in the courtyard. Her throat had been cut.

"I'll take care of this," Mrs. Pleasant told the men. The other women had fled. "You can rely on my discretion." She removed her housekeeping apron and covered Malina's face. "No one will ever know you were here tonight. Your wives need never know."

Teresa Bell's hands reached for Lizzie's neck. Lizzie gasped and pulled away, but Mrs. Bell had caught hold of the chain of her necklace and held her fast. "Such a strange coin." Her face was very close to Lizzie's. Lizzie could feel the heat of her breath, could see the raspberry stain like blood on her tongue, the pores of her skin clotted with powder. "Is it very old? I never saw its like," she said.

"I really must be going." Lizzie opened Mrs. Bell's icy fingers by force and stood. Won't you promise to stay away from Mrs. Pleasant, Mrs. Putnam had begged her, and if the question were put to her again, put to her just now, she would return quite a different answer. Despite every effort, her words came out with a tremble. "I must get back. Everyone is so worried about little Jenny. Please take me to her at once."

"Did I scare you? I apologize."

"Not at all." Lizzie managed to govern her voice, though not her legs. They shook and she sat again. "Why do you keep her on?"

"Keep her on?" Mrs. Bell smiled so her teeth showed. They were small and perfectly graduated, like strung pearls. "You don't understand a thing, do you? Old Mrs. Pleasant does what she likes. And Mr. Bell, if he has a fault, it's loyalty. He'd never turn on her."

"Who was the murderer?"

"She never said. Mr. Bell knows, of course, seeing as he was there."

"Why have you told me this?" Lizzie asked.

"Because you're a white woman. And so am I."

"Then why won't you take me to Jenny?"

"I will, of course. Are you worried about her? She's just upstairs, asleep."

Lizzie felt her heart rattling against the cage of her ribs. Mrs. Bell's face was too composed; her tone of voice too even. It had all been a performance, and Lizzie had been taken in. "You're lying, then. She's frightened to sleep by herself. What have you done with her?" She remembered Mrs. Bell's face the first time they had met, her courteous, placid voice. My mother set me out on the windowsill in a thunderstorm, she'd said.

Now Mrs. Bell's face showed annoyance, perhaps—surprise, at least. Something swam through the bright glass surface of her eyes. She picked up the painted canary, wound its key. "We played with this music box here until she dozed off. I lugged her upstairs. I see my word isn't enough. I'm happy to show you."

There was a sequence of tinny chirping, then a strangled cry. The automaton froze into place, its beak open in silent alarm.

Lizzie followed Mrs. Bell to the back of the house, where a spiral staircase coiled its way from the basement to the third floor. A glass dome capped the staircase; as a result, the house was slightly brighter here. The light fell directly on a newel post that supported a statue of a woman carved of dark wood, and holding up a lamp. Of course, she was insufficiently clothed. Lizzie would have been surprised to find her otherwise.

They started to climb. The spiral of the stairs formed a murky well at its center. Lizzie watched the well deepen as she rose; it gave her a vague vertigo.

The gas was not lit on the second floor, and the curtains throughout were drawn, so once they left the skylight it was darker than ever. Mrs. Bell fetched a lantern, then opened a small door, too small to lead to a room; Lizzie would have guessed it led to a closet. "The whole house is stuffed with passageways and peepholes," Mrs. Bell said. "There's not a room you can know yourself safe from spying eyes. Mrs. Pleasant designed it. This is the shortest route." She stepped inside.

Lizzie forced herself to follow. The space was low at the entry, but opened at the back into a narrow, window-less corridor. The air was still and smelled of dust. Lizzie saw Mrs. Bell's light receding in front of her. Mrs. Bell made a turn and the light went out. The space was narrow enough for Lizzie to hold the walls on either side. She imagined they were narrowing further. She made the turn herself and could just see Mrs. Bell's light again. She hurried forward. The light went out.

Lizzie listened for Mrs. Bell's footsteps but heard nothing. She groped forward and hit another wall. No one knew she had come here. She and Mrs. Bell were apparently alone in the house except for the drunken servants. *Quite* alone. No one would ever come to look for her.

"Mrs. Bell," she called. "Mrs. Bell!" She hit the wall in front of her with her fists. The knocking echoed about her. "Mrs. Bell!"

She decided to go back. They had made only one turn. They had left an open door. It was hard to set her feet on a floor she could not see. She was moving slowly, far more slowly than when she'd had the light. She told herself that this was why it took so long to get back to the turn. Eventually she was forced to acknowledge that she had missed it. She turned back again.

Her eyes were beginning to adjust, but the beating of her heart made the corridor seem to pulse about her, as if with each heartbeat she were being squeezed. In the dis-tance she thought she saw a tiny orange pin of light, like an afterimage of sun. Shadows now appeared, impossible without light, and therefore illusions. She held one hand across her face to protect her eyes and groped forward with the other toward the tiny mirage of brightness. Before entering this corridor she would have said the house was silent; now her straining ears heard no end of creaks, paddings, scuttlings, and shiftings, the worst of which were her own footsteps. Her hip hit something on the wall to her right, something round and cold, which she shrank from at first, and then realized was a doorknob. She twisted it and fell into a room. In the dim light she could make out heavy velvet curtains. She ran to these and wrenched them open. The fog was still too thick to see out, but she could now see inside.

She was in a bedchamber, all done in reds. On a stone pillar by the window was a statue of a woman on a horse. She carried a bow and wore only a quiver of arrows, the strap of which fell between her breasts. There was a vase with raised figures of men and women. Lizzie had to bend close to see. They were riding each other in positions she found hard to credit. She made herself look away.

A picture hung on the wall to her left. It showed a dark woman in a white dress. She lay on a grassy hill, one hand tucked into her own bodice, the other lifting an apple toward her mouth. Her shoulders were carelessly bare, her skirt had fallen away from her ankles; clearly she thought she was alone. But the shadow of a cloaked man stretched across the grass beside her. His legs were elongated in the manner of shadows. He stood watching her, just a step outside the gilded frame. It was a dreamy scene, but full of foreboding.

Another picture showed an older, fattish woman in

modern dress. Her hair was in disarray, but not seductively so. There was something about her so out of place that Lizzie moved to look more closely. The woman in the picture took a step toward her. Lizzie's throat closed over and then opened. It was a mirror, of course, enormous, nine or ten feet across, with grapevines carved into the frame and painted in red, gold, and green. "You're such an idiot!" she told her reflection, who seemed unsurprised to hear it.

The bed itself was piled with cushions, puffy coverlets, and knitted shawls in such chaotic profusion that Lizzie couldn't immediately tell whether it was occupied or vacant. The bedding lay in mounds and curves. She put a hand hesitantly onto one such drift; it collapsed when pushed. If she had touched someone in the bed this would have finished her. She would have screamed or fainted or died. It was a narrow escape, but the bed was empty.

The knob on the door to the outer hallway was made of white china and painted with a woman's eyes and apple-red lips. Lizzie walked across a carpet whose edges were embroidered with roses, and turned the knob.

Mrs. Bell was waiting in the hallway with her lamp.

"Right through here," she said, as if she and Lizzie had never been separated.

Lizzie wanted nothing more than to run for the staircase, the mule, the Ark. But a person who has freely chosen to spend her days asking rich people for money is no coward. She governed her spirited imagination and followed Mrs. Bell down the hall, down a second hall, and into a room at the very end.

SEVEN

The room at the end of the hall was a nursery, although not just now in use. There was the smell of trapped air, and sheeted forms that suggested chairs, chests, rocking horses, phantasms. There had been some testimony about the Bell children at the William Sharon–Allie Hill divorce trial. Lizzie couldn't quite recall it and couldn't imagine how it had been relevant. She did remember a cartoon from the *Wasp* at about that time—Mrs. Pleasant, dressed like Gilbert and Sullivan's Buttercup, but with a basket of babies. "In my youth when I was young and charming, I practiced baby farming," the caption had read. She remembered Mrs. Bell telling her there were six children, but some of them grown.

In one corner was a small bed. Mrs. Bell stepped toward it and her light fell on Jenny Ijub, lying on her back under a tumbling-blocks quilt. The bedding had been pulled over her, but incompletely, so that Lizzie could see the brown shoulders of her dress, the dirty toes of one stocking. She had a finger in her mouth and there was a high flush on her cheeks.

She was asleep. For the second time in as many hours, Lizzie felt relief shoot through her. She knelt on the floor and touched Jenny's face, drawing a finger along the brow of one closed eye. Beneath the lid, the eye flickered, then stilled. Lizzie shook her shoulder gently and then less gently. "Jenny. Jenny Ijub. I've come for you."

The little girl didn't move. "I gave her something to help her sleep," Mrs. Bell said. "She was so agitated. It wasn't healthy." Dust spun about Mrs. Bell's lamp, swirled across her powdered face.

Lizzie leaned in and smelled camphor on Jenny's breath. She shook Jenny harder. Was it possible to come into the House of Mystery and not go away drugged? *Don't eat or drink anything.* She herself shouldn't have had the cordial. She felt fine, but it had been incautious. She wedged her arms under Jenny and pulled her closer.

Jenny came awake all at once, kicking and striking out till Lizzie released her. Her body relaxed then, but her features remained pinched and her voice was strung with tears. "I won't go back," she said. "You're not the mother of me."

Lizzie didn't want a quarrel in front of Mrs. Bell, with whom she was still angrier than she could say. She didn't want to take the time to overcome Jenny with reason and gentleness. Neither did she want to carry her forcibly from the house. She had a happy inspiration. "I'll take you to the ducks, then."

Jenny regarded her, suspicious but sleepy. Her pupils were black points in the brown eyes. Her hair was wild and blown about her head. One ear stuck out. Lizzie smoothed the hair to cover it.

Jenny indicated Mrs. Bell. "Can she go, too?"

"*May* she go," said Lizzie. "No, we've taken too much of Mrs. Bell's time already."

"All right," Jenny said. She fell asleep again.

Mrs. Bell stood above her, half lit by the lamp she held and half in shadow. She didn't look at Lizzie and she didn't say a word. On a shelf behind her, a row of expensive dolls stared into the middle distance of the room, seven painted skulls, seven tiny Cupid's-bow mouths. This made Lizzie think, inevitably and guiltily, of Jenny's broken doll.

Lizzie couldn't see that these dolls had ever been played with. She'd had three dolls herself as a child and never played with any of them, not liking their compulsive smiles, their lumpy bodies, the emptiness of their lives. Without her to pick them up, move their arms, and speak their voices, they were nothing. It was too much to ask. And then they had stared, of course, much like Baby Edward. Their eyes had never closed.

"You lie there until you calm down," she'd said to them sometimes, to justify her neglect. ("Lizzie keeps her dolls just like new," her mother told people, with obvious approval.)

Lizzie searched the floor for Jenny's shoes. She took them in one hand and lifted Jenny into her arms. She recognized the smell of Jenny's hair, sweet but spoiled, like stale cake or those candies in Chinatown that came in a thin wrapping of rice paper that you ate along with the sweet. "We're most grateful for your kindness," she told Mrs. Bell stiffly.

"My pleasure." Mrs. Bell's voice matched Lizzie's, note for impeccable note. Her face was as vacant and unused as the dolls'. "Do call again."

Jenny was an awkward load. The steps seemed steeper descending, the bottom of the well a terrifying distance away now that Lizzie had no hand free for the banister.

There was a portrait on the wall next to Lizzie where she paused to rest. She assumed this was the likeness of Mr. Bell. If so, he was a balding, handsome man with a sharp nose and white side-whiskers. His eyes were very, very blue. Mrs. Bell's portrait hung next to him, life-sized and wearing fewer clothes than you might expect of a mother of six. In her arms she held a tiny white dog with a smashed flat face. Its color was incontrovertible.

Behind Mrs. Bell and the dog was the grandfather clock from the entryway. The time in the picture was just past two, an artful reference to Mrs. Bell's age at the time of the sitting, or so Lizzie supposed. The longer hand was just past twelve. XII, in fact, but what difference did that make?

If Lizzie had seen these things on the way up, her magical juncture might have begun in wandering lost and frightened in the dark. This would have been an awful way to start the rest of her life.

Of course, if she'd seen her signs on the way up, they would have come in the wrong order.

Lizzie shifted Jenny in her arms and continued down the stairs. At the bottom she paused to look up. Mrs. Bell stood with her lamp in the darkness of the floor above. The lamp lit her face from below, gave her a ghoulish tint. It occurred to Lizzie that she really should have asked Mrs. Bell to thank Mrs. Pleasant for the chickens, but it seemed unbearably awkward to do so now. She passed the real grandfather clock and went out the door.

EIGHT

*T*he not-white terrier was delighted at the chance to ride in the buggy. Lizzie knew she should go straight back to the Brown Ark, where everyone was worried most to death. Jenny was asleep and could hardly appreciate an outing. But Lizzie had promised her one.

Besides, Lizzie thought she could use a little time to compose herself before facing her magical juncture, not that she believed in such things, not that the appearance of the clues hadn't been all too neatly arranged in the House of Mystery. It didn't feel like the hand of fate; it felt like the hand of Mrs. Pleasant. Still, Lizzie was tense and nervy; the morning had been too much.

So she turned right instead of left and drove out to Golden Gate Park, letting the mule pick the pace, giving the hacks for hire a wide berth, so as not to risk a meeting with Mr. Finney. A road to Ocean Beach was being constructed. South Drive swarmed with laborers. The fog was burning away, exposing a watery sun, reluctant and cold.

If Jenny had been awake, Lizzie would have taken her to the new Children's Quarters and maybe bought her a ride on the merry-go-round. She would have stood with the mothers, watching from the balcony of the Sharon building. Lizzie had not seen it yet herself, but the orphans at the Ark had been guests there twice and come back talking of painted horses and maypoles.

The original plan for the William Sharon bequest had been a huge marble gate with the senator's name cut into it. As if he'd donated the entire park instead of merely an unnecessary portal, the outraged papers had said. The park commissioner had persuaded the estate into the Children's Quarters instead—croquet sets, tricycles, ice cream fountains, donkeys, and goat carts. A happy memorial, then, but a curious consequence, to turn Senator William Sharon into Saint Nicholas when his case hadn't even been settled yet. Allie Hill had accused him of adultery, and his spirited public defense was that he'd paid her five hundred dollars a month to share his bed and never once considered marrying her.

Lizzie stopped the buggy at Alvord Lake, where a tribe of mallards had settled the past autumn. She was sorry not to have bread. She'd noticed how children who themselves had nothing enjoyed the chance to be generous. She'd seen dreadful bullies who, when given a handful of stale biscuits and a mob of ducks, suddenly developed a fine sense of justice. It was wonderful to see them trying to feed every

Sister Moon

duck, no duck more than the others, taking special pains to see that the littlest got a share. That would have been worth waking Jenny. That would have been a treat. "We're here," Lizzie said, shaking Jenny until her eyes opened.

She could not find one of Jenny's shoes, so she carried her to a park bench and held her there in the pale sunlight, listening to the mild griping of the mallards. The dog dashed about on the lawn, where, when next Lizzie looked, it had found something nasty to roll in.

It was not yet eleven in the morning and Lizzie was already exhausted. Each duck cut a small wake in the water, V-shaped, spreading open like a wing. The sun struck these waves so that the surface of the water was crossed with brief veins of gold. At the lake edges, the reflections of trees floated and undulated. It was all so beautiful. She shook Jenny again. "Ducks," she said.

Jenny scarcely opened her eyes. "Not those ducks," she answered. Even asleep, even drugged, she was not relaxed. She lay in Lizzie's lap, curled up tightly, and one elbow dug into Lizzie's thigh.

Lizzie had so many things to think about. She tried to impose some order on the recurring images of fog and red wallpaper, the spiral staircase, black passageways, a murdered girl in a yellow dress. She'd had an adventure, no doubt about it, and it hadn't been pleasant. Ever since her first visit to the House of Mystery she'd chafed at her usual life. She'd been impulsive, discontented. She'd drunk daytime wine and been rude to dead people. She'd been the object of occult concern, and honestly, it was time to admit she'd enjoyed it.

But this morning she'd been frightened. She couldn't

153

think of Malina Paillet without distress and she couldn't think of Mrs. Pleasant with pleasure. The party was over, and all Lizzie wanted was her same old corner in the cinders. You can be anyone you want, Mrs. Pleasant had said, and what luck! Lizzie wanted to be her old, unintrusive self. Her magical juncture must be made to take her right back home.

She was done with Jenny. She was done with the House of Mystery. She had no curiosity over Mr. Finney. She was merely the treasurer, merely involved in donations, and these other matters would be well handled by other people.

Jenny's breath was fragrantly medicinal, wet and warm on Lizzie's neck as they returned to the buggy. Lizzie had never said they wouldn't be going back to the Brown Ark eventually. Obviously there was no choice for it. She'd honored her part of the bargain by producing ducks. As she clicked her tongue at the mule she told herself that it was cruel to keep the staff in suspense when Jenny had been safely found. Besides, she was tired of staggering about Golden Gate Park with a drugged child in her arms.

Back at the Ark, their appearance was greeted with great relief, quickly mastered. Jenny was carried, still sleeping, to her bed. Dr. Kearney was sent for, to confirm that she'd taken no lasting harm from the adventure.

Nell remained with Lizzie to ask many questions. In the face of Lizzie's evasions, Nell was persistent. She couldn't understand how Jenny would have known the way to the House of Mystery, or how Lizzie had known to look for her there. She couldn't understand how Lizzie could have been so careless as to lose one of Jenny's shoes. "It doesn't matter that only one has been lost," she pointed out. "Two will have to be purchased." She took exception to the impulse to take Jenny to the park instead of bringing her back to begin her punishment. Truancy was not tolerated at the Brown Ark, and most runaways were not treated to outings. It wouldn't help Jenny's popularity when the other children heard. Lizzie had no children herself and no sense of how often a firm hand was required. It was easy to be too sympathetic; more mothers had ruined their children with indulgence than with neglect.

And while Lizzie was out larking, the Chinese boy had arrived. He could not be run off. He responded to any attempt to dislodge him by falling to his knees and praying loudly. It appeared to be the Lord's Prayer, Nell was able to pick out a word here and there, but aside from that he seemed to speak no English. She did allow that he was very clean, still he must be sent back at once, and they were all depending on Lizzie to manage this, since it was Lizzie who'd encouraged him to come in the first place.

None of the scolding offended Lizzie; she imagined it was mostly on the mark. It made her miss her mother. She'd been far too hard on her mother recently. Lizzie was so lucky to have belonged somewhere and to someone. Sleeping in one's own bed was one of the most agreeable sensations she knew. Sad to think how foreign it was to the wards.

She imagined Jenny, waking up this afternoon, or this evening, or sometime in the night, to find herself back in the Ark, and resolutely erased the image. Would Jenny even remember having seen the ducks? "I won't be going to the House of Mystery ever again," she told Nell, who hadn't asked and was, of course, made even more suspicious by the declaration.

"Well, goodness, why should you?" Nell agreed. "Why would anyone?"

NINE

*J*enny continued to sleep. In her dreams she heard
Maud Curry's voice. "They found her in a Chinese
opium den," Maud was explaining authoritatively. "Kidnapped and drugged. At least that's what she says. But who'd
want to kidnap her? Me, I don't believe a word of it."

Jenny held very still. She kept her eyes closed. If she
was going to wake up back at the Brown Ark, then she would
just not wake up at all. She was curiously contented. She
told herself she was still in the house with the woman so sad
and so beautiful she was almost a princess. They were waiting there together for Mrs. Pleasant. You'll see I don't forget you, either, Mrs. Pleasant had promised.

The day passed, and every time Jenny opened her eyes
enough to see where she was, she shut them immediately. A

bowl of potato soup was left for her, but she didn't wake up to eat. Night came again and Maud was beside her on the bed, pinching her, shaking her hard. Her voice was so close Jenny could smell it, a boiled-egg and licorice smell. "You listen to me," Maud whispered fiercely. "Little Jenny Ijub. Are you listening?"

She shook Jenny again. "I know where you really went. You ran away to old Mrs. Pleasant. And she didn't want you any more than we do. Do you hear me?" She took the lobe of Jenny's ear between her fingers and squeezed. "Say it," she told Jenny. "Say out loud that nobody loves you."

Jenny tried not to wake up, but Maud's fingernails were cutting into her ear. At first it was an ache she could ignore, but it quickly grew sharper and more painful. The pain hooked Jenny like a fish, hauled her out of her secret contentment, gasping, into the open air.

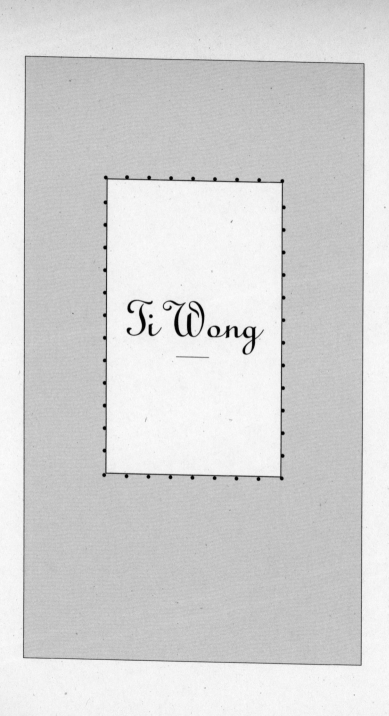

Ti Wong

Lizzie had looked in on Jenny that afternoon while Dr. Kearney was at her bedside. Dr. Kearney was a thin man, unusually tall, with almost no hair on his face. His shoulders were hunched, his spine permanently curved from years of leaning down to talk to people. He was considerably younger than Lizzie, but he was a man and a professional, so she never felt the advantage of it. Yet she was quite fond of him. For all his nervous energy and towering height, he was soft with the children. He read widely and with great enthusiasm, though never novels.

"No damage," he assured Lizzie. "All serene." He spoke past her. "Let the child sleep as long as she likes." Lizzie turned to see Nell behind her in the doorway.

"The Chinese boy is in the kitchen," Nell said. Dr.

Kearney was still talking, so Lizzie could pretend not to have heard. "When she wakes, don't be surprised if she has no memory of this adventure at all," Dr. Kearney was saying. "Don't be alarmed."

"*This* one has no memory of any adventure," Nell said. "Or so she claims."

"And entirely plausibly." Dr. Kearney began to put his instruments back into his bag. "A German doctor has published a series of investigations on memory. I was just reading about it. A Dr. Ebbinghaus. He set himself the task of learning four hundred and twenty sets of sixteen-syllable lines. Unrelated syllables. *Völlig sinnloses Material.* A fatiguing investigation. All marvelously scientific."

"I'm sure," said Nell. She disappeared from the doorway. Conversations of this sort about studies of this sort were no doubt a very fine thing for those with nothing to do, she'd told Lizzie often enough on similar occasions. This was, of course, the category into which Lizzie fell.

"How interesting," Lizzie said. She accompanied Dr. Kearney out of the room, inviting him to continue. It did interest her, but mostly she was using him for cover. She wished to escape from Nell without confronting the Chinese boy, since she saw no reason he couldn't stay if he wished to.

And she certainly had no desire to communicate his unwelcomeness in some sort of extended charade.

Besides, Lillie Langtry had just adopted a small Chinese boy; they were all the rage in the more fashionable homes.

Most important, Nell would not manage to send him away herself. She was more softhearted than she sounded, and better able to delegate unkindness than to deliver it. If Lizzie could avoid her now, then Nell would simply wait until the next time she saw her. If that didn't happen for a week or two, if it could be delayed until Ti Wong was no longer making his first unfavorable impression, then Nell would be just as content to keep him. Lizzie had only to lie low, keep her head down and wait for this happy result. The first step was escaping the Brown Ark unnoticed.

"Dr. Ebbinghaus found that he could impose a rhythm on his syllables as a memory aid," Dr. Kearney was telling her. "Actors learn the words of many plays over the course of their careers. I've seen mention of monks in the Dark Ages who couldn't read, but could recite the entire Bible. I don't think it was uncommon. I myself could recite poetry by the bushelful when I was a boy. 'In Xanadu did Kubla Khan a stately pleasure-dome decree.'"

"'Where Alph, the sacred river, ran,'" said Lizzie encouragingly. They were approaching the front door. "'Through caverns measureless to man.'"

"'Down to a sunless sea.'"

It was her father's favorite poem. Perhaps her father had also imagined himself inside Xanadu; perhaps he responded only to the music. He had a sentimental side, little as Lizzie had seen of it. But now the words reminded her of her own recent wander through the darkness. Less grand in the flesh. Less grand when it didn't rhyme, didn't sing that song with the vowels. Less grand when cut to fit *her*.

Lizzie wished Dr. Kearney would keep his voice down, but his enthusiasm for Ebbinghaus was growing with every sentence. He reached for the doorknob. "'Obliviscence' is Dr. Ebbinghaus's term for forgetting," Dr. Kearney said heartily. "Don't you find that's often the more interesting topic? Isn't 'obliviscence' a lovely, drowsy word?" and then they were finally outside, walking through the sand, with only steps to go.

He untied his horse, gave Lizzie a lift in his rig to the streetcar. "How I do carry on!" he cried in apology as they parted, but she assured him she wouldn't have him any other way. She caught the streetcar home and slept all afternoon. She spent the next few days calling on donors, determined not to return to the Ark until she was sure the Chinese boy was well settled in.

TWO

That Wednesday, Lizzie called at the Putnams'. Odd Wednesdays were Mrs. Putnam's regular at-home days and Lizzie was resuming her regular, pre—magical-juncture life down to the tiniest particular. Erma was visiting from Sacramento with the new baby, and Mrs. Mullin, like Lizzie, was obligated to attend. Lizzie was eager to show everyone her same old self, boring as ever, and keeping quiet about her real thoughts, just the way they liked her best.

She sat in the Putnams' conservatory, a fashionable room with a terra-cotta tile floor and curtains of dotted muslin. A fern grew in a bronze planter at the end of the sofa next to Lizzie. It was so large that one frond tapped her shoulder whenever she moved her head.

Outside, the sky darkened. A light rain flicked against

the windows, giving the room a contrasting coziness. The baby fussed. Mrs. Putnam took him from Erma, bounced him on her thighs, floated him on her fat, rustling skirts until he quieted. "Isn't he precious?" she asked, and Lizzie supposed that another time he was bound to be. He hiccoughed, his heavy eyelids flying open, startled, with each spasm. "Isn't he the precious man?"

"He is just so precious," Mrs. Mullin said. "Erma, he's a little rosebud!" Mrs. Mullin was wearing a dress of gray wool, with a white collar that sprang up around her thin neck. From certain angles her head seemed suspended above it like an impossibly balanced egg.

Blythe appeared, pushing a cart with their afternoon tea. Blythe was a widow with two adult sons who'd worked for the Putnams fifteen years now. When she left the room, Mrs. Putnam would say that they thought of Blythe as one of the family. Mrs. Mullin would add what a charity it was to keep her on, when a Chinaman could be got for so much less. Cheap Chinese help was one reason wives in San Francisco society were considered so spoiled.

Lizzie's own contributions were equally unvarying. "How are the boys, Blythe?" Lizzie asked, just as she always did, as if they weren't, in fact, grown men.

"I've no complaints, Miss Hayes," Blythe said, but in her absence, Mrs. Putnam would know better. The boys were badly behaved, shockingly extravagant. They would be the ruin of poor Blythe if not the actual death of her.

Blythe brought Lizzie the tea tray. On it were biscuits with almonds pressed into the tops and arranged like petals, and buttered toast with lime marmalade. Lizzie circled the spoon in her cup so it made a rough music against the china, like the tongue of a crude bell. She turned to Erma. "Think how many times you and I played at this. Tea parties with water for tea and wooden blocks for tea cakes. In this very house. Why are children in such a hurry to grow up?"

"Babies," said Erma complacently, "are God's very best idea." And that quickly the coziness was gone. Lizzie felt excluded from the sentiment, as though she were still playing make-believe while everyone else had gone on and done the real thing. She would never have a baby, nor would she be anyone's baby ever again. She had a tactile memory of her mother's hand on the back of her head, following the brushstroke down her hair, and was overcome with self-pity when it turned out to be the fern. Poor Lizzie had no one of her very own. She sat back and the fern frond groped at her bosom.

Outside the melancholy ticking of rain, inside the murmur of women's voices. Blythe was one of the family, but ever so much more expensive than a Chinaman would be. Children were God's very best idea, except for Blythe's, who would be the death of her. Mrs. Mullin had met a Mr. and Mrs. Derry while attending a lecture on the customs of Japan. "In Japan, they consider it impolite to finish the food on your plate!"

"Not really! Do you hear, Lizzie?"

"They won't take a gift unless it's offered three times! The first two are considered mere politeness."

Lizzie helped herself to another biscuit. What a nightmare fund-raising must be in Japan!

According to Mrs. Mullin, the Japanese were an exceptionally clean, respectable race, who only looked like the Chinese. The way you could tell the difference was that the Japanese were extremely sensitive to beauty. Sunrises and waterfalls and the like, they couldn't get enough of them. The Chinese didn't care so much for nature, which is why they were so good underground.

But the Derrys were a nice, refined sort of people, and they lived on Octavia, close to the Bell mansion. They'd told Mrs. Mullin that in the days before the Sharon trial had made Mrs. Pleasant such a public figure, large groups of Negroes used to gather at the House of Mystery for voodoo ceremonies. This would happen only on stormy nights and when Thomas Bell was away. "How those women carried on in his absence! They counted on the noise of the wind to cover the drums, but it didn't hardly do the job," Mrs. Mullin noted. "As if thunder rolls in rhythm!"

Mrs. Putnam's teacup floated to her mouth. She spoke from behind it. "I hope you've kept your promise and not seen that woman again." Everyone turned to look at Lizzie. "I'm forced to tell you there's been talk." Her voice *sounded* forced. It sounded tired, upset. "Ever since the séance your name has been linked to hers. A strong public disavowal right then and there would have settled the matter."

"I'll make one here and now. I'll have nothing more to do with her," Lizzie said. The room was warm with tea and approval. Poor Malina Paillet, who never got to be warm again. Drums and the moon and a young dead girl about whom no one cared. Red rooms and painted mouths. Statues of naked, pleading women. Good-bye to all of that, and not the tiniest touch of headache.

In fact, after her declaration, things got even better.

As a reward for being the same old Lizzie, Mrs. Putnam invited her to join them for the Saturday-evening promenade. Not this week, when they had a dinner to go to, but weather permitting, the next. Happy Lizzie! She loved the Saturday-night Market Street parade. Saturday afternoon was for women and fashion. Lizzie could go to that alone, but she had no interest. Saturday night required an escort.

And then things got better yet. The baby made a series of gaseous noises and began to smell. The nursemaid was hovering nearby. She was thin and drained-looking, a woman whose hands, when empty, drooped exhausted from her wrists. Mrs. Putnam handed little Charles to her. His odor receded down the hall, up the stairs, and behind the nursery doors. There was no further talk of what a rosebud he was. Lizzie drank her tea in utter contentment.

THREE

Then, after all that stalwart normalcy, that very Sunday, as she was leaving St. Luke's, she met Mr. Finney out with his hack. He tipped his hat, exclaimed unconvincingly on the coincidence, and offered her a free ride to the Ark or her home, wherever she was headed. In full sunlight, his eyes, behind his glasses, were bluer, but mottled as pebbles.

As part of being her same old self, Lizzie had determined never to see Mr. Finney again. Someone else could deal with the mystery of Jenny Ijub, though it had seduced her initially by being so like a story, with its medieval jousting and Irish wives as tiny as fairies. But she was resolved to leave it now unfinished, had never found Jenny an agreeable little girl. If there were a wealthy father, someone else would have to produce him.

Lizzie's mood of the moment was elevated. She'd just heard an improving sermon with many particulars worth considering at her leisure. "Making a home for Christ in your heart" had been the basic text, and she'd planned to spend the afternoon examining and redoubling her efforts to do so.

Instead, Mr. Finney. After the first shock, she was not frightened of him. It was daylight; there were plenty of people on the streets. He made the offer so courteously. There was a nasty, gritty wind, and a ride, even in an open hack, would be nicer than walking. She could see that the only way out was through. She asked to be taken to the Brown Ark, since there was no reason he should learn where she lived and she very much doubted the ride would be free.

Sure enough, Mr. Finney had a proposition to make. He began by telling her how much he admired her. His opinion of her was exceedingly high. "I see I didn't snow you for a minute," he said. He was relaxed, affable. He really was very good-looking, in a scholarly way, because of the spectacles, but easy in his movements and manner. Lizzie was proud to be seen with such a presentable young man. She rerouted some of her disapproval of him to herself for this ridiculous vanity.

He twisted around in his seat, scarcely tending to the horse, but it seemed to manage without him. "You didn't snow me, either," he continued. "I know you still have the child."

"I don't," Lizzie said, which was a lie on a Sunday and saddened her greatly. The wind boxed her ears. So she quickly tempered it with something true. "I do know where she is." In spite of her resolute uninvolvedness, she found she couldn't stop there. "What do you want with her?" she asked.

There was a suspenseful moment while she waited for the answer. She expected to hear about abandoned women. Romance and betrayal. Summer heat. A child born unwelcomely. *Babies are God's very best idea,* except when they're not. She could practically do the story herself, though the interest would be in the names and details. But a carriage was passing them; Mr. Finney had turned around momentarily to drive.

When he could, he turned back. Why, nothing, he told her. He didn't want the child at all. He was pleased to think of the good care she was getting with the good ladies of the Brown Ark. He gave Lizzie a gorgeous smile, revealing his tiny incisor like a fang. There was a sudden strong gust of wind, which took the yellow feather from her hat. Lizzie watched it fly away.

Not what the girl was accustomed to, Mr. Finney added darkly. Lizzie turned to look at him again. When he saw she was looking, he shook his head sadly. No, it was her mother wished her returned. Mr. Finney observed that a well-brought-up lady like Miss Hayes would have only the highest opinion of motherhood. Probably Miss Hayes's own mother was a saint. But Miss Hayes mustn't be picturing a natural mother with a natural mother's feelings. "Truly," Mr. Finney finished, "a great shame that God don't deny motherhood to women of cruel and grasping disposition." He seemed to be losing his Irish accent. It faded in and out of his speech now, as if he couldn't decide on his heritage.

It made Lizzie wonder whether he needed the glasses.

At just that moment he took them off. He pulled a hand-kerchief from his pocket; it snapped like a flag.

"But the child's mother could take her at any time," she pointed out. "I don't understand what she needs you for. I don't understand the need for lies and subterfuges."

The horse wandered to the side of Gough Street and stopped. In the resulting silence, Mr. Finney muted his voice. "Ah, but then there's Mammy Pleasant. She paid the mother good money for the child. She mustn't know the child's been taken back."

"She bought the child?" Lizzie asked. How would that happen? Was the child for sale to anyone, or had Mrs. Pleasant simply made an irresistible offer? She imagined Mrs. Pleasant coolly covering the face of a murdered girl with her housekeeping apron. What wouldn't the woman do? She resolved yet again not to play any part in Mrs. Pleasant's machinations.

"I imagine it pleased her to buy a little white girl." Mr. Finney's voice was prim. He wiped one eye with his hand-kerchief, dabbed at it. "I'm afraid some sand has blown into my eye," he said. "Might I impose upon you, Miss Hayes, to look?" There was nothing of Ireland in his accent now, but there might have been a whisper of Australia. "Please. I can feel a stone the size of a goose egg rolling about in there."

Lizzie could see no way to refuse him, not with his eye so obviously streaked with red. He leaned down to her and she leaned forward. The brim of her hat touched his face. They were almost close enough to kiss.

The eye he held open was swimming with tears. Through them Lizzie could see a pinpoint of dust. She took his handkerchief and touched it away. Inside her leather gloves, her fingers shivered. "I thank you," he told her. "You're a lady who doesn't shrink from a rough task. Many would have fainted."

He blinked several times, then returned to the topic under discussion. He didn't know what the bill of sale had been, he said, but he'd been offered thirty dollars for the quiet restoration of child to mother. Now, for that same thirty dollars, he would tell the mother he'd been unable to locate the child. He would pretend that Lizzie's trick had fooled him, as it might, after all, have done. He asked for no additional sum, because it sat so much better with his conscience to leave the girl where she was. He would have the thirty dollars he'd already all but earned, and he would have peace of mind as well. Everyone would be happy who deserved to be. He would prefer cash.

The horse urinated loudly. The noise went on and on. It was a sound Lizzie usually found comforting—the same sound as when you poured yourself a hot bath, the lullaby sound of rain on stone. Now it seemed merely coarse. This was an ugly request to come so close after a moment of some intimacy. Could he have dreamt for one instant that she would agree? The particular sum he requested had the touch of Judas in it.

"I have a small independence," Lizzie said coldly. She didn't credit a word he said. "But I'm not a wealthy woman."

The horse stamped its foot. Mr. Finney reached the whip to her shoulder, sketched down her arm with it. It didn't actually touch her, but Lizzie felt her face grow hot. "I begin to see the pattern of our friendship," Mr. Finney said. "And it's you denying me every little thing I ask."

He was flirting with her! "We're not friends," Lizzie said, climbing from the hack to the street. There was nothing flattering about this, she told herself, but she had to make the point sternly. She waited to feel as insulted as she'd been.

Mr. Finney's voice was increasingly soft. "That choice belongs to the lady, of course. But it disappoints me to hear you say so.

"Twenty-five dollars, then." He was clearly a man with a tender heart. "It's worth five dollars to me just to keep Mammy Pleasant out of it."

"I couldn't scrape together more than ten," Lizzie said haughtily. She meant it as a refusal. He took it as an offer. He said he would come to the Brown Ark the next day to get it. He picked up the reins and clattered away, abandoning her on Gough Street like the sharper he was.

Apparently neither age nor position nor blameless respectability protected a woman from the mockery of a man who'd attained none of these. Apparently he thought her so old and neglected that she would respond to any cheap attention. Even worse was the way she had done so. Lizzie stood looking after him, touching her gloved hands to her cheeks. She was angry, but she was also flushed and unsettled. She'd just been blackmailed and it was her very first time.

The wind had grown stronger. It hissed through the lattice of telegraph wires, rattled the ash cans, tossed single sheets of newspaper about like confetti, spit sand into the air. It lifted her dress and breathed on her ankles; loosened her hair from its pins and beat her around the face with it. She clutched her hat to her head.

Rabbi Voorsanger came around the corner. Usually his face was wreathed in his own cigar smoke. Today the wind was carrying the smoke away.

From an upstairs window Lizzie could just hear the chords of an accordion. They resolved themselves into "Santa Lucia." The rabbi's steps were light, and timed to the music. He danced his way down the hill, beard and coat flapping, until he disappeared into a crowd of people.

FOUR

So instead of making a home for Christ in her heart, Lizzie spent the afternoon thinking about Mr. Finney. First she thought that she could simply not be at the Brown Ark when he came. Let the matter of the Chinese boy have an extra day to settle itself. Let Nell be the one to send someone to send Mr. Finney off.

Then, having given the matter a troubled night, she'd realized that the right thing, however distasteful, however uncertain in result, the Christian thing, however it prolonged her involvement in the continued, messy saga of Jenny Ijub, would be to return the girl to her mother. She should meet Mr. Finney as planned and she should ask who Jenny's mother was and how to find her.

Perhaps she was not such a bad mother. Lizzie had no evidence beyond Mr. Finney's word that she was, and Mr. Finney's word was clearly insufficient.

There was, of course, the fact that she'd sold her daughter. Could a mother sell a daughter she loved? Lizzie thought that if she asked the Chinese boy this question, he would surely say yes. He would know of wonderful mothers who'd done just that. Apparently the woman cared enough for Jenny to offer thirty dollars for her return. Thirty dollars was probably a fortune to such a woman.

It had begun to rain that night and was raining hard by morning. Lizzie didn't usually go to the Ark in the rain. But when Lizzie made up her mind to something, it was made up. Jenny must be returned to the mother who wanted her back. This meant that Lizzie must first meet with Mr. Finney.

By lunchtime she'd forgotten Mr. Finney even existed.

While she was still dressing and making her plans, the Chinese boy arrived to fetch her. Ti Wong was a round-cheeked child, short and solidly packed, who looked younger than his eleven years. Of course, the Chinese calculated age differently. He told her he was collecting whatever board members he could. Mrs. Hallis, the Ladies' Relief and Protection Society president, and Mrs. Wilson, the ex-president, were already in the buggy. Nell said they were needed at once since some of the wards were ill.

His English turned out to be excellent, a fast, bitten-off staccato, but easy enough to understand and with a good vocabulary. Lizzie learnt later that it had improved wonderfully the minute Nell stopped trying to get someone to run him off.

One boy was especially ill, Meredith Penny, newly arrived from Santa Cruz. Ti Wong had himself helped Nell move Meredith in the night to the sickroom, and he told Lizzie that the boy had been too hot, with a too light, too shallow pulse. "Wood floating on water," he said. And when she didn't answer, added as if in explanation, "a Fu pulse."

The rain turned to a downpour. The mule stared curses at them, its ears set at an outraged angle. Lizzie took the seat in the front of the buggy and tried to hold an umbrella over herself and Ti Wong both. It was more polite than it was effective; he was already drenched. By the time they reached the Brown Ark, Ti Wong's teeth were chattering and his hands trembled the reins over the mule's back.

They drew up beside Dr. Kearney's rig. His bay nickered at them, gleaming wet and miserable. Ti Wong went to stable the mule and change his clothes. Lizzie and the other board members joined Nell and Dr. Kearney in the sickroom.

Meredith Penny was eight years old, Mrs. Lake told Lizzie later. He had plans to be a fireman. "I can't interest you in medicine, then?" Dr. Kearney was asking as Lizzie entered. He was seated by the bed in a chair that was too small for him, his knees high as a grasshopper's. He had his watch out; his hand cupped Meredith's wrist. "You have the look of a doctor to me."

Meredith allowed as how he might be a doctor.

"A doctor meets the nicest people," Dr. Kearney said.

In the parlor he gave the women his diagnosis. Diphtheria. Lizzie's feet were wet and her neck was cold. She didn't know whether the latter was from rain or terror. The storm was painting the parlor windows with water and sand, so that the room grew darker with every gust of wind. "Oh, my Lord," Mrs. Hallis said. Her hands were gripped together and still they shook. "Oh, my Lord."

Dr. Kearney put the Brown Ark under immediate quarantine. Lizzie sent Ti Wong out in his dry clothes into the storm to nail the yellow warning card onto the front door and stable the doctor's horse.

The other children were released from class and told to wait on their beds until Dr. Kearney could see them. By the end of the morning, Jenny Comstock, age fourteen, Ella Louisa Gray, age five, Harry Whinery, age five, and Kate Hanley, age seven, had all been sent to the sickroom. Six days passed and they'd been joined by Tilly Beacon, age twelve, Mansel Bennett, age eleven, Mattie Lorenzen, age seven, Elizabeth Jane Comstock, age fourteen, Alexander MacPherson, age five, George Maxwell, age nine, and Edward Reed, age twelve.

In later years Lizzie often felt she remembered little of those dreadful days. She had been too tired and too terrified to take it in. Just as often, she felt she could never forget it. One child after another became listless and feverish. Some of them complained of sore throats, more did not. Their cheeks were the color of burnt roses, their lips slowly turned blue. Only the unaffected cried; the sick were too busy breathing.

Every woman on the board with no small children of

her own arrived to help. When they slept, they slept on the sofas in the tower room and the parlor and on chairs beside the children's beds. They did manage to contain the disease within the Ark itself; no cases were reported in the rest of the city.

Bartholomew Fitton's father attempted to remove him from the Ark. He stood on the porch, a small, fat, desperate man in a straw hat, shouting at Nell so that all the children could hear. No power on earth would force him to leave his son there to die, he shouted. He tried to shoulder Nell aside, but she would not move. The police took Mr. Fitton away. A gun was found in his breast pocket; the officer then posted at the door told them so. This officer had his own children and wouldn't accept so much as a cup of tea from inside.

Meanwhile, the Comstocks, whose twins were already showing signs of the disease, made a tent for themselves in sight of the sickroom windows. They appeared under these every morning, waiting. Mrs. Lake would open the windows. "All serene," she would call, so they'd know their children had lived through another night.

Meredith Penny was moved again, this time into a private room. Lizzie sat with him for hours, soaked in the general smell of sickness and the particular smell of this sickness—an unmistakable sort of wet mouse odor. When she'd been without sleep for more than a day, Lizzie had moments that returned her to her mother's deathbed. She stroked her mother's arm. She brushed her mother's hair. Her father's death was much more recent, but sudden and unexpected, a heart attack, and without the awful vigil.

No one had really gotten to know this child. She tried to hold his twitching hands, she talked to him, she sponged his forehead. All the while, his eyes bulged from their sockets; his breath rasped in his throat like a crow cawing.

She ran out of things to say. She didn't know what songs he might like, or what stories. She wanted to talk to him about him, to give him a whole story of himself. This is what you love, she wanted to say. This is what you're good at. These are the foods you like to eat. Here's something you said when you were five. But she didn't know him at all.

On the seventh day he seemed better, and she waited hopefully for Dr. Kearney to tell her this was not her imagination. Dr. Kearney shook his head, leaning down to her softly. "This is the worst for me," he said. "When it's children and there's nothing for me to do." Meredith Penny's fever rose higher and higher, until it carried him away. He died, and Lizzie and Mrs. Hallis and Dr. Kearney and the Reverend Phillips watched him do it.

Later that morning Nell found Lizzie hiding in the cupola. "You need to eat and you need to sleep," Nell said. Grief made her even fiercer than usual. "We're only getting started," she added, because she was no one for the comforting lie.

Lizzie was hungry, but she couldn't make herself go back downstairs. I'll never sleep, she thought, but she did, though she rose four hours later, unrested. In that same four hours, Lena Heath, age ten, had been sent to the sick-room.

The rain of days before had passed. It would have suited Lizzie better than this calm blue, this high, indifferent sky. She went to the kitchen to make herself some coffee. She turned at the slippery sound of Mrs. Lake's shoes.

"He's with his mother now," Mrs. Lake told her. "That's what I try to hold in my mind. The child falling asleep in his mother's arms. There's rejoicing in heaven today." This surely should have been a great comfort, but Lizzie could not make it so. She was too tired. She had another bit of a cry and then washed her face, combed her hair, and returned to the sickroom.

A week later, the sick included Ella May Howard, age twelve, Franka Haun, age six, May Isabella Miller, age twelve, Dock Franklin Cole, age eight, Bartholomew Fitton, age five, and Harry Ambrose, age eight. Mattie Lorenzen was dead, although Dr. Kearney had performed a tracheotomy to try to save him. So was Ella Louisa Gray, the first child in her class to learn to skip.

On February 22, Nell woke Lizzie from an afternoon nap. "Ti Wong," she said simply, and Lizzie rose to follow her down the stairs to the private room for the dying. Miss Stevens had arrived already and stood by the boy's bed.

His appearance was an enormous shock, just when each of the women would have said she was far past shocking. They'd not thought of him as one of the children. No one had ever asked him how he was feeling. Nell's face was wet and melted at the eyes, soft as dough. "He never complained, the lamb. He did as he was told and he never complained. Just yesterday I sent him to the basement for clean blankets. He must have already been deathly ill. Running up and down those flights of stairs. If only we'd sent him right away as I wished. Just a few weeks with us will be enough to kill him."

Ti Wong did not appear to be conscious. He lay with

his fingers opening and closing as if he could catch his breath in his hands. "The policeman's gone for Dr. Kearney," Nell said. "I only hope he can be found."

Lizzie leaned down and tried to speak to Ti Wong. Beneath the thin surface of his lids, his eyes darted about like minnows. She picked up his hand, hot in hers, still grasping spasmodically. She felt his wrist; his pulse was unsteady, intermittent. A Fu pulse, Lizzie remembered he'd said with casual eleven-year-old competence. She was the one who'd let him stay. She was the one to send him out to stable a horse in his last suit of dry clothes. This one would fall to her account.

The other women returned to the other patients. Lizzie sat with Ti Wong. She prayed to God to spare them both. God makes no bargains, her mother had told her often enough, and a woman with a dead child knows this better than anyone. But Lizzie had never gotten out of the habit. In return for Ti Wong she offered God Ti Wong. Give us back this valuable child, she prayed, and I promise to value him. I promise him a valuable life. Not as a servant, but as something requiring education, a minister or a teacher.

She knew this promise would be hard to fulfill. She stood by it. Let the very difficulty of it speak to her desperation. Ti Wong's breath slid in and out of his throat with a sound like sandpaper. He lived on a ribbon of air, which spun down to a thread. His face went from blue to black. His hand went from hot to cold. Two hours passed, and then three.

Then came a long moment when he didn't breathe at

all. Lizzie was on her feet, ringing frantically for the other women, when the trough of his chest finally rose.

"He's dying," she told Nell, who arrived first. "If Dr. Kearney's rig isn't already outside, then he's too late."

She couldn't take her eyes off Ti Wong's chest. She was hardly aware of Miss Stevens, arriving with towels, alcohol, a knife, a child's silver whistle, until she spoke. "We'll have to do it ourselves," Miss Stevens said. "I'll do it. I've watched Dr. Kearney three times now."

If she hadn't offered, the procedure might have been discussed. It was possible the terrified women would have talked about it and talked about it until it was too late. Lizzie was overwhelmed with gratitude. Wonderful Miss Stevens with her science projects and her dissections. Her wonderful young eyes and her steady heart. Ti Wong began to convulse. His chest was an empty bowl.

Lizzie held him by the arms. She had to climb onto the bed to do this, hoist her skirts and straddle the boy. Nell took hold of his head. Miss Stevens put the knife to his throat. She paused then, with her eyes closed. "Yea, though I walk through the valley of the shadow of death, I will fear no evil," Lizzie said. She spoke loudly for Ti Wong to hear. Nell joined her. ". . . for Thou art with me." Miss Stevens made her first cut.

"Hold him still," she cried, because the child had jerked and struggled. Blood flowed from his throat, pooled in the cup of his neck. "I can't see what I'm doing," she said then, sharply. "There wasn't so much blood for Dr. Kearney." Lizzie let go of Ti Wong's arms to towel the blood away with both hands. It came too fast, ran from his neck like water from a spout, seeped into Lizzie's sleeves. Miss Stevens had slit his throat.

Lizzie stopped wiping the blood away and tried to hold it back instead. Miss Stevens pushed her hands aside, made a second blind cut. There, amidst the blood, Lizzie could see a thin white shining reed. Miss Stevens impaled it on the point of her knife, rotated her wrist. With the other hand, she slid the whistle down beside the blade. Ti Wong's chest rose at once, his breath singing a long, high, hysterical note, twice, three times. His face grew pink again and his fists relaxed. He slept while Miss Stevens held the whistle in place with her fingers and Lizzie kept the blood back with soaking towels and her hands.

Five minutes later Dr. Kearney rushed in and found them there, Lizzie still astride Ti Wong, afraid to move. What a picture they must have made, Lizzie thought later. Miss Hayes and Miss Stevens drenched in gore, two Lady Macbeths up to their elbows, their hands inside Ti Wong's neck, and Ti Wong singing in his sleep like a bird. The doctor was impressed all the way to speechlessness by the sight of them.

It was something to remember, something to carry with them out of the horror, that they had behaved with courage and competence. When a thing needed doing, they had done it. Miss Stevens was the heroine, of course, but Lizzie had also come through. Ti Wong survived diphtheria and the Ladies' Relief and Protection Society both, and had the scars to prove it.

The next day Bartholomew Fitton, George Maxwell, and Elizabeth Jane Comstock died within hours of one another. It was a dreadful, unspeakable day.

These proved to be the final diphtheria deaths. Of the fifty-seven children residing in the Brown Ark at the time, twenty contracted the disease and six of those died. The other fourteen recovered their health—"Children are resilient," Dr. Kearney said—but the agony of loss was slow to recede.

FIVE

For many months afterward, every moment of pleasure for Lizzie was quickly followed by feelings of guilt. Where before she'd wished to return to her normal self as a matter of principle, now it was a matter of need. Another magical juncture she must find the strength to refuse. But how would she ever enjoy her dinner, her book, her Saturday ride again? She lost weight, though not to the point of being thin. She couldn't sleep. Ti Wong was the only subject on which she could allow herself to be happy.

What a bright boy he turned out to be. She loved to hear how he'd wheedled Nell into letting him make popcorn or taffy. If any of the other children asked, Nell said it was too much mess. But Ti Wong was her pet, her favorite.

When he was still abed, letting Lizzie read him Sherlock Holmes mysteries and recovering his voice, she had told Nell that they needed to give more thought to his future. Nell was surprisingly agreeable, even to this. "What would you like to be when you grow up?" Lizzie had asked him.

She herself had already decided he'd be a doctor. A Fu pulse, he'd told her. Dr. Kearney could surely be co-opted into this project. He would see the value in a doctor who spoke Chinese but was trained in Western medicine, none of that hocus-pocus of spinning needles.

Ti Wong had answered he wanted to be a Pinkerton, but that could be changed. Would have to be changed. The Pinks wouldn't take a Celestial.

And then, just when some routine was finally returning—classes, fights among the boys, quarrels among the girls all resumed—just when it seemed things could, in fact, go on Minna Graham came to the breakfast table, complaining of a headache. The light was dreadful bright, she told them. Her eyes hurt. She asked to go back to bed. Nell was too tired to deal with it. She suggested that Minna, unable to contract diphtheria and largely ignored during the epidemic, now wanted attention. This was agreed to be just like Minna Graham. She went so far as to break out in large red spots.

Measles, Dr. Kearney said. Two weeks later seven of the children, including Jenny Ijub, had rashes. New cases continued to appear throughout the month. Fortunately the strain involved was a light one. The new epidemic recalled the tragedies inevitably to everyone's mind, but didn't repeat them.

SIX

Next came an epizoetic. More than half the horses in the Turf Gallery and the Fashion Stables on Sutter Street contracted distemper, as well as twenty of the horses in the Bill Bridges Stable, thirteen in the Hopkins Stable, and four in Roe Allen's Stable on Market Street. Citywide some three hundred horses were affected. A chloride of lime mixed with carbolic acid was recommended for use about the barn. For horses themselves, potash and licorice root were to be applied in a paste directly onto the swollen glands in the throat.

The symptoms, case by case, were mild, but the aggregate was not; the streetcar companies were all but crippled. Yet under these adverse circumstances Myrtle Rolphe managed to get to Chinatown. Unaccompanied by police or clergy, with the proprietor protesting her every step, Miss Rolphe walked into the bowels of an opium den. With one hand she held a lavender-scented handkerchief over her nose to protect herself from the seductive fumes. With the other she seized one of Jesus' straying lambs by the ear and dragged him to safety. The incident was less than twenty-four hours old, and Lizzie had already heard the story five times at least.

Ti Wong could not hear it often enough. He was so obviously in love with Miss Rolphe. It made Lizzie very sad. Such an open display, such a hopeless object. She thought of Diego Estenagas, her Spanish prince. Only unrequited love lasted forever. Poor Ti Wong would spend his life desiring pretty, charitable white women who liked him only for his faith.

SEVEN

*A*lthough all the women at the Brown Ark carried the diphtheria tragedies with them for the rest of their lives, on Mrs. Lake there was an immediate and peculiar impact. She began to insist that Ti Wong had brought the disease from Chinatown, even though Meredith Penny had obviously arrived from Santa Cruz already ill, even though there'd been no other reported cases in San Francisco and a deadly plague in Santa Cruz.

Not that it mattered, Mrs. Lake was quick to assert. No one was blaming anyone. But. Still. Lizzie thought Mrs. Lake was suffering from not having saved anybody with an emergency tracheotomy. Miss Stevens was handling herself better.

There was another factor contributing to Mrs. Lake's imbalance. An unrelenting series of plagues is always

bound to carry a biblical portent. But San Francisco had
already been hearing for some time that Armageddon was
coming.

One afternoon back in October, when Lizzie had
been eating a lunch at the Brown Ark, by invitation of
course, she'd brought up the rumors of the appearance in
Nevada of an Indian Messiah. He was reported to be
preaching of the coming of a new world, a world without
white people, which was even now floating in the heavens,
drifting eastward from the Pacific toward the plains. When
the new world landed, the whites would be destroyed, while
all the dead Indians and herds of dead buffalo would be
resurrected. The Messiah asked His followers only to be
honest, peaceable, and chaste. He was said to perform
miracles. This was all, in Lizzie's mind, very Christian,
which made it hard to dismiss.

Miss Stevens had responded to Lizzie by telling the
table how, in August of 1872, the Indians in Lake County
had begun to perform the Misha Dance, prompted by the
appearance of a monstrous fish in Blue Lakes. They'd
feared the end of the world was at hand, Miss Stevens said.
Her tone of voice was amused, as if these fears had, in fact,
been demonstrably mistaken.

The real subject of this conversation was Mrs. Maria
B. Woodworth. Mrs. Woodworth was an evangelist, called
on by God in spite of her sex. She'd arrived in Oakland after a triumphant tour of the Midwest, set up a tent, and
begun a series of revivals. Here are just a few of the things
people said about her:

"Genuine, old-fashioned Methodist religion" (Dr.
Lewis Kern).

"I like it the best of anything I ever saw in the way of a religious meeting" (I. H. Ellis).

"The same low order which characterized the African Voodoo, and the Indian Medicine Man" (Charles Wendt, Unitarian pastor).

"Mental debauchery" (*Tribune* editorial).

Mrs. Woodworth's technique was charismatic to the point of mesmerism. Her followers fell often into ecstatic trances, during which they lay as if dead. These trances could last for hours or days, until those who experienced them came to at last, weeping and seeing angels.

Oakland doctors wrote letters to the papers, expressing concern about the effects of undiluted religion upon the weak-minded. Lizzie had read an article about one Albertson Smith, who, after attending one evening, was convinced he could fly. He leapt from the upper deck of the Oakland ferry, crashed onto the dock, and was taken into police custody.

But Mrs. Lake had actually gone to one of the winter meetings, and brought back a cautiously neutral report. The audience had by then swelled from an initial twenty-three Doom Sealers, as her followers were known, to several thousand. "It was all brimstone and the fiery pit," she'd told Miss Stevens, Lizzie, and Nell. "Babies were crying. Women were screaming. Half the crowd was singing one hymn, the other half another. People of every color there, and all treated exactly alike. Outside, the wind, howling and snapping at the tent. I couldn't hear Mrs. Woodworth at all, I could only just see her, standing at the altar with her arms raised in the air and bodies all around her feet. There must have been twenty of them or more, stiff and lifeless as logs.

"Then, just when I was wishing I hadn't come, just when I was thinking something cynical and worldly, I noticed my hands beginning to shake. They were all atingle, dancing around at the end of my arms, and I couldn't control them. And then it was my legs and I slid to the floor as gently as if I were swimming through water. One of the men cupped his hands through the air above me, as if he saw the water, too, and I were being baptized. 'Now you'll see something beautiful,' he said. Then everything went black except for one light I thought was a star, but it turned out to be the top of the tent." She offered to take Lizzie along next time. "You'll see that she has a power not easily explained," Mrs. Lake said.

But Lizzie thought it didn't sound quite the place for Episcopalians. She was joined in this sentiment by the bishop, who, in November, had issued a general instruction to stay away from women who preached. "Much good can be done by women in a quiet way," he'd said. "There is no need to make a public parade out of praying for the sick."

Privately Nell and Lizzie agreed that Mrs. Lake was among the more susceptible of God's creations and had never had a cynical or worldly thought in her life. "I'd like to see anyone try to make me see angels," said Nell, and Lizzie would have liked to see this, too.

Then Christmas had come and gone, and it was late January when Mrs. Woodworth had her vision. She'd seen a mountain of water rise out of the Pacific and fall on the three cities of Alameda, Oakland, and San Francisco. She'd pleaded with God, asking Him to spare the cities if ten righteous men could be found within them. His answer was that all the righteous should move immediately inland. His judgment on the unrighteous would take the form of a tidal wave.

This vision was shared by several of Mrs. Woodworth's followers, who added their own details. The wave would hit on April 14, 1890, just after Easter. Chicago would be simultaneously destroyed, and also Milwaukee. Europe would be plunged into war. The Doom Sealers petitioned the governor, asking him to read the Book of Jonah, set aside a day for prayer, and remove all prisoners, monies, and securities in the San Francisco area to high ground. They published pamphlets. They quit their jobs, sold their homes and belongings, and left the city.

This was the context in which Mrs. Lake had her pupils praying at all hours, searching their souls for hidden sins as if it were an Easter egg hunt. They were studying the Dark Ages, and she played a dreadful game of tag for which she'd enlisted Ti Wong. She told him to walk up and down the aisles of the room, touching the students—boys and girls both!—at random on the shoulder. Everyone he touched was to go stand at the back of the room. When the game was over, a quarter of the class remained in their seats. The others were dead. It was an aid to understanding the great plagues of Europe. Mrs. Lake claimed she'd asked Ti Wong to participate because the plague came first from China.

Such a cruel lesson, so poorly timed, so unlike gentle Mrs. Lake. The game had given Minna Graham nightmares; she'd been one of the last children touched. In her dreams, a great black bird circled her head and landed on her shoulder. She heard the rustle of its feathers in her ear and awoke crying, saying that it was pecking at her eyes. All the girls in the room with her were in a state. Mrs. Lake was sent off to the spa in Pope Valley to take the waters until she was herself again.

EIGHT

Nell felt strongly that among the many ill-advised features of this game must be counted the encouragement Ti Wong had been given to touch the girls. She marched him up to the cupola, where Lizzie was sorting through recent donations, so that Lizzie could talk to him about this. Someone had actually donated a used pessary. Lizzie swept it quickly underneath a cotton skirt.

She had no intention of discussing the matter of touching white girls with Ti Wong, but since he was standing before her, waiting, she tried to think of something else to discuss.

"I go somewhere for you?" he asked. "Fetch something?"

"No," Lizzie answered. "I don't need a thing," and

then she reconsidered. Somewhere here, on one of the tabletops, she had left the address Mrs. Pleasant had given her for headache medicine. She had tried to go once, but had not been able to communicate with the druggist, was not even sure she'd found the right place. She'd come away with candied ginger, pretending that was what she'd wanted all along, although she had no idea what to do with it, and eventually threw it away even though she could see it would never, ever spoil and maybe she would need it one day. It had represented a failure.

Now she rose and moved the stacks of books, the almost empty bottles of ink, the letter openers, the agate paperweight, the watch face with no innards, and a faded pincushion, filled with sawdust and shaped like a strawberry. Instead of seeds it was studded with glass-topped pins, and underneath was Mrs. Pleasant's scrap of paper. Lizzie read the address aloud. "Could you find this place?" she asked Ti Wong.

"I know this place," he said. "Hall of Joyful Relief."

Myrtle Rolphe had been very clear and quite insistent. Ti Wong would run any errand, she had said, except those that took him into Chinatown. His uncle and aunt were apparently resigned to his Christianity now, and to his new home at the Brown Ark, but they could always change their minds. Any new boat could bring additional relatives, or people who claimed to be additional relatives. Then poor Ti Wong would be taken away and forced to worship idols.

But surely he would be safe enough if he and Lizzie went to Chinatown together. They would take the mule and then walk. Fresh air was always good for growing boys.

For many years a rumor had persisted that Chinatown existed as a false façade over a large underground city. Beneath the streets, the Chinese residents had dug a maze eight stories deep, where opium was smoked, slave girls hidden, gambling and tong wars pursued with Oriental implacability. In these tunnels a new race was feared to be evolving. These new, underground Chinese were said to be even more able to withstand hardship and deprivation than the originals. Someday they would come boiling out of their holes like ants.

There was another persistent rumor—that white women were kidnapped on the streets of Chinatown and kept as slaves in the dark below. Tell the proprietor I sent you, Mrs. Pleasant had said, Mrs. Pleasant about whom it was sometimes whispered that she sold white babies to Chinamen. From Lizzie's point of view there was just enough danger in a trip to Chinatown to make it a pleasure and not so much as to make it an adventure.

The Hall of Joyful Relief was located on Washington Place. The streets were crowded and noisy, dark and narrow. It had rained in the night, the water rushing down California Street to puddle in the alleys and reflect the red and gilt of the balconies above. There was the smell of fish and incense. Ti Wong led Lizzie past a barbershop, where a man bent over a customer, reaching into his ear with a little black pick, then past a grocery, where sugar cane stalks leaned like fishing poles against the walls. Racks of plucked chickens hung by their necks in the windows. On the sidewalk were buckets of live crabs and turtles.

A white man emerged from an alleyway, winked at Lizzie rudely, and walked by. Nothing about him suggested that he was a gentleman. They passed a restaurant whose odors she had never encountered before and could not identify, but made her mouth water anyway. On Dupont, thin, reedy music floated down from an upper story. One huge golden tooth swung from the balcony railing of a building where, presumably, a dentist worked. On the next balcony over, Lizzie saw an old man smoking a pipe and staring back at her. They passed a house flying the dragon flag of China and a large sign in English that read: "Chow Loon, 4 family Parental Tablet Society."

A woman with wooden soles and ankle bracelets walked by, her bracelets ringing, her shoes clapping. She wore rouge in a large red oval that covered her face, and her hair was oiled a shiny black. All San Francisco knew of the sad lives of Chinese slave women. The sight made Lizzie take hold of Ti Wong's sleeve. He turned to look at her. She thought he might imagine she was trying to keep him, instead of her intention, which was to keep him safe. She let go.

In the window of the Hall of Joyful Relief, a row of green bottles caught the sun. Each bottle held a horned toad, pickled and standing on its head. The druggist sat at a table, writing something for another man who stood and dictated in rapid Chinese. When Lizzie and Ti Wong entered, the druggist held up one hand to silence them before they spoke. Lizzie watched him write. He held the brush upright with his thumb and index finger, but moved it down the page with the little finger. After he finished, the two men talked together briefly.

Then the druggist turned to Lizzie. "Tell him," Lizzie

said to Ti Wong, "that I want a tea for headache. Tell him Mrs. Pleasant, the colored woman from Octavia Street, said he would know what to give me."

She was embarrassed to have come. The bottles of toads did not look scientific to her. She had no faith in the enigmatic learning of the Orient. If their religion was primitive, wouldn't their medicine be the same? She could just hear the bells of St. Mary's tolling the hour, a reproachful, Christian sound. And yet, as administered by Mrs. Pleasant, the tea had seemed to help. To ignore actual experience was also a form of superstition.

The druggist reached over and took hold of Ti Wong's clipped hair. He rubbed it with his fingers. Lizzie felt his disapproval. He touched the scars on Ti Wong's throat. Next he reached past Ti Wong to Lizzie, grasping her wrist, pressing for her pulse. He spoke extensively in Chinese, then disappeared into the back of the shop, and returned with a paper envelope filled with dried leaves and flowers. He held up four fingers. Four cups of tea? Four cents? Lizzie turned to Ti Wong, who managed the purchase for her.

"What did he say to you?" she asked Ti Wong when they were on the street again.

"That Mrs. Pleasant very smart," said Ti Wong. "That you have many headaches."

It had been a much longer conversation than that, but Lizzie didn't question him further. On the corner of Dupont and Washington, a bearded man sat at a table covered with red cloth on which were placed several painted boxes. He called to Ti Wong, reached into one box, pulled out a paper, and read from it. He laughed, and all trace of expression left Ti Wong's face. They walked on.

"Do you know that man?" Lizzie asked.

"Fortune-teller. Friend of uncle."

"What did he say to you?"

Ti Wong fluttered his fingers along the scars on his neck as if he were playing a flute. Lizzie didn't think he knew he was doing so. She wished it to be a cheerful mannerism, but feared it was a nervous one.

"My fortune," he said. He wouldn't look at her. "That Jesus boys be swimming soon, but Chinese boys stay happy and dry."

NINE

After living at the Ark in quarantine for so many weeks, Lizzie had been surprised by how hard it was to return to her solitary house. She'd thought she couldn't wait for her quiet breakfasts again, with only the newspaper for company, for her own bedroom and her own bed, but sleep eluded her. Or so it seemed, though she must have dozed sometimes, because one morning she remembered a dream. She was in a boat with a blue-eyed man who turned out to be Mr. Finney. He stood. "Save me," he said. He stepped onto the water and sank slowly, as if into mud—up to his knees, up to his waist, up to his shoulders, out of sight.

Lizzie had forgotten about Mr. Finney, and also about Jenny's mother and her own plans regarding them. Currently she had no appetite for schemes of any kind. God would do as God would do. Why meddle? Besides, she'd no way to contact Mr. Finney.

In fact, she could think of nothing worth getting out of bed for. Donations had more than doubled during the epidemics, while the number of wards had significantly dropped. Many of the survivors had been removed at the first chance by relatives. They would not be back until the specter of death faded from everyone's mind. As a consequence there were beds and shoes enough for everyone. The larder was stocked. Lizzie didn't suppose the budget had ever been so healthy.

Take a rest, everyone told Lizzie, take a trip. Just when she hadn't heart enough for either.

She lay one morning, hardly moving, under her mother's quilt, a pattern like a shackle of rings in blue and white. The white was turning to yellow and the fabric was beginning to fray. A large spider web filled the corner of the bedroom window. Lizzie couldn't see the spider, but on the sill beneath the web lay the dry, hollow corpses of two flies. The window and the curtains needed washing. Nothing was as it should be. What kind of world was it that required the deaths of children? What kind of magical juncture was that?

Are you happy with your life? Mrs. Pleasant had asked her on that first afternoon in the House of Mystery, and ever since the question, and only since the question, the answer had become no. How did she used to do it, take such pleasure in small things? How would she ever be able to do so again?

If there had been someone to bring her breakfast, Lizzie wouldn't have gotten up at all. She would have asked for tea, blankets, a fire, a story with dragons in it—a story out of someone else's childhood—or a lullaby from the same. But there was only the constant weight of Baby Edward, watching her lie there as if dead, when anyone could see she was anything but.

Finally she was too hungry. She went to the kitchen without combing her hair and made herself a poached egg on toast. Nothing spoiled food the way eating alone did. Flavors flattened, textures coarsened. Chocolate turned to copper. Chewing became audible and then thunderous. Lizzie looked back on her childhood in this very house, and it seemed to be all solitary meals, brought to her room on trays. She could not recall that she had eaten anything hot more than once or twice in her life before adulthood.

She decided to call on Mrs. Wright, who liked to tell stories and had few chances to do so. Lizzie had grown quite fond of her during their incarceration together. A visit would be an act of charity and, like all the best acts of charity, good for them both.

She found Mrs. Wright sitting in her chair in her bedroom at the Ark, facing the window, the curtains tightly pulled. There was little light in the room, and a cloying, medicinal smell, like fermented cloves. Mrs. Wright spoke before Lizzie had a chance to announce herself. "Did you have a nice time in the country, dear?"

Lizzie had talked of going to the country. "I haven't left yet," she said. She had no energy for holidays.

"You should. Birds and trees. God's poetry. Nature triumphant. Of course, at my age the words bring that bit of a chill. Nature is as nature does."

"Nonsense," said Lizzie. "You're in bloom." After all,

Mrs. Wright couldn't see herself. Perhaps she would believe this.

"Nonsense back to you." Mrs. Wright's voice was made of salt.

Lizzie went to open the curtains. The clouds hung low and unbroken. The light was sullen and turned everything it touched green.

She pulled a chair into place beside Mrs. Wright and described the light to her. "I feel that way myself today," Lizzie finished. "Colorless, sunless." It was an intimate revelation. There was no reason for her to trouble Mrs. Wright with it.

"I expect you're just tired. You should buy yourself something. Ask Mr. McCallum at the Bank of California. He'll give you a draft on my account." Mrs. Wright waved her hands as if Lizzie had protested. "You know how I love to see you in something pretty." She felt for Lizzie's lap, patted it, found her hand and squeezed.

She'd drifted again. Lizzie was glad to see that she'd landed in a time when she had money and could be with someone she loved. "I'll do that," Lizzie said. "It's very kind of you."

The orange cat appeared outside. It was stalking something small, a rat perhaps, or a mole. The cat slid along the sand with focused, watery grace. Lizzie, whose heart was all with the world's little victims, could do nothing but refuse to watch. She looked instead at the lowering sky. "The city feels different to me now that I'm out in it again," she said. "It's grown around us so quickly I don't often notice, but I see it fresh just now. Like a scab laid over the past. I remember when this was all sand and chaparral. I remember those gold and silver horses the Spanish used to ride. They were so beautiful. You never see those now. Of course, you remember it better than I."

"Mostly I remember mud," Mrs. Wright said, "with empty whiskey bottles sunk into it like cobblestones to make a sidewalk, and the way the fires kept on coming, one right after another." She sucked on her false teeth with a wet, hissing sound, turned her face to Lizzie, her eyes white and veined as Florentine marble. "The land didn't want us at first. We were the persistent ones, had to be. So bring on your tidal waves. We'll survive them all right."

Well, if nothing more than endurance was required, Lizzie decided she could do it. It occurred to her that probably some Indian woman about her age had once stood in these very sand dunes and thought the same thing. How many white people can there be? How long can they stay? How much can they change?

Still, some things do endure. All around us, all inside us, something ancient manages to survive. The cat had come up empty. It sat, licked at the bottom of one paw, and then turned its head so that Lizzie saw its blunt muzzle outlined against the sand.

The
Good
Manners
Club

———

ONE

$\mathcal{M}$ary Ellen Pleasant was called to testify on Allie Hill's behalf six times during the years of the Sharon divorce case and was never cross-examined. Shortly before her death, she gave an interview in which she explained this fact. William Sharon had offered her $500,000 to quit the case. "Take the money," he'd said. "Go away and be Queen of the Niggers."

She'd refused the offer and the insult, but told him she would speak of both if his lawyers ever came after her on the stand.

Mrs. Pleasant was widely believed to be paying Allie Hill's expenses, but what the trial really cost her was her reputation. The main thing Mrs. Pleasant was charged with was baby-farming. This was irrelevant to the Sharon case, but went to character. Mrs. Pleasant had connections with foundling hospitals and prostitutes. She could tell any fun-loving man of influence and property that he'd had a child; he'd have no way of disproving it. She had a reckless uncon-cern for getting the correct baby into the correct family.

One day Thomas Bell was called to the stand to testify for Allie Hill. On May 1 of 1881, Sharon's lawyers claimed, Allie had been to the graveyard, casting spells and burying socks. Thomas Bell was called to refute. He distinctly re-called that Allie Hill had been at Octavia Street all that same day, making doll clothes for Viola and Marie.

"How many children do you have?" Sharon's attorney asked on cross-examination.

The question was objected to as irrelevant.

"Thomas Bell claims to remember the exact day of Miss Hill's visit, though it happened three years ago," the lawyer argued. Surely they were entitled to test his memory a bit on other matters.

The question was allowed. Mr. Bell proved unable to answer. It might be six. It might be seven. He was flustered. "Take your time," the attorney said. "Use your fingers."

Mrs. Pleasant's baby-farming, Sharon's lawyers went on to argue, was so pervasive, the House of Mystery itself wasn't safe from her.

In later cases, those concerning the Bell estate, the origins of the Bell children were thoroughly discussed. Friends, tradesmen, physicians, psychics, spurned lovers, and dismissed servants were all called upon to clarify the inner workings of the household, though clarity was never the result of this mass of contradictory testimony.

One servant who did not testify, but was testified about, was a young woman from Panama named Bella Stercus. She'd come to work for the Bell family in 1879. The broad outlines of her story, as told by others, were supported decades later by the testimony given in the Teresa Bell estate case.

Bella Stercus was the oldest of seven children whose father had died and whose mother could no longer manage to feed so many. She came to San Francisco with little money and little English. One of the hands on her boat, pitying her, had told her to find Mrs. Mary E. Pleasant on Octavia Street and say she needed work. She arrived with only the clothes she was wearing, but she spoke of bringing all six of her siblings to America. Mrs. Pleasant liked her spirit.

"So you've experience with children," Mrs. Pleasant said. Her Spanish was slightly better than Bella's English; between them they managed to understand each other. She engaged Bella to act as nursemaid for Fred Bell, who was now four, and Marie, who was two.

Bella had never seen anything like the House of Mystery. When she first lived there, she walked on tiptoe through the dark halls, the white rooms. The house was as silent and dim as the bottom of a pond, though the lamps and mirrors and bits of glass sent random sparkles into it like flickering fish.

The fact that Bella could hardly talk to anyone made her feel invisible, a ghost from the nursery. The staff was mostly white and she was unused to white people. After a day spent with the two white children, her own face in the mirror seemed murky, strange, all wrong, even to herself.

It was a quiet house, but sometimes she could see that things were going on. Doors and curtains would be closed. A murmur would run through the dark halls. She would take the children onto the lawn and reporters would shout questions she didn't understand through the wrought-iron gate. Once she discovered a man digging in the arbor and had to call Sam from the stables to chase him away. Later she was told that many people thought Mrs. Pleasant had a cache of diamonds buried somewhere in the yard. Sam liked to say that anyone who couldn't get to the Comstock came to dig for treasure on Octavia Street.

Nelson Brady, the colored groundskeeper, did tricks with the shadows of his hands for her. He made wolves, roosters, and angels. "Bella, Bella," he said. He was using her Christian name, or else he was telling her she was beautiful. Either was awfully fresh, but since she didn't know which it was, she didn't take offense.

Fred and Marie were placid and dimpled, easy children to care for, and yet they exhausted Bella as her own siblings never had. She went to bed as soon as the children did, and sank into sleep as if she were drowning. She dreamt of boats with feathered sails, trees that had her mother's eyes. The fog of San Francisco entered her blood, thickened coldly around her heart.

One day Mrs. Pleasant stopped Bella in the hall. She motioned for her to come into the kitchen. There, Mrs. Pleasant fried bread while Bella watched, and gave it to her, sprinkled with sugar and cinnamon. To know that someone had seen her, cared about her, cooked for her and just for her, was the first warm thing to happen to Bella in San Francisco. This was the moment she thought she would survive there. By eating that bread, she ceased to be a ghost.

Nelson Brady walked by the window, and Bella felt herself coloring. "Married," Mrs. Pleasant said. Bella looked at her without expression. Mrs. Pleasant struggled for the word. "*Esposa*," she said, and Bella found she had understood the first time, after all.

Her English improved. She forced herself to speak it, even to the children, who didn't care. She tried to make sense of the household. The children were alternately petted and ignored. Mrs. Pleasant made all the decisions regarding them and seemed also to handle the finances. When Mrs. Bell needed money, she made the request to Mrs. Pleasant, who spoke to Mr. Bell about it. This seemed odd to Bella, but she assumed it was American.

Mrs. Bell and Mrs. Pleasant were clearly fond of each other, in a stormy, door-slamming sort of way. When Mr. Bell was traveling, which was more often than not, Mrs. Bell trailed Mrs. Pleasant about the house. Mrs. Pleasant was never idle. Bella would hear them in the hall, and the mere sound of women's voices would make her so homesick for her mother she would need to sit down until the fit passed.

But she was better at concealing it. "You're looking well," Mrs. Pleasant said to her one day. "It's good to see you bloom so. Now I know you've settled."

Then a new child arrived, not a baby, but a girl one year older than Fred. Her hair was dark as a shadow, her arms thin where Marie's and Fred's were plump, her eyes brown where theirs were blue, her manner nervous where theirs were steady. Mrs. Pleasant brought her into the nursery and introduced her as their new sister. Her name had been Viola Smith, but now would be Viola Bell. No one suggested that Bella's wages would change with the addition of a third, more difficult child.

Bella often drew pictures for the children to color. She was good with a pencil and favored the birds and flowers of her homeland, which, she told the children, were as bright as spinning tops. She coaxed Viola to the table with paint pots of red and pink.

Two days after Viola's arrival, Mrs. Bell looked in on them. "Up!" Marie said, holding out her little creased arms. "Lift me up!"

"Are we having ice cream, Mama?" Fred asked. Sometimes Mrs. Bell's visits meant special treats.

"Are we having ice cream, Mama?" Viola repeated. Her eyes were wide.

A year later Viola was still there. She was a smart girl, quicker than Fred or Marie, though perhaps merely older. She bossed Marie about, dressed her as if she were a doll, managed her at mealtimes, put her down for her nap. Marie adored her.

One day Bella gave Fred and Viola each a sugar drop for learning a poem and one to Marie for sitting quietly while they recited. Fred's poem was "The Rainbow" by Wordsworth. Viola's poem was "The Fairies," by William Allingham. When they finished, Marie clapped her hands. Then she began to cry.

"She dropped her candy," Viola, who'd already eaten hers, suggested. She knelt. "Pick up your foot, Marie," she said. "Hold on to my shoulder." She ran her fingers along the floor so that they came up dusty. It was quite a performance, and then, at the end of it, Bella found the candy in Viola's pocket.

Bella was disturbed by the incident. On previous occasions she'd also found Viola bossy, deceptive, selfish. And little Marie was thoroughly in her sway. So when Mrs. Bell asked Bella's opinion of Viola, Bella gave it. Viola was a cunning child. Bella was worried about the influence this might have on Marie.

That same afternoon, Mrs. Bell took the children to the back lawn. The sun was high and warm. The children were rosy and glassy-eyed from their naps. Everyone was relaxed and had no reason to be afraid. Mrs. Bell put all three into the hammock together. "Swing me," Fred demanded. He was now six years old. Viola was seven. Marie was four.

"Let me see you holding tight first." Mrs. Bell checked all six hands. "Don't let go," she warned, tugging especially at Marie's fists to make sure she wouldn't. Then she'd given the hammock a push. The children swung out and back. "Higher," said Fred. "Higher, higher!" Mrs. Bell pushed the hammock again. The children were laughing. Marie and Viola knocked heads, but they laughed even harder at that. "Higher," Viola said. They were laughing so hard their mouths were stuck open.

Bella saw Viola's hand lift to her forehead, touching herself where Marie's head had hit. Just then, Mrs. Bell gave another push, harder, her hand under Viola's bottom. Which came first, the shove or Viola's hand on her forehead? Bella remembered it first one way, then the other. They came so close together. She could never settle it in her mind.

The hammock turned over, spilling all three children onto the grass. Viola flew the farthest, but Marie hit the hardest. Bella heard a sound she thought was Marie's arm breaking. She ran to pick her up, wings in her throat. Marie's face had twisted into an expression of shock; her mouth was a sharp, lipless roundness from which no sound came. She stood up, holding both arms out, which was how Bella knew the arms were whole.

Bella picked Marie up and turned to look at the other two children. Fred was still laughing. Viola lay on her back, the color gone from her face. Her eyes stared up at the blue sky, where the hammock swung upside down and empty, into the blue and out and in again.

Viola's hip had cracked and shifted; her leg had been jarred out of place. She was carried to bed, where she stayed more than a month.

After that Viola was given a jump rope and Bella was told to see that she used it. It was a ridiculous request, and Bella didn't understand. Viola could no more jump rope than she could fly. Mrs. Pleasant engaged a piano teacher, and this made more sense. But Viola was no longer treated as a daughter. In spite of her infirmity, she was given many chores and little affection. Mrs. Bell often called her down the steep spiral staircase only to send her back up on some errand. She seemed determined to proceed as if Viola had never been hurt.

A governess was hired for Marie and Fred, but not for Viola. "She's one of Mammy's," Mrs. Bell told the governess in Bella's presence. She suggested that Viola affected the limp. "A real cunning child. Don't you be taken in."

Bella heard her own words coming back at her. She

played the scene in the hammock through again, but now she decided Mrs. Bell had purposefully thrown Viola onto the grass. Bella had complained about her, and just that quickly Mrs. Bell had addressed the problem.

Bella had never pitied herself for being in service. She never tried to imagine having a house like the one on Octavia Street, which was more than big enough for her entire family and all their friends as well. She never tried to imagine having servants to cook and fetch for her. She'd heard that Mrs. Pleasant had been born to slavery, and found her rise a wonderful thing, but Mrs. Pleasant was an exceptional woman. Bella herself was saving money to bring her brother Eduardo to San Francisco. If Mrs. Pleasant would only hire him, too, Bella thought, she could be content.

And yet she pitied Viola. Not only crippled, but so fallen from favor as to become a servant in a house where she'd once been a daughter. It was hard to see, horrible to contemplate.

And all Bella's fault. How could she have condemned a child over a piece of candy? She found Mrs. Pleasant on the staircase and forced herself to speak. The portrait of Mrs. Bell watched her from the wall, white diamonds and milky eyes.

Bella was frightened of her own words. She was right to be frightened, because they spun up the staircase to the floor above, where Mrs. Bell heard them. She called down. "My own mother stripped me and set me outside the window to freeze!" Mrs. Bell hovered over the landing like a golden hawk. Her voice was tight and shivered. "I never would hurt a child." She came down to Mrs. Pleasant. "Never. See how everyone conspires against me?" She began to cry.

Mrs. Pleasant embraced her. Her face was half hidden by Mrs. Bell's shoulder, but it did not look friendly. "Mrs. Bell loves children," she said. "How cruel of you. You don't see how she suffers every time she sees Viola. All this time, and you hardly know us."

Bella was dismissed to the nursery. A few days later, she was dismissed for good. Mrs. Pleasant told Bella there was a position open in the house of Mrs. Washington. "Fred and Marie are too old now for a nursemaid," she explained, ignoring the fact that there was a new baby in the nursery, a tiny bald girl named Robina.

A family friend took Viola to Los Angeles, where she stayed more than a year, undergoing a series of unsuccessful operations on her hip. When she came back, Bella was gone. Mrs. Pleasant had given her an excellent reference. But Bella felt she could no longer be trusted with children. She confided the whole guilty tale to Nelson Brady, then used the money saved for Eduardo's passage to return to Panama.

Q: Now, what is it that impresses—is there anything special that impresses your recollection as having been there in the year 1881?
A: Yes: my injury impresses me very clearly.
Q: How did that happen, Miss Bell?
A: Well, I was thrown out of a hammock.
Q: Explain under what circumstances you were thrown out of a hammock, that happened to impress you.
A: Well, Fred, Marie and myself, we were in the hammock—we usually got into the hammock in

the evening, because it was a little warm during the day, and my mother was swinging the hammock, and I think she swung a little bit too high, and we were all flung out, and I happened to be swung the furthest and dislocated my hip.

Q: Dislocated your hip?

A: Yes.

Q: And from that injury you have never recovered?

A: No, I have not.*

*Transcript from Viola Bell's suit for heirship in the estate of Teresa Bell.

T W O

What with the plagues and the winter storms and the impending tidal wave, everyone's mind was on charity these days. Mrs. Pleasant sent more baskets of food and also, just for Jenny Ijub, two used dresses and a piano teacher. The dresses were hand-me-downs from the Bell girls. Too fine, really; the staff disliked seeing Jenny dressed so, as if she were at a party instead of living an orphan's life. It was bound to produce envy in the other wards.

But the piano teacher was conceded, however reluctantly, to be a good thing. Someday Jenny would have to support herself. The dental offices were always looking for pianists, and all they needed was someone able to play loudly enough to mask the sounds of screaming. Piano lessons were a very practical plan.

Next, the charity bug bit young Maud Curry, who decided to devote herself to helping Jenny get adopted. Maud had reached a pious age and was bothered, for religious reasons, by Jenny's continual good fortune. She remembered Jenny's stories—lemon sticks, ponies, parents—but had honestly forgotten that she herself was the author. The result of this combination of remembering and forgetting was that Maud thought of Jenny as a dreadful, unrepentant liar.

Why would God dress a dreadful, unrepentant liar like a princess? Maud decided to be an instrument of the Lord. She picked a group of girls—Melody Miller, Tilly Beacon, Ella May Howard, Coral Campbell—and charged them with informing Jenny whenever her manners were wanting, or her appearance, or her attitude. They called themselves the Good Manners Club. Two of these girls had the special status of being diphtheria survivors.

The staff was touched by this display of selfless concern. "I was afraid the other children would be jealous," Mrs. Lake said. "Instead they've made quite a project of her." And from Nell: "She's certainly lucky to have such friends."

Jenny ate her dinner one evening surrounded by well-wishers. "She shouldn't be taking such big bites, should she, Maud?" Tilly Beacon asked.

"No, indeed."

"Don't cut your bread, Jenny. You should break it with your hands," Melody said, when Jenny hadn't even touched her bread yet.

"And everything after the soup is eaten with a fork."

"I know," Jenny said. She wasn't hungry. The chicken she'd just eaten wedged in her throat until she was afraid it was stuck there forever. She took a gulp of milk to try to force it down.

"I'm just making sure." Maud took a prim bite of cheese. Her angel-colored hair was growing out. It curled in lovely rings around her shoulders. Soon Mrs. Lake would cut it back to dandelion fluff, weeping as she did so. "You sound a little conceited. Good manners are spoiled if you're stuck-up about having them."

"We shouldn't be able to hear you drinking," Coral said.

At bedtime the girls gathered around Jenny's bed to discuss her classroom performance. "Your hair was untidy," Melody began. "And you should thank Miss Stevens when she corrects your sums."

"No one else does," Jenny said.

"No one else makes so many mistakes."

"Let me see your hands," Maud instructed. She flipped them from one side to the other. Her own were hot and sticky. "Go wash them again. All the pretty dresses in the world won't help if you don't keep yourself clean."

Jenny went back to the basin. Her feet were bare. She could feel grains of sand beneath them on the wood floor, and there was a sound like buzzing flies in her ears. She poured some water, dipped her hands in. As she rubbed them together she looked out the window. She could see the barn, the wood just turning to silver in the moonlight. Across it lay the long, pointed shadow of the Ark's tower. She took as much time as she could, but whenever she looked back down the row of beds, there was the group of girls on hers, still waiting for her. Jenny had a loose tooth and it was disgusting, they were agreeing, the way she kept poking at it with her tongue. She would have to be made to stop.

The piano teacher was named Miss Viola Bell. She had the largest, darkest eyes Jenny had ever seen, and also a twisted leg. She needed a crutch to lower herself onto the piano bench and to rise. When Jenny sat beside her, Viola's skirts brushed Jenny's legs. They were cold and damp. Matron didn't like her much. Jenny was still deciding.

"I'm forced to wonder about the character of any young woman from that house," Jenny overheard Matron telling Miss Stevens. Jenny could see that Viola was hearing, too, although she pretended not to.

"We always start with middle C." Viola tapped the key quietly, and then louder—*pim, pim, pim, PIM*. They were using the piano in the basement schoolroom while the rest of the children played outside. Matron was in the hall, but the door was open.

"I'm forced to wonder how she'll have the time to practice and still do her chores and her schooling, too," said Matron. "Of course, there's no point if she doesn't practice faithfully. You must tell me at once if she falls behind in her schoolwork."

"Curve your fingers," Viola said. She took Jenny's hand and made it into a claw. She shook it at the wrist. "Relax a little." She showed Jenny how to play a scale.

What she wanted first was even fingering. She wound a metronome to demonstrate. She and Jenny clapped along.

"Don't love any of the notes more than the others," she said. "Every note needs just the same amount of time to breathe."

"I don't love any of them." Jenny didn't mean to speak. It just came out.

"I see," said Viola. She gave Jenny an appraising look. "Don't hate any of the notes more than the others, then."

Jenny had left her with the wrong impression. In fact, Jenny liked the way Viola's hands felt, working her fingers into proper shapes. Viola told Jenny what to do, but not in a bossy way. "Like prancing horses," she said of Jenny's fingers. She pranced her own on the keys in a lively tune. "Two-minute waltz," she said. "You could soft-cook an egg to it."

Jenny could see that, in order to practice, she'd have to come down every day and be by herself. She was happy that Mrs. Pleasant hadn't forgotten her. She thought it was going to be nice, learning to play piano.

THREE

The board of the Ladies' Relief and Protection Society threw a soirée to honor those of its members who'd lived at the Ark and worked so bravely throughout the epidemics. Lizzie's depression had not lifted, but she could hardly refuse to be fêted. The party was at the home of two delightfully ready patrons, Ethel Crosby and Margaret Cole, whom she wouldn't insult for the world. She wore her coin necklace and her apricot silk, but under her corset her heart felt pricked with pins.

The Putnams lent her Roscoe so she could drive over and leave early if the evening proved too much. They continued very pleased with her, as if she'd chosen to stay away from everyone they disapproved of for all those weeks instead of having been put under quarantine. Still, Lizzie had had no plans to do otherwise; her conscience was clear.

As she left her house, an evening fog was beginning to swirl into the streets. The city had a magical, underwater feeling. Horses' hooves echoed in the wet air, and cold currents streamed past her, visible as ghosts.

At Ethel Crosby and Margaret Cole's she listened to any number of fine speeches. The tracheotomy in which she had assisted was repeatedly detailed; she was honored for her patience with Meredith Penny, for the grisly clothes she'd washed, the hands she'd held, the prayers she'd offered. Lizzie didn't suppose she'd ever been the object of so much approval. She felt uncomfortably exposed, yet cautiously pleased. She would never like being noticed, but she *had* done well, so that was the part that pleased her. Everyone had done well.

It was a nasty surprise, then, when she stepped outside for some air, for one moment of privacy, to have Mrs. Hallis follow merely to say something unkind. "I was astonished to learn," Mrs. Hallis began, "that we're sheltering a child for Mammy Pleasant. Your decision, I'm told."

"We had the space," Lizzie said. "In my opinion. The little girl had nowhere to go. She's a nice little girl."

"I'm sure that's all true. I'm sure you were full of good intent. You always are." Somehow Mrs. Hallis managed to make this uncomplimentary. "But none of this falls to your area of concern. And now you've created a situation. What is Mrs. Pleasant most known for? Baby-farming. What do we deal in? Babies. We can't for a moment be seen as one of Mrs. Pleasant's operations. We'd never recover from the scandal. The Ark would close forever."

Mrs. Hallis was a Methodist with the face of a Botticelli. She believed in culpability, which was not the philosophy of most people with such lips. "When we act," Mrs. Hallis had asked the ladies during her installation as president, "why should we not hold ourselves responsible for remote consequences as well as immediate?" This was laudable, but hard.

"I wouldn't have brought it up tonight of all nights," Mrs. Hallis said. "I did plan to wait. But Miss Cole asked about it. If word is already out to the donors, the circumstances are dire."

"The circumstances are imaginary!" Lizzie said. "Mrs. Pleasant came to the Ark only the one time when she brought the child. I don't know her at all, if that's what you're implying."

"I'm relieved to hear you say so. Of course, I believe you, I know you wouldn't lie. And yet, Miss Hayes, we run a charity based on public support. We must consider appearances as well as facts. And my cook, Hop Tung, says it's common knowledge that you run her errands in Chinatown."

Lizzie was so shocked by this she didn't immediately respond. The shock was followed by resentment. She was being watched and talked about. Her neck grew hot, and then her cheeks. Her hands were cold. The image of Mrs. Hallis questioning her Chinese cook about Lizzie's affairs made her first frightened, then humiliated, and then angry. So they'd all only been pretending to admire her all evening, when really she was the object of a campaign of whispers that reached even into their kitchens.

"Am I being dismissed?" she asked. Her voice cracked like ice across the last word.

"Of course not. I only tell you as a friendly warning."

Lizzie couldn't manage another sentence. She left the porch and then the party without a word to anyone, even her hostesses. She woke the next morning with a sickening silver headache on which all the tea in China could have no effect. It had been a great mistake to leave her bed, she decided. She wouldn't make such an error again.

Three days later Mrs. Putnam called. Lizzie roused herself sufficiently to dress, but there was no food in the house, nothing to offer by way of hospitality. The newspapers were piled unread on the parlor settee. There was dust.

Mrs. Putnam took it all in. "How was the party?" she asked. Probably she'd already heard how hastily Lizzie had left. Probably the information was already circulating up in Sacramento through Erma. Soon the governor would know or, at the very least, his Chinese cook.

Lizzie had this bitter succession of thoughts. But Mrs. Putnam's face was too kind. Lizzie chose to confide. When she got to Hop Tung, Mrs. Putnam shook her head. All was unfolding just as Lizzie's mother had feared. If her advice at the séance had only been instantly taken! How disheartening it must be to rouse oneself to Contact only to be ignored.

Not that Mrs. Putnam was ever one to lose herself in regrets. "The past is only useful as a guide to the future," she said briskly. She proposed that Lizzie immediately be seen with respectable people. She proposed the long-promised, long-delayed Saturday-night promenade.

"You can invite that Mrs. Wright you're so taken with," she offered, which made it impossible for Lizzie to refuse. Though she'd lost the taste for it herself, it would be such a treat for poor Mrs. Wright. The Putnams would fetch them both.

The usual Saturday-night route was a loop that could be walked in either direction—Market to Kearny to Bush to Powell or Powell to Bush to Kearny to Market. Whatever the weather, the streets were full of people. The Salvation Army band sang at one end of Market Street, while at the other, groups of young men gathered to smoke cigars and watch the wind lift the ladies' skirts.

You might see anyone in San Francisco on a Saturday night. You could buy stocks or snakes. You could buy a pig or a paste necklace or a paste guaranteed to dissolve warts. The Crockers might be walking in one direction and their servants, off duty, in the other. Fast Irish women passed slow Spanish men. There were sailors from the ships of every country in the world and soldiers from the Presidio. There were sweethearts and zealots and labor agitators and mesmerists; there were black Gilbert Islanders, huge Kanakas, turbaned lascars, tattooed Indians, Chinese with their long hair fiercely loose, Italians in fussy shirts with blue sashes. And the whole scene flooded with so much lamplight it was as if they were all onstage together. The very sidewalks seemed made of light.

Lizzie held Mrs. Wright's arm and tried to describe it aloud. She recognized Mrs. Hallis out promenading with her husband and two married daughters; they nodded briskly to each other. She saw Myrtle Rolphe freezing out a young man with a fast smile and a gold tooth.

Mrs. Putnam began to talk about the phantom fire engine. The story was getting a good deal of press. A Mr. Tomkinson was suing the fire department for damages sustained on Third and Folsom when a recklessly speeding engine had chased his horses. His driver had lost the reins, smashing his buggy into splinters against a telegraph pole. Mr. Tomkinson was asking for one hundred nine dollars and seventy-five cents in compensation. There were more than a dozen credible witnesses.

Only there'd been no fire on this occasion, and none of the city's many engines had been at Third and Folsom. After an investigation so exhaustive that Chief Scannell was forced to retire to the country under a doctor's care, acting Chief Sullivan concluded that Mr. Tomkinson would have to apply for compensation to a supernatural agency. Mrs. Putnam was both pleased and horrified to think there were whole engines of ghosts clattering down the stone pavement on Folsom, carelessly sounding gongs and spooking the horses.

"When you think of all the men who've died fighting fires in San Francisco," Mr. Putnam noted. "Really, the wonder is there aren't more of these incidents."

Mrs. Putnam was forced to agree. "But what do you think it means?" she asked. "Is the manifestation a random occurrence or is it a warning we should heed? What a time for omens this has been! Can you ever remember another such, Mrs. Wright?"

Mrs. Wright had been squeezing Lizzie's arm for the

past few moments. She answered loudly and quickly. "Stuff and nonsense. One of the engines was out and everyone is lying about it to avoid payment. These events can always be readily explained if you remember what liars people are. Especially when money is involved.

"These witnesses you refer to—was there anything supernatural in what they observed? The baying of invisible hounds? The scent of unearthly roses?" Her voice was innocent, but Lizzie could tell Mrs. Wright was goading the Putnams.

Lizzie found Mrs. Wright's rock-solid disbelief extremely comforting. She might shift about from past to present, but Mrs. Wright kept her feet on the ground. It was also slightly rude. Mrs. Wright did not know the Putnams well enough to contradict them so loudly. Nor was her version appealing to them. "That would involve a massive conspiracy to conceal the truth," Mr. Putnam pointed out. His posture was stiff, his tone formal.

"Someone somewhere would be bound to talk." Mrs. Putnam turned to Lizzie. "Don't you think so?"

Lizzie found that she had no opinion on the subject of supernatural fire engines. Naturally, this pleased no one.

The Putnams began to walk faster, and the distance between the two couples increased. This gap was quickly filled with other people. It could not have been the Putnams' intention to abandon her, but suddenly Lizzie couldn't see them anywhere.

A group of Italian sailors walking together, arm in arm, created a phalanx against which Lizzie was forced to give way. A gaunt and rheumy-eyed man staggered drunkenly toward her, only to find his path blocked by a bosomy, theatrical woman with a serious overbite. "Even today, the women of ancient Egypt are remembered for their beauty. What did they have that you don't have?" she asked Lizzie. She extended her hand. In it was a small box, inlaid with an ivory ibis. "Something tiny enough to fit in this box. Would you like to open it?"

Suddenly, inexplicably, the woman and the question filled Lizzie with dread. Why had the woman picked her? Did she look the sort to open a box with no idea as to its contents?

Lizzie tried to walk past without answering, and the woman intercepted her again. "Go ahead. Open it."

Lizzie began to sweat in the cold night air. She moved to the left, pulling Mrs. Wright along so rapidly she careened into a man with a huge black beard and a white top hat. There was the fleshy sound of collision, the smell of whiskey, a small reproachful noise from Mrs. Wright, a large irritated noise from the man.

"What are you afraid of? Only yourself," the woman with the box shouted after Lizzie.

Lizzie saw the opening of a narrow alleyway and guided Mrs. Wright into it and out of the crush. Several moments were spent in apology and explanation. Mrs. Wright's hat had been knocked askew and Lizzie straightened it. They began walking again, forward into the alley. Only then did Lizzie look up. The bright glow of streetlamps was gone, and she found herself in a place she'd never been. She was on Morton Street.

The sounds of the Saturday-night promenade fell

away, leaving only their own footsteps. On the left were a
dozen small cottages, each with a shallow bay window. In
every window a woman sat idly, a smile painted on her lips,
and her eyes both staring and unseeing. Instead of dresses,
these women wore simple wrappers that would fall away at a
touch. Their hair was pinned up in a way that suggested its
coming down. The wrappers were in different colors, but
otherwise the women looked exactly the same—dark hair,
white skin, red mouths.

The dread Lizzie had been feeling doubled, but now
she knew what she was afraid of. She feared recognizing a
face, some girl they'd sheltered at the Brown Ark. The
women were like dolls, waiting for someone to pick them
up, move their arms and legs, animate them. She could not
take her eyes off them; the women refused to look at her.
She thought that what she was seeing was sex, but that it had
been made to look like death.

Lines of men drank from flasks and bottles as they
waited their turns. In the presence of Lizzie and Mrs.
Wright, they fell utterly, eerily silent. A man left one of the
cottages, a very young man with barely a beard. When he
spotted them he reversed direction and walked ahead so
they would see only his back. "Get out of here!" a man who
looked to be Lizzie's age snapped at her. "What can you be
thinking?"

This late in her life, it was doubtful Lizzie would ever
know what physical passion was. She blamed no one for
this; there were things she could have done if she'd chosen
to do them. As an adolescent she'd conducted her own
solitary investigations until somehow her mother knew.

There was a period when Effie had been told to tie her hands together every night, but it lasted only a few weeks, only long enough to make the point. "I know you're a good girl," her mother had said, and Lizzie had chosen to be one.

Once, when she was nineteen, Teddy Sprague had pressed against her in the backyard of his house by the large rhododendron. Later she wished she'd pressed back, but at the time she was merely embarrassed. Perhaps if she'd been beautiful, if he'd spoken first, if it had been more like something in a book, she might have behaved differently. Instead she reacted instinctively. It was a revealing instinct, the instinct of no. Lizzie had instantly known that any shared embrace would leave her feeling exposed, observed. The inner woman would not allow the outer woman to look so foolish.

She'd often told herself she didn't really mind; she could do without. Other women seemed to dislike it often as not. There was plenty of excitement to be found in music and in books, even a bodily excitement. And then there were so many other pleasures to be had—water on her skin and in her throat, the taste of crab legs with melted butter, the smell of lemons and horses and the sea, the touch of velvet and satin, hills of poppies, Beethoven, blackberries and olives, sneezing and stretching in the sun. She would not allow these ecstasies to seem any bit less than they were. She loved them. The pleasures of the flesh were a gift from God.

None of this belonged on Morton Street. Lizzie tried to imagine a looking-glass alley where men sat in windows and waited for women with money. She pretended she was entering a door, making a selection, demanding who and what she wanted. Money on the dressing table. The man like a puppet in her arms.

The fantasy was ludicrous. And upsetting. She didn't have a word for the combination of horror and thrill and buffoonery and sadness it gave her. What did men feel when they did such things? Whom did they pretend to do them to? Why must they do them at all?

"What's happening?" Mrs. Wright asked. "Why have you stopped talking? Where are we?"

"Lizzie!" Mr. Putnam's footsteps sounded behind them. "Where do you think you're going?" He seized her by the elbow.

"Mrs. Wright was getting knocked about by all the people," Lizzie said. "I was looking for somewhere less crowded."

"I'll take Mrs. Wright's arm, then," Mr. Putnam said. "Neither of you should be here." He led them back to Kearny Street and Mrs. Putnam.

"What were you thinking, Lizzie?" Mrs. Putnam asked.

It wasn't a question, so Lizzie didn't answer it. Inwardly she was annoyed at the fuss. Wasn't she a grown woman, and perfectly able to look at the realities of life? At the same time her hands were shaking and she couldn't make them stop.

"We were on Morton Street," Mrs. Wright announced to the whole staff the minute Lizzie returned her to the Ark. "Of course, I didn't see a thing."

"How very distressing," Mrs. Lake said.

"How interesting," said Miss Stevens.

Nell fetched them all a glass of wine and a piece of cold apple pie to help them recover. No experience could have brought more ready sympathy. These are real women, Lizzie told herself. This is where I live, with God, first of all, and then these real women in this real world.

FOUR

$\mathscr{B}$ecause she had continued so listless, because since the quarantine had lifted and she'd learnt that Mrs. Pleasant was a communicable disease, she had spent less and less time at the Brown Ark, Lizzie was not immediately informed of Jenny's piano lessons. She heard of them finally from Ti Wong.

She'd dropped by to give him the new Conan Doyle and was told he was upstairs cleaning the tower room. "I suppose it will be good for his English," Nell said amiably. "Go on up," just as if Nell were happy to see her, were the most agreeable of women. How Ti Wong had charmed her merely by almost dying!

Nell had no way of knowing, of course, that the book Lizzie had brought contained cocaine injections, a wooden-legged convict, and a pair of hideous twins. Even Lizzie hadn't read it yet. Although Doyle's previous stories had garnered little excitement and mixed reviews, this was beginning to change. Lizzie felt that combination of validation and annoyance the early reader feels toward anyone coming later. It dampened her own enthusiasm slightly.

Ti Wong was not cleaning the room at all, but was seated, dreamily looking out the cupola window to the street, when she entered. "I saw you coming," he said. "I saw your tiny, tiny hat."

He smiled when she held out the book. "You read to me?"

"We'll read it together."

"Okay." Yet he showed no inclination to start. Lizzie settled herself on the horsehair couch and opened the book invitingly, but he stayed at the window. "Very high up," he said.

"Yes."

"Ocean far away."

"Yes, indeed. You're not worrying about the prophecy, are you? God doesn't work that way."

"Story of Noah," Ti Wong pointed out. "Story of Red Sea."

"God doesn't work that way *anymore*," Lizzie told him, but Ti Wong said she was not being as scientific as Mr. Holmes, and even to her own ears it was unconvincing.

Although San Francisco continued largely uninterested, over in Oakland, Mrs. Woodworth's crowds were still growing. When her tent was shredded by high winds and collapsed on the worshippers, it was replaced by a new one, specially made to hold an audience of eight thousand, nine hundred. No evangelist had ever required a space so large before; Mrs. Woodworth asked God's forgiveness for the hubris of it. Her humility was restored by her unfortunate husband, who opened a concession booth and sold lemonade and peanuts to the believers.

Recently the meetings had been attacked by hoodlums and, in consequence, by baton-swinging policemen. The noise of benches being smashed and the hoarse shouts of fighting men were added to the general din. A boy was cured of Saint Vitus's dance. A man was cured of a gambling addiction. Flora Briggs, a fourteen-year-old girl attending a meeting with her four-year-old cousin, fell into a faint and lay on the altar unnoticed for hours. When her uncle tried to fetch her out, he was thrown from the tent by burly men singing hymns. Her doctor told the newspapers he feared the girl's health was permanently weakened by the dampness and the excitement. "If you went to one of Mrs. Woodworth's meetings, you'd see it's just a circus," Lizzie told Ti Wong.

"We go?"

"Certainly not. You'd catch a chill. Or get arrested." But that made it sound too exciting; she was beginning to want to go herself. She tried to stop. "The music is horrid. You're safe here, Ti Wong. I promise. Why would God spare you from diphtheria only to drown you?"

"You think Miss Bell goes to revival?"

"What do you know of Miss Bell?"

Ti Wong pointed down through the window and Lizzie stood to see. There was Viola Bell, papers under one arm and crutch under the other, struggling through the sand up to the Brown Ark door.

"So Mrs. Woodworth can make her walk," Ti Wong explained, just as Lizzie was asking, "What is she doing here?"

Lizzie went downstairs and listened through the open door while Jenny did her scales. When Miss Bell told her to, Jenny walked her fingers on the keys. She marched them, trotted them, galloped them according to Miss Bell's instruction. "Some people play by imposing their will on the instrument," Miss Bell told her. "Others think only of letting the piano sing through them. You must think about what kind of pianist it will suit you best to be."

From outside, Lizzie could just hear Maud's voice.

"Red lion, red lion,
Come out of your den.
Whoever you catch
Will be one of your men."

Nell found Lizzie listening in the basement. "A message arrived for you," she said. "As if we didn't have enough to do without delivering your mail." She handed the note over, and climbed the stairs in a great show of breathlessness.

Lizzie opened the envelope with her fingernails.

"Mr. Finney would be honored if Miss Hayes would consent to meet him in the Grand Court of the Palace at one o'clock Monday, this. He will wait all afternoon in hope."

So, Mr. Finney wanted his money at long last.

Of course, Lizzie courted further scandal by appearing in a public place with a young man who was no relation of hers. The Palace was as public as a place could get—see and be seen. Still, she must endeavor to do what was right. She remembered how Mrs. Pleasant had said she was too concerned with appearances. No doubt it was true. And what seemed right to Lizzie now was that little Jenny be returned to her mother, in spite of Mrs. Pleasant's efforts to separate them. There was surely an irony in this, Lizzie thought. I am no agent of Mrs. Pleasant's, she told an imaginary (and chagrined) Mrs. Hallis. Lizzie was trusting her instincts.

Any remaining doubts were dispelled by Sunday morning's sermon. Like a sign from God, the subject was Abraham and Isaac. Lizzie had never liked this story, and even less the related one of Hagar and Ishmael. Why does Ishmael matter so much less than Isaac? she'd asked once in Sunday school. It was the sort of question bound to occur to a child who feared her parents would rather have lost their five-year-old daughter than their newborn son. Lizzie was probably ten at this time.

God doesn't have favorites, her Sunday-school teacher had answered. And He blessed and protected Ishmael. But His covenant for Isaac was made before either was born.

As if God wouldn't know both were coming. Lizzie was not satisfied, but she let the matter drop. If she quarreled with the Sunday-school teacher, her parents were bound to learn of it. Sunday school is not a place for questions, her mother would say. It was, instead, a training in unquestioning faith.

But what Lizzie had really meant was, Why does Ishmael matter so much less to Abraham? She knew all children were precious to God.

This morning, the Reverend Pilchner reminded them that the sacrifice God suggested to Abraham was the one God would actually make. In fact, the mountain in Moriah where Abraham's son had been spared was very close to the place where Christ was crucified. The sacrifice of a child, then, was something God asked only of Himself. It was beyond man and meant to be so, which interpretation helped Lizzie like the story a great deal better.

The fine weather of the weekend persisted into Monday. Lizzie took the streetcar to the Annie Street entrance with its fine marble walls. She had decided on a two-o'clock arrival as a test of Mr. Finney's patience. She couldn't help hoping he wouldn't pass.

Light spilled into the Grand Court through the dome; sunlight, but sieved softer and more golden by the amber glass. The setting was one of opulence: purple tablecloths, silver sugar dishes, vases of cut crystal. The acoustics of the Grand Court were designed for privacy. Hushed conversations bubbled through the room, indistinct, but various as birdsong. Lizzie was unlikely to enjoy the social aspects of the occasion, so she took a deliberate moment's pleasure in the setting. She didn't often get to the Grand Court, where deals were made and men undone over cocktails.

Mr. Finney was waiting for her. He rose. She had never seen him so nicely dressed. Although his shirt was still a coarse linen, frayed at the cuffs, and his dress coat was thready at the elbows, there was nothing in this to reproach. On the contrary, a gentleman showed good taste by never dressing above his income.

"I'm having champagne," he said. "I'll get you a glass."

Lizzie turned to the waiter, a white man; the colored waiters had never been rehired. "I'll have a cup of tea. And a sandwich, please. Whatever you recommend."

He withdrew at once, and Lizzie and Mr. Finney looked at each other across the table. "Mr. Finney," she said straight off. She wanted no inconsequential pleasantries, nothing that would prolong the meeting. "I need you to tell me the identity of Jenny's mother. And anything else that would help me locate her. I'm determined to see them reunited."

"Right to it." Mr. Finney smiled at her fondly. "You're a businesslike woman. I admire that. I admire you more every time I see you. It's the way you look, Miss Hayes. So proper and churchy, and all the time one of Mrs. Pleasant's own. You do it to a turn."

"Please honor my request," Lizzie said. She struggled with her tone of voice, which somehow settled on lifeless. *One of Mrs. Pleasant's own.* But why argue with such a man? Why argue with anyone? It was only appearances, after all, no truth to it.

He removed his glasses, rubbed them against his sleeve, and replaced them. She remembered leaning toward him to dab the grit from his eye, so close she could feel the intermittent warmth of his breathing.

"Well," he said. "Right to it, then. It embarrasses me mightily to have to begin by admitting that bit about Jenny's mother was a lie. I don't know who she is. Need drove me to it. Debts and creditors. I'm usually quite an honest man."

"I'm sure," said Lizzie. She stood, forcing him to stand as well. "Then we've nothing more to say."

"But I *have* learned the name of the child's father."

They sat again. Mr. Finney was relaxed in his chair. He appeared as comfortable as if he were in his own dining room, sipping his champagne, gesturing with his free hand. "What's that worth to you?"

He appeared to think it worth a lot. He so obviously thought himself in the position of advantage today. Lizzie noted this, and it made her anxious.

Her tea arrived, and her sandwich. She let the waiter withdraw, then took a small bite. Cold tongue. Chewing it helped calm her. She swallowed. "I imagine it's worth a good deal more to the father than to me," she said, casual and self-possessed. "Why not appeal to him?"

"Sadly, he's dead."

"Are there other relatives who might be made to feel their responsibility?"

"There are indeed."

"Then go to them."

"Look here," said Mr. Finney. His aura of sincerity intensified. The air was thick as smoke with it. "I only want a fair cut. My information was hard come by. You were willing to pay me ten dollars just to leave the child alone. How much more valuable is this?" He took a pen from his pocket, called the waiter over and asked for a piece of paper. The hotel stationery was heavy and beautifully monogrammed.

"Now I'm writing the father's name," Mr. Finney

same. Or so we judged. The thing is that you can never know about the father for absolute certain. Even your own father, you can never be sure."

"You're not strengthening your case."

"Your mother was dead. Men suffer from loneliness more than women. If you knew what that was like, you'd find it forgivable. You don't strike me as an unforgiving woman." He raised his glass to her and her forgiving nature. The bubbles careened through his champagne.

She was composed enough now to pour her tea without having her hands shake, busied herself with the cream. She did so not because she wanted tea, but to demonstrate how wide of the mark he'd shot. She didn't entertain this preposterous lie for a moment, and showed it by turning to him a face as unperturbed as pond water. That he expected payment for this insult! "Secondly, I just happen to get the care of her. A remarkable coincidence!"

Mr. Finney leaned in. She saw his face reflected in a silver teapot, the nose as big as a potato. When she looked back up to his actual face it was less handsome as well. There was a sheen of oil on his forehead, drops of champagne in his moustache. In the golden light, his eyes were the color of mud. She was amazed she'd ever thought him nice to look at.

"No coincidence," he said. "Mrs. Pleasant brought your sister to you. She knew what she was doing. She was tidying up. I worked for her once, she's a great tidier."

"She's not. Quite the opposite. That's thirdly. Fourthly my father was too old."

"He was old. The—event—didn't proceed smoothly, or so I'm informed. And yet not too old, as it happened."

Lizzie didn't remember that she'd ever been more af-
fronted. This had the brief charm of novelty, and then
she'd had more than enough. She left, her tea untasted,
her sandwich barely touched, and the bill to fall to Mr.
Finney's account. She strode through the tables and past a
group of women, which now contained Mrs. Hallis. Mrs.
Hallis stood and Lizzie acknowledged her. She hoped
faintly that this marked the first moment she'd been seen.
She hoped Mrs. Hallis hadn't watched while Mr. Finney
passed his *billets-doux*. But it no longer seemed a large concern.

When she stepped into the white sunlight of Annie
Street, she decided to stroll along Market for a while before
catching the streetcar. She thought that Mr. Finney might
have followed her, but he hadn't, which was too bad, because while she was walking she thought of a fifthly and
sixthly she could have delivered, but she felt no temptation
to go back.

She passed a street vendor who tried to lure her into a
game with cups and a pea, but she'd had quite enough of
that sort of thing. He would hide the pea under one of the
cups and she would find it or she wouldn't; none of that
would be the point. All the while, just like Mr. Finney,
he'd be sizing her up: How much did she have, how much
would she play, how much could he take? How great a fool
was she?

FIVE

$\mathcal{A}$ disciplined imagination is a useful tool in avoiding unpleasant thoughts. An unbridled imagination carries you straight to them. Lizzie went home and read three novels, one after the other, no daylight between, and no recollection of any of them. She then helped six other ladies dust and scrub St. Luke's in preparation for Easter week. She attended two piano recitals, one in the afternoon and one in the evening. She called on donors. And when she'd finished all this, less than two days had passed since her meeting with Mr. Finney.

The weather turned unusually warm, and Miss Stevens seized her chance to take the littles on a picnic to Ocean Beach to see the rock formations. "Which is strongest," Miss Stevens would ask the littles, "air, water, or stone?" and then show them the smoothly carved pools, caves, and keyholes. This always came as such a surprise to children and could be made to carry some valuable life lessons as well.

She sent Ti Wong to Lizzie with a note. Would Lizzie like to go to the seashore? Miss Stevens needed another adult to chaperone and everyone else was busy. Lizzie was never busy, but Miss Stevens was too polite to say so.

The beach was crowded. There were men in wool swimming costumes, although the water was far too cold for actual swimming. They waded and their feet turned an unappetizingly fishy blue. Women protected themselves from sudden bursts of sun and wind with colored parasols. An Irish couple had made a windbreak of a bedsheet and were charging people a penny apiece to shelter beside it. There was a cart selling chips of ice and bottles of beer. There was a long table on which Charlie the Bird Man had arranged his canary cages. Charlie's canaries walked tightropes, sat in chairs, and fired tiny cannons triggered with strings. One canary flew into the crowd, landing on hats, picking out pigeons for Charlie to pester for money.

Like so many other men in San Francisco, Charlie had been unlucky in love. He'd been robbed on his honeymoon night, as he would tell anyone who'd listen, robbed by his bride. "She took my money, my clothes, my heart," he said, in Lizzie's general direction. His tone was accusing. "All she left me was the birds."

He sent a canary to Lizzie's shoulder. It took hold of her earlobe in a bite so gentle it was almost a kiss. The littles surrounded her, pleading for the bird themselves, reaching out their fingers enticingly, driving it deeper into her hair. It murmured in a way that tingled on the curve of

Lizzie's neck. Charlie whistled, and the bird came back to him, just like a dog.

Ti Wong had made the boys a red kite with paste and paint, wood and newsprint. It was shaped vaguely like a falcon, which Charlie said would agitate the canaries, so Miss Stevens sent the boys far down the beach to fly it. They ran along the sand, throwing the kite into the air, but were unable to keep it aloft. Eventually it fell—like Icarus, Miss Stevens pointed out—into the sea and dissolved. When pulled in, only the crossbar remained. The boys threw it back and reeled it in repeatedly, a sort of fishing game, but requiring no patience or experience. They played tag with the waves, dashing in and out, until they were wet to the knees and beyond.

Jenny dropped her sandwich. "Now it's a *sand*wich," Miss Stevens told her gaily. "Brush it off, dear. A little grit won't hurt." She explained that birds needed just that additional grit as an aid to digestion.

Lizzie had determined to pay Jenny no special attentions. Instead, she found herself aware of Jenny's whereabouts at every moment. Lizzie traded sandwiches with her and ate the sandy one herself. Jenny did not say thank you. If only Maud were there! Maud would coax her into better behavior.

They all went to climb the stairs to the Cliff House. From there they turned to face Seal Rocks. "Actually," Miss Stevens said, "those are sea lions, not seals. You can tell by the ears, which are smaller. And their flippers are larger than a seal's would be." She'd brought opera glasses so the children could see nature close up and detailed. The sea lions lay in the clefts of the rocks. Now and then one would slide languidly into the water, then somersault back onto the rock, its spotted fur newly polished by the water.

"The Costanoan Indians used to tell a story about Seal Rocks," Lizzie told the children standing nearest her. Nobody encouraged her to continue, but nobody moved away, either. "One day a beautiful woman appeared on the beach here to two little girls. She warned them of an attack by sea from another tribe across the bay. To protect them, she gave them three wishes.

"First they wished for a great fog so the boats of the enemy would be lost. Then they wished for a great storm so the boats of the enemy would be destroyed. Then they wished to turn the rival warriors into sea lions. And that's the real reason there are sea lions on the coast here." How many cultures told stories in which everyone was saved through the cunning of little girls? What a shame the Costanoans were gone now, little girls with all the rest of them.

"I would have wished for more wishes," Matthew Burton said, the way children always do, always will. And then, "Wouldn't the third wish have been enough? Why did they need the first two?" Matthew was Miss Stevens's ideal pupil, methodical, logical to a fault.

Jenny passed Lizzie the opera glasses. One of the sea lions yawned. Through the glasses Lizzie could see a fishy flotsam in its throat. The sea lion closed its mouth and turned its head so that it seemed to look right at her. Its eyes were soft as a cow's. Lizzie lowered the glasses and the sea lion didn't turn away.

Out past Seal Rocks, on the horizon, a boat with a white sail floated sleepily. An orange-and-blue hot-air balloon drifted over the water. Sunshine dazzled off the windows of the Cliff House in short, sharp flashes that made Lizzie worry about headache. She looked upward instead, to Sutro Heights and the line of white plaster statues on the bluff.

Without asking permission, the children were already running up the hill and scrambling down to the cove on the far side of the Cliff House. Over the noise of the ocean, the sea lions, the gulls, they could later claim not to have heard anyone calling them back. This left the women with no choice but to follow. The descent was steep.

In spite of a large, enticing peanut stand by the cliff face, it was less crowded here. A dangerous undertow kept people out of the water, and the littles were sternly warned of this. Other children, children who'd come with their parents, were begging for peanuts, but the wards of the Brown Ark knew better than to ask. Lizzie saw Jenny pick up some discarded hulls, look hopefully inside.

The tide had spit seaweed and slivers of wood onto the sand. Some of the wood was blackened and might well have been all that remained of the *Parallel,* a schooner that had foundered just off Point Lobos a year or so before. The *Parallel* had been loaded with dynamite. They'd heard the explosion way back at the Brown Ark, and it had broken every window in the Cliff House. Miss Stevens explained how a sound could break glass. Like magic!

Lizzie stationed herself between the children and the water. This was a precaution, but it also allowed her a chance to be alone. She wanted to imagine the things the ocean hid, fish with bulbous eyes, forests of coral, clams the size of bathtubs. She wanted a moment in which to feel her life for what it was, an inconsequential bit of noise at the edge of something deep and vast.

She picked her way through a scramble of sand verbena, its leaves thick, flat, and coated with salt. She disturbed several small crabs, sand fleas, and a darkly colored sea gull with a red bill and a black tail. It leapt away, skimmed along the water, rode the updraft just above the foam. Lizzie knelt and pressed her palm into the wet sand. She rose and wiped her hand on her skirt. Water seeped into the pools her fingertips had made. Down the beach she could see Jenny collecting a handful of broken mussel shells.

A young man and woman strolled by arm in arm. "Is she yours?" the woman asked Lizzie. She'd seen how Lizzie watched Jenny.

"No," said Lizzie. Too quickly. "No. She's an orphan."

"How sad," said the man. "Such a sweet little girl."

Close to the waterline the tide had carved a tunnel through the rocky cliffs. This inspired the boys into pirate games. They'd forced the girls inside and were devising tortures, when Miss Stevens caught on and set the prisoners free. Lizzie saw her emerge, a boy's ear in each of her hands.

Miss Stevens called the children together. "Which is strongest, air, water, or stone?" she asked them. The gulls screamed themselves hoarse.

The children returned to the Ark, tired and chapped from the sun and wind. Their clothes were scratchy with salt and sand; the ocean continued to boom distantly in their ears. Jenny had a coiled hermit-crab shell clutched in her fist. She brought it near her face to see how far down into the ink of the coil she could see. She wondered if there was anyone hidden inside. Her fingers smelled of seaweed. She breathed the odor in again and again.

When she went to put the shell into her wardrobe—a box that apples had once arrived in—Maud Curry was sitting on her bed, waiting. "What have you got?" she demanded. "Give it to me. And go wash your hands and smooth your hair. No wonder no one adopts you. You smell."

The
Ogre
Mother

ONE

Lizzie went straight from her day at the beach to Mrs. Putnam's Wednesday at-home. She cleaned up in the Putnams' bathroom and joined the ladies in the conservatory. Everything was as it should be. Erma had returned to Sacramento with the children—Lizzie was so lucky not to have children! Erma had aged ten years for every child—the sun was shining, the biscuits had raspberry jam fillings, and Mrs. Mullin took the seat under the fern.

A tall vase near Lizzie was stuffed with fresh-cut branches of lilac. They smelled wonderful. Mrs. Putnam had dressed in a harmonious plum. She took her usual chair and told Lizzie she'd met a family whose daughter went to the Sacred Heart Convent in Oakland. This was the same school Marie Bell attended. The prohibition on seeing Mrs. Pleasant apparently would never dampen Mrs. Putnam's need to discuss her.

Mrs. Putnam had learnt that Marie was a taciturn child, but that, in itself, spoke volumes. She was often visited by Mrs. Pleasant, but never by her father or mother. Mrs. Pleasant was also thought to have chosen the school, since she was a practicing Catholic and the Bells were not, though Mrs. Pleasant did occasionally appear also on the donors' list at the African Methodist Episcopal church. Say what you would, that woman took care of her own.

Marie was a pale, plump girl with hair like straw and cheeks like strawberries. "Not the beauty her mother was, I'm told," said Mrs. Putnam, "but that might be all to the good." Beauty was perilous to girls just as often as it was advantageous, and while Mrs. Putnam was not one who liked to pass judgment, it must be remembered that Marie did not have the sort of mother who could guide her to respectability.

Poor Marie was not even lively. "Everyone who knows her can tell," Mrs. Putnam informed Lizzie, "that something is terribly wrong in that house." Meanwhile, she had it on good authority that Fred Bell, the oldest boy, had been sent to military school in the East, but he'd run off with a dancer, or else he'd been expelled for setting a fire. Either way, it was awful, and he was back in San Francisco, but not at the House of Mystery, as his father refused to speak to him.

"There was some testimony about the Bell children during the Sharon trial," Lizzie said. "But I can't quite remember it."

"Oh, I paid no attention to the Sharon trial," Mrs. Putnam said. "No one I know did."

"A degrading business. It reflected so poorly on the city. Why can't the papers publish the nice things people do?" Behind Mrs. Mullin, the fern was a fountain of green feathers rising from her head like the war bonnet of an Indian. "And the way they persisted in printing every sordid detail! As if decent people cared to read such things!"

On the street outside, a man was shouting at his horse or his wife. Mrs. Putnam put down her tea and moved to close the window. She stood between the dotted-muslin curtains in a dazzling cone of sunlight so that Lizzie could hardly see her. This gave her voice an oracular authority. "It was when Mr. Bell was called to the stand," she said. "This was during the first trial. Five, six years ago. Sharon's lawyer—"

"William Barnes, it was then," Mrs. Mullin offered helpfully.

"Mr. Barnes said that one of the Bell twins was actually the daughter of a German Jew working at the Palace as a maid—"

"Until she became the Bell twins' wet nurse."

"She was not a married woman. She gave her baby to Mrs. Pleasant, who promised to find a loving family. But then, Barnes said, Mammy Pleasant palmed Bertha's baby off on Thomas Bell and let Bertha nurse her right in the Bell home. Tricked that old coot into thinking he was the proud father of twins."

"Mrs. Pleasant denied every jot of it, but she refused to say where Bertha's baby had gone. The Bells sued the *Alta* just for publishing the testimony. They said it was libel to the family—"

"Until they dropped the suit," Mrs. Mullin noted. "They didn't want a lot of lawyers poking around the House of Mystery!"

Lizzie remembered it now. "How old would that baby be?" she asked, even though she knew the answer would be too old. Jenny could certainly be Jewish, with her dark hair and dark eyes.

"Oh, goodness, I don't know, dear. Seven or eight, I suppose." Mrs. Putnam returned to her seat so that her voice came again from her mouth and not from a pillar of fire. Inevitably her credibility suffered. "It was Mr. Barnes's contention that Mrs. Pleasant manufactured the whole case against Sharon. Paid every witness. Forged the wedding contract. Coached poor, dim Allie. Hoodwinked Mr. Bell along with everyone else."

"She doesn't feel about family the way we do. No colored person cares about blood."

"How could they?" Mrs. Putnam asked. "In all fairness, it's a matter of history, not race. Sold away from your mother and denied by your father. A white man, let's face that fact. That's why she does that baby-farming, shuffling children into any old family. Why should she care who belongs to whom? Whoever cared for her?" She paused a moment, shaking her head from the pity of it.

"They do say one of the Bell children is colored." Mrs. Mullin's eyes were big and round, and she blinked them slowly. "But no one knows which."

And Lizzie went on saying nothing. She didn't, as was customary, pay with stories of her own. She told no one about the red bedroom, the nursery with its staring dolls, or the murder of Malina Paillet, much as they would have loved it. She didn't mention Jenny Ijub or Mr. Finney's preposterous accusations, much as they would have hated it. She wasn't even sure why she kept silent. In spite of her protestations, her interest in the Bell family had become proprietary; her position, implicated. Listening to these stories made Lizzie feel guilty.

Something had begun to nag at her, something she'd remembered only just now, just here in the Putnams' house. She turned it over and over in her mind, tried to worry or argue it away. It kept resurfacing. Wood floating on water. Lizzie's imagination was tougher than she was, exactly as her mother had always contended.

Blythe came in and Lizzie watched her collect the tea things. The cups were British, gold handles and tiny blue forget-me-nots. The pot was from China, very fat and painted white with blue willow trees, temples, and doves. The tea inside was a black Ceylon. "How are the boys, Blythe?" Lizzie said, forgetting she had already asked.

"I've no complaints," Blythe answered.

Lizzie stood. "I think I'll go say hello to Mr. Putnam."

Invading Mr. Putnam's library was not her usual routine, and she saw it noted, but it was unimpeachable, so she wasn't stopped. He was reading the paper. Some men grew more corpulent as they aged. Mr. Putnam was the sort who shrank. Folds of skin lay across his neck as a result of his slow disappearance.

The curtains were closed here, so it was much darker than the conservatory. Mr. Putnam read by the light of a small bright lamp. Lizzie's father used to do the same. Lizzie's mother had said he kept the curtains closed to fool himself into thinking it was late enough in the day for a drink. A glass of port sat on a mahogany table, close to Mr. Putnam's right hand.

He stood up politely. "Why, Lizzie," he said. "What a pleasant surprise. But you look tired."

Lizzie *was* tired. She sank into a seat across from him. He returned to his chair. The room smelled strongly of books, a smell she loved above all things, and the usual male odors of liquor and old cigars. The same as in her father's study. Many months after her father's death, Lizzie had moved into her mother's bedroom. She changed the rugs, the curtains, the position of the bed (her mother was a great believer in Dr. Crittenton's analysis of magnetic fields and healthful westward orientation during sleep). It was hard at first, but the room was large, with good light, and now it was hers.

In contrast, she'd entered her father's study only once since his death, when she met there with the family's solicitor, Mr. Griswold, and heard the terms of her father's will. There'd been an ashtray on the table with some parings of her father's fingernails in it. Lizzie supposed they'd been thrown out by now, but not by her.

Her heart quickened. She picked up a tasseled cushion, held it in her arms across her chest, against that beating. "Mr. Putnam," she said. She had trouble going on. She started again. "Mr. Putnam."

"Did you wish to see me about something particular?"

In the glow of the lamp Mr. Putnam's face took on a yellowish alarm. Lizzie knew him well. He didn't mind talking to women if he could stick to rehearsed compliments. He fancied himself good at these; he imagined women enjoyed them. An old-fashioned gallant.

But a genuine conversation was sure to tax him. It was unkind to force one on him. She waited while he took a sip from his drink, then spoke quietly. "Some time ago you said that someone had told you the sorts of foods Mrs. Pleasant served at her table. I was wondering who that someone was."

Mr. Putnam's expression intensified into one of trapped horror. Lizzie, who'd merely hoped to set her mind at rest, was surprised. This was a bad result; she shouldn't have come.

Paradoxically, it had a calming effect on her. His reaction was so extreme; it was as if he had taken her anxiousness away and added it to his. She was able to set the pillow back, breathe more evenly. "I was wondering if it was my father," she said. There. She'd thought it, she'd said it. No way to unmake this moment.

He responded with a fit of coughing. Lizzie fetched him water, but he'd already gulped his port, which made him sputter all the more. She waited through this, making small noises of concern and sympathy, the same she would make to a nervous horse. Really, she thought, she had her answer. If this answer hadn't raised other questions she would have taken pity on him and excused herself. He kept sneaking looks at her, hoping she had done so.

But when he finally responded, his voice was nothing but kind. "What brings these questions, my dear?"

Why lie? The Putnams were her parents' oldest friends; she'd known them all her life. "I've been told I have a sister.

A half sister. Actually, I think I'm being blackmailed. Please don't tell Mrs. Putnam. She'd be so distressed."

As was he, of course. "Oh, my dear!"

"So you can see I really must know the truth. Sparing me won't spare me now."

Mr. Putnam stared at the empty glass in his hands. He poured himself another two fingers. "May I get you something?" he asked.

"No," said Lizzie. Eventually she would have to rejoin the women. Nothing would rouse their suspicions faster than liquor on her breath. Best to see this straight through straight.

"You must never tell Mrs. Putnam I've said a word." Mr. Putnam shook his head morosely. "I can't tell you how I wish you didn't know. Mind you, I don't believe that part about a sister. I never did. I told your father so.

"What mischief could he get up to, at his age? It was a fleecing, wolves to a lamb. He was a good man, Lizzie, or there'd have been no point. Your mother was already dead. A man—a man is different from a woman. He installed the child in the country, down south where you used to camp summers."

Down by the big trees. Lizzie remembered trunks like houses, a stream that dried by July, pine needles covering the ground so your feet sank when you walked. High, windy cliffs over foam. This all arrived in a moment, a flood of smells and sounds.

"There was a weathervane," she said sadly. "Carved like a flock of flying ducks. It clacked when the wind blew. Every year my father let me repaint it. I used to love doing that." She was so astonished she could feel nothing else besides.

"He made one condition. It was as much to protect you, Lizzie, as himself. The mother was a grasping, mendacious woman, not at all fit to raise a child, and he saw she would only increase her demands once she'd made a start. So he said he'd refuse all support if she ever contacted him again. He swore if she came even once to see the girl, he would cast them both off. After his death, we were forced to do that. Is she the one blackmailing you? She can't prove any of it. You pay her nothing."

"It's not the mother. Do you know where she is now?"

"I don't know anything about her. Which is as much as I wish to know."

"How does Mrs. Pleasant figure in?"

"Mrs. Pleasant helped arrange a nursemaid for the child. Is she the one blackmailing you?"

"No."

"But she's in back of it. Got to be. Who else? That child is not your sister, Lizzie, and no one says she is, excepting a couple of women who were born telling lies. Don't you pay a single cent. Mrs. Pleasant knew your father a long time, since the first days when she cooked at Case and Heiser and he supplied the meat. She made it her business to know the up-and-comers, and she found the way to work him."

"Your mother was a saint. How she suffered!" Mrs. Putnam stood in the doorway. Lizzie didn't know whether she had just arrived or had been standing outside for a while, hearing every word.

She shut the door and came into the room with her wide plum skirt sweeping the floor like a furious pendulum. Lizzie had never seen such a set of high red blotches on her cheeks. "When poor Harriet came all the way back from the grave to warn you! When I learnt that Mrs. Pleasant was making her afterlife a misery as well as her life!"

"Your father was a good man, Lizzie," Mr. Putnam repeated. He looked appealingly at his wife for confirmation, for forgiveness. "Lizzie already knew," he told her. "She came asking."

The color went down in Mrs. Putnam's face. She shifted with visible effort into briskness and efficiency. "*You're* a good man," she said. "Better than I ever deserved, and don't I know it. But you talk too much. This hasn't a thing to do with Lizzie, and it would hurt her mother horribly. I thank God she's dead! The past must bury the past.

"Now." She gave Lizzie a quick nod. "We're all done in here. Mrs. Mullin is waiting in the conservatory, wondering what we've all got up to, and you know what a gossip she is. You just pinch some color into your cheeks and come sit with us, Lizzie, as if nothing has happened. Let poor Mr. Putnam finish his port in peace. Look how you've upset him, but I entirely forgive you and none of this need ever be referred to again."

Mrs. Mullin's suspicions were indeed roused. They expressed themselves as a series of questions as to how Lizzie had found Mr. Putnam. Fortunately they were easily answered. To every delicate probe, Lizzie responded that Mr. Putnam had seemed in good spirits.

Meanwhile she tried to organize her own thoughts and feelings into clear, useful sequentiality. These are the things she thought and in this order:

First, it was a shame she didn't care more for Jenny. She preferred a girl like Maud, someone kind and thoughtful, someone lively, someone you could talk to who'd talk right back. Why couldn't it be Maud? Jenny seemed more Baby Edward's sister than Lizzie's, tight-lipped and disapproving.

And if Jenny really were her sister, wouldn't Lizzie instinctively feel something more for her? Mr. Putnam was quite right to point out that even if her father believed her to be his, she might still very well not be. Novels, even the history books, were littered with women who lied about such things. And for each one caught out, there must be a dozen never doubted.

Jenny had shown up at the Brown Ark, and on Lizzie's day there, too, so Mrs. Pleasant must have arranged it all. But did this make it more or less likely that Jenny was her sister? Lizzie tried to remember whether she'd been specifically asked for, the way Mrs. Pleasant's baskets of food were specifically directed to her. She wasn't sure, but clearly there were schemes within schemes.

And yet Mrs. Pleasant had asked nothing from her beyond Jenny's place at the Ark. She'd left Jenny off and that had been that.

Did it even matter whether Jenny was Lizzie's sister? Her father's acknowledgment certainly attested to the possibility. He had behaved in such a way as to make it possible. Everything else was mere chance. Surely, one's moral responsibilities were not determined by chance. As Mrs.

Hallis said, there were immediate consequences to behavior and there were remote ones. Why distinguish between the two?

What moral responsibilities? Lizzie's behavior was not at fault here. Jenny was well cared for at the Ark, where everyone was more than kind to her. She had the prettiest dresses of any ward there. She had piano lessons. She had food and a bed and good friends. Any obligations Lizzie might or might not have were thoroughly discharged.

And what kind of a name *was* Ijub?

And all the while, Lizzie kept up a polite discourse on the weather and Blythe's children and Mr. Putnam's high spirits. It was a bravura performance, supported by Mrs. Putnam, who kept the conversation easy and prompted Lizzie if she ever seemed about to forget her lines.

Outside, two men and a woman strolled by. They'd come up the hill, were laughing and panting, loosening their scarves, unbuttoning their coats. No such thing in San Francisco as going out for a little walk.

The woman wore a soft hat with a black veil folded back. She had a yellow rose pinned to it, not a rosebud, but a full round bloom. It gave Lizzie a start. She actually jerked in response.

"Are you cold, Lizzie?" Mrs. Mullin asked, but Lizzie couldn't answer, because she had just realized that her father must have attended Mrs. Pleasant's Geneva Cottage red-invitation, men-only parties. What else would make her mother such a saint?

Maybe her father was a good man. Mr. Putnam said so, and he would know. Maybe they really had been forced to set Jenny aside, if Jenny's mother was so thoroughly bad.

Mr. Putnam had said this, too, though he'd also claimed to know nothing about Jenny's mother. Mr. Finney had said the same thing once and followed it with the same retraction.

In any case, Lizzie had always thought her father a good man. But he was most certainly, most incontrovertibly, a man with a terrible temper.

"What's wrong?" Mrs. Mullin asked.

"She gets those dreadful headaches," Mrs. Putnam said. "Lizzie, I expect you'd better lie down."

But Lizzie had already risen. "I must go," she said. She tried to think of a reason to offer, gave it up. She left the house without her gloves. Blythe had to run after her.

Everywhere Lizzie looked, the color yellow sprang at her. There was so much of it. Sunshine on windows. Buttons on coats. The golden wattles dripping with their fabulous golden spikes of blossoms. It would be a terrible thing to be a young girl dead and missing the springtime.

Lizzie went home and drew the curtains in every room but her father's study, which she didn't enter. A letter from the Brown Ark had been delivered in her absence. She opened it and read:

My dear Lizzie,

I hope this finds you well. My own health is excellent although I'm aware of those wishing otherwise. The vultures gather, but I'll disappoint them as long as I can. I won't tell you their names. Last night's soup had a peculiar taste, but

I make nothing of this, I put it down to careless-
ness in the kitchen. I remember when the food
here was always done to a turn. I had a new pair of
knitted slippers, but someone seems to have
taken them. I won't tell you who or this letter
might not be sent.

The dog has disappeared and no one will tell
me why. I'm reminded of the day my dear friend
Millicent Peterson died. We were told she fell
from her horse, but her dog vanished the same
hour. Dogs do find ways to tell us things, don't
you know? If they're let. I remember how that
terrier used to bark at everyone. I always knew
when someone was coming through the yard.

I hope you'll think it safe enough to visit
when you return,

Sincerely yours,
Mrs. Wright

with a postscript from Miss Stevens, serving as secretary:

P.S. The dog is fine and Mrs. Wright petted it
only yesterday. She is most unwell, as you can see,
and I think it cruel that she must spend her de-
clining days in this endless drama of poisonings
and murder. Now she wishes me to add that she
has instructed her bank manager to provide you
with additional funds should you need them. She
believes you've not come to see her because
you're on a European tour. It would be a kindness if, when next you speak, you thank her for

the money. Otherwise she will worry at us end-
lessly, convinced she's been robbed. I wonder if
her impulses were so generous when she actually
had funds, although it is tenderly done; I take
nothing away from her genuine benevolence.

At about four o'clock Lizzie heard the foghorn. When
she looked outside around dinnertime, she couldn't see
across the street. It didn't necessarily follow that no one
could see in. She left the curtains drawn.

T W O

"Wake up." Maud's face floated white as paste in the dark, and behind it Melody's face, and behind that, Coral's. When Jenny sat up she saw that Ella May and Tilly were also there. The whole Good Manners Club. Maud's voice was a hiss. "Come with us."

They made Jenny go first up the stairs. "Shhh!" Melody told her once, although she was already making as little noise as an Indian. They went up one flight and then another, until they were in the tower room.

"You're not afraid to be here, are you?" Maud asked.

Outside, the fog was so thick that no lights shone through. "No," said Jenny, with a sense of being trapped. She knew there was no right answer to that question. Maud excelled at questions without right answers.

"You need to toughen up," Maud said. "When you're adopted, you'll probably sleep by yourself. You can't be such a baby about it. None of the rest of us mind the dark."

Jenny thought she didn't mind the dark, either. What she minded was being shut up. But even that was all right, because she knew the door didn't lock. She needed only to wait as long as she could, letting the other girls go back to their beds, and then go out again. She could go anywhere she liked, out to the barn with the dog and the mule, or into the downstairs parlor to sleep. Or out to the street. She often went for walks when she couldn't sleep. As long as you were wherever you were expected when morning came, no one knew. Jenny took a seat on the settee that smelled of dead horses. The door shut with a click.

The room was cold and stank of dust and the bitter Chinese tea Miss Hayes drank. Jenny's breath was coming as fast as if she'd run up the stairs.

She didn't hear the girls, but they would wait for her. She couldn't leave yet. She must stay still as long as she possibly could. The silence pressed against her ears until it turned her pulse into a metronome.

Jenny put her hands on her knees and played scales over them. Two minutes, she told herself. An egg cooking. She kept her hands arched and tried to keep her fingering even. Give every note the same time to breathe. Instead she found herself playing faster and faster, lost track of when the egg was done.

She rose and picked her way through the clutter of charitable donations. There was a stuffed squirrel with its tail raised, and a hat rack with dangerous points on which she scratched her arm. There was a broken music stand,

and a large cracked vase for umbrellas. Jenny reached the door and turned the knob.

It spun like a pinwheel. She panicked. She grabbed the doorknob tightly, pulled with both hands. The knob rattled in its socket, could be wiggled this way and that like her loose tooth.

Maud must have known it was broken, or arranged for it to be broken. Generally the boys stayed out of things between the girls, but Duffy Phelps would do anything Maud wanted, and Mrs. Lake said he was a wizard with a hammer, could fix anything. The thought that the boys might have known what Maud had planned was a special humiliation for Jenny.

By now she was gasping for air and unable to speak. No one would hear her, anyway. She stumbled back to the settee and flung herself onto it. Her face was already hot with tears, and now she began to weep with her mouth open, making faces that stretched her cheeks. Whenever she took a breath there was a noise like barking. She wiped her nose on the hem of her nightgown, because she had nothing else, and then fell asleep.

She awoke cold as well as terrified. She found a woman's dress, velvet with the hem kicked out, smelling of mothballs. She pulled its skirt over her as she lay on the settee. The pulse in her ears was deafening and yet she was convinced that something hungry was in the room with her. There'd been a rustle, the tick-tock of claws, only her heart was too loud for her to hear this.

She rose. Whatever was hungry retreated with a scrabble, but it would be back when it saw what a little girl she was. She was exactly what something hungry would want. Jenny had to get out. She crept to the nearest window.

Outside, the world was gone. There were no stars, no scrub, no sand, no city. Nothing above and nothing below. A vast and milky ocean rolled against the glass.

T H R E E

$\mathcal{T}$he next afternoon Lizzie heard the front door chime. She was expecting no one. Before she could reach the door, it chimed again. When she opened it, she found Miss Viola Bell standing on the doorstep. She refused to come in. She was wearing a coat of blue wool, pinned at the throat with a large, garish brooch. Inside the coat she looked small and cold. "Do you know what's happened?" she said. "Do you care?"

The fog from the night before had dissipated, but the air was clingy and carried the echoey sounds of horses and wheels. The bit of yard in front of Lizzie's house was trellised. Few blossoms; it still looked wintry, but there was one branch of jasmine, and some sleepy bees.

"How nice to see you, Miss Bell," Lizzie said. "Please come inside. What are you talking of?"

Viola shifted on her crutch and her sheet music fell. Lizzie stooped and retrieved it. "The Mockingbird's Song" was the top sheet, "a piece for Teacher and Student." "I'm talking of Jenny. Who was found this morning, standing on the ledge outside the cupola window. She'd been there all night, in her thin little nightdress, with nothing but yards and yards of air beneath her and the cold, hard ground. If she'd fallen!"

"*Please* come in," Lizzie said again.

Across the way she could see her neighbor's boy in the window, watching. He had his jaw tied up for toothache, and a cat like a shawl on his shoulders.

Again Viola refused. Her voice was thready, her color poor. "Do you see that she could have been killed?"

Lizzie did not. "I don't understand," she said. "Jenny's so happy at the Brown Ark. Happy and safe."

"Happy?" A bead of spit appeared on Viola's lip; she wiped at it with the fingers of her cotton glove. Her dark hair was twisted into her hat, which was of a simple black felt that any shopgirl could have bettered. "How should she be happy? It would be one thing, if she'd never known anything but poverty. But to be petted one minute and cast aside the next. Don't you think that's the cruelest thing can be done to a child?"

It was possible, of course, that Jenny had talked to Viola about her past, but then Jenny didn't talk to anyone about anything. "What do you know about Jenny?" Lizzie asked.

"I know she's not *happy.* I went to the Brown Ark for our lesson. I was told she'd been put to bed and the doctor sent for. I asked the matron for your address and came here. I want you to know I hold you responsible. If she'd died you'd be responsible for that, too." Viola's voice had started low and gotten angrier without getting louder. Her fist gripped the handle of her crutch so tightly that it shook.

"Why am I responsible?" Lizzie asked. She had her own ideas, of course, but she didn't see how Viola could share them. Lizzie had calmed considerably since the day before; another sleepless night avoiding thoughts of her father had spent her. But now Viola was upsetting her again. Lizzie wished Viola would come inside, was afraid the neighbors would see, was afraid she would fall.

Viola tossed her head. The sunlight hit her brooch, making it sparkle threateningly. "Mr. Finney asked me to remind you about his money, if I ever had the chance. We're to be married." She said these last words as if she was aware she shouldn't be saying them but unable to deny herself the pleasure of it.

Now Lizzie wished there were only Jenny to worry about. "I hope you'll be very happy," she said automatically, and then, "I'm afraid he's a dangerous man. I'm sorry, I must say it. You're so very young."

Viola's brooch was a twinkling rose at her throat; her eyes were bright as glass. "I know he's not been a good man," she said. "We tell each other everything. He repents it all."

"You read the Bible together," Lizzie suggested. Your love will save him. She could imagine the potency of that, Mr. Finney, so handsome, so sincere. *Save me.* If he'd offered that aspect to Lizzie, she doubted that even she, twice Viola's age, would have successfully resisted. She had never understood Jane Austen's Fanny Price. "I've seen a different side of him."

It was the wrong thing to say, only confirmed Viola's special intimacy. "I'm sure you have," she said proudly.

Lizzie felt the press of dead air she associated with Baby Edward. The silver color in the corner of her eye, the taste in her mouth, the sickening spin of Viola's brooch. "It was you, then, told Mr. Finney about my father."

"Yes."

"What else did Mrs. Pleasant say about him?" Lizzie closed her eyes and there were tiny fairy lights on the inside of her lids. She pushed the headache firmly away. She couldn't have one now, not with Viola's heart open before her and matters of such delicacy still to be discussed. The usual terror approached, but Lizzie refused it.

"Mrs. Pleasant said nothing. She has a book with names in it, dates, and such like. I saw it last week, just for a moment. I can't show you, but I don't lie. I want the money for Mr. Finney because he has debts to settle before we can marry, but I didn't do it for that. I did it for Jenny. Someone has to watch over her."

Viola's voice had quickened, while Lizzie's mind had slowed. "I believe you," Lizzie said, her words unintelligible. She made a greater effort, achieved a moment's normalcy. Then it was gone again, bees buzzing, lights popping, the silver stain spreading over the world.

But no headache sent by anyone for any reason would stop Lizzie. She was speaking without thinking of it; the pain would come, no doubt, but she'd have what she wanted when it did. "I need to know what else Mrs. Pleasant has in her book about my father." The silver film soaked into Viola's eyes, her hair. Lizzie's hands were made of snow. "Things from long ago. I'll pay you to look again."

"How much?"

"Fifty dollars."

Viola was trembling. She was angry or ill or tired from standing for so long. Lizzie felt the power leaking from her own legs. She couldn't do anything more. She pulled the door shut without waiting for an answer, so that Viola wouldn't see her when the pain hit.

Doggedly her imagination fetched up images of Malina Paillet, but all in silver now. Drops of silver blood fell on silver silk. The sharp slice of a silver moon. Her head falling away from her neck. Silver roses wilting on her wrist. "You have only the beauty of youth," her angry suitor told her. He caught her by the hair.

Lizzie was lying on the marble of the entryway with no recollection of how she'd gotten there. She wondered whether Viola was still waiting outside, but she couldn't lift herself up to go see.

FOUR

*L*ater Lizzie managed to reach the sofa in the dayroom, where she spent the rest of the night. She threw up twice, but by morning her headache had receded and she felt it only when she turned her head or sat or stood quickly. She would have liked to stay in bed for the day. But sometime during the ebbing, Viola's initial words had finally penetrated. Little Jenny had spent the night on the cupola ledge in her nightdress, and she might have been killed.

Lizzie washed her face with the coldest water she could stand. She dressed and caught the streetcar on Van Ness and walked the rest of the way to the Ark. The leaves of the silver-dollar eucalyptus were green on one side, silver on the other, so that a breeze made the stands of trees shimmer like water.

Lizzie knew the name of this tree because her father had taught it to her. He'd liked taking her for walks. "You don't complain about the hills," he said approvingly. "You don't chatter on about nothing."

He didn't always talk himself, but she liked it when he did. He was less guarded in what he said than her mother was, not so determined to make a lesson out of everything. Here in San Francisco, where the money grows on trees, he would start off, so that once as a girl she'd asked him which trees the money grew on, and the silver-dollars were the ones he'd named. He'd also said he could remember a time when there were no trees in San Francisco at all, but never, ever a time when there was no money.

He'd liked to tell stories that illustrated the lunacy of the madly rich. He was appalled by them, but proud as well—only in San Francisco.

Mr. Crocker's spite fence.

Layman's medieval castle.

Stanford's mechanical birds.

How many of these men had been at Mrs. Pleasant's parties with him? How many had pretended later not to know her, or one another, either?

Her father had also told her of Dr. Toland, a man who kept his dead wife in a glass-topped coffin in his office. What kind of a story was that to tell a child? Her mother was horrified when she heard. You'll give the child nightmares, she cried, so frightened of Lizzie's unruly imagination. You always underestimate her, Lizzie's father had replied. Lizzie had been so proud to hear him say that.

The story hadn't bothered her a bit. Lizzie asked to be

kept under glass herself, which amused her father. But it struck her as a sensible precaution, just in case she wasn't dead after all, to leave a window through which she could get someone's attention.

The dead woman under glass put her in mind of the women on Morton Street. Against all her best efforts, she saw her father waiting in line there, making a selection, the woman like a puppet in his arms. Her mother at home, telling Effie to tie Lizzie's hands at night.

At the Ark, she found Nell in the parlor laying newly crocheted doilies over the backs of the threadbare chairs. The older girls must have been learning to tat. The doilies were round with scalloped edges and in no way improved the appearance of the room. Dubious finery piled on faded finery.

"Still abed," Nell said, without Lizzie's even asking. "You just missed Dr. Kearney coming by for a second check. He says she's fine. But not talking, not our Jenny. We ask her, Just what were you playing at out on that ledge in the dark, and she won't say a word."

The line of Nell's mouth changed from tight to soft; her cheeks sagged into pockets. "The lamb," she added. "Poor Maudie hasn't left her side since we found her. I thought my heart would stop when I first saw her, her nightdress flying in the wind like a kite, holding on to the window with those tiny fingers. Her hands were so cold I thought they'd crack when we opened them. We were in a state, all right."

Since Jenny wouldn't talk, Ti Wong had taken it upon himself to investigate, Nell added. Nell herself guessed it was simple high jinks of some kind, a game gone wrong.

But Ti Wong had been carefully through the tower room, and in his opinion, the door was jiggered. He'd also found a hidden pessary. That had taken some quick talking on Nell's part; she wished Lizzie had been there to see that!

The embroidered wisdom on the wall behind Nell had been changed again. Now it read:

> *How small, of all that human hearts endure,*
> *That part which laws or kings can cause or cure!*
> SAMUEL JOHNSON

A square of light fell from the one small window at the end of the room onto the floor. There was a row of empty beds and then one with Jenny in it, awake and sitting up. On the bed past Jenny, Maud lay asleep, facedown across the blankets, her golden curls spilling off the side of the mattress. What a vigil for a young friend to keep! There must be *something* about Jenny to inspire such devotion. Lizzie was determined to find it.

She spoke in a whisper so as not to wake Maud. "Are you all right now, little Jenny?"

"Yes," Jenny said. Her eyelids were swollen as if she'd been crying. Her hair was a tangle that would have to be painfully addressed when she was feeling better.

"I'm glad." Lizzie tried to think what to say next. She had so few ideas she settled on what she was really thinking. "Does it seem to you that we're anything alike?"

Apparently the question was too ridiculous to be worth answering. Jenny looked at her briefly, then looked away.

Lizzie sat on the side of her bed. The headache stabbed once, then stopped. "I like ducks and you like ducks." Lizzie counted on her fingers. "That's one. I used to play the piano when I was a little girl. That's two."

"You're not a little girl." Jenny lay back on her pillow. Now Lizzie saw a bruise on her neck, up by her ear, a scratch on her arm. Her fingernails were torn and must have hurt.

"Not anymore. But I was once. I like stories. Do you like stories?"

"Tell one," Jenny said. She turned her huge dark eyes to Lizzie. She was missing a tooth, right in the front of her mouth. Lizzie saw the gap when Jenny spoke. She would have the smile of a jack-o'-lantern if she ever smiled at all.

Telling a story was the perfect way to have a conversation with someone who refused to talk.

Once upon a time there was a king and a queen, and they had a daughter. They'd wanted a child for many years, and when the baby came she was the answer to their prayers. Her skin was snowy white with just a hint of apples. Her lips were red; her eyes were blue, and bright as stars. She was the most beautiful baby anyone could remember ever seeing.

But one night while the king and queen slept, an ogre took the child from her cradle and replaced her with a child of its own. In the morning the child in the cradle was wrinkled as a walnut, had eyes that crossed, and little pointed teeth. "This is not my child," the queen said, but the king was not so sure. Perhaps the child had fallen ill during the night. He sent for the finest doctors in the kingdom, yet no one could restore the child's beauty.

The ogre child grew every day. It was wicked as well as ugly. When the mother fed it, it bit her and then drank the blood instead of the milk. "This is not my child," the queen said, and when the king again refused to listen, she crept out into the night to find her daughter.

She walked for many days. Her shoes were soft and wore through at the soles. Her feet were soft and began to bleed. She came to a forest and in the forest was a stream and into this stream she put her bloody feet.

She was used to being served and cared for, not fending for herself. She hadn't eaten in quite some time.

So the queen was hungry as well as footsore, and there, beside her toes, trapped in a small pool, was a large silver fish. She picked up a stone to kill the fish, but before she could the fish spoke. "Put me back in the stream," it said, "and if I can ever do you a kindness, I will."

"How can a fish do me a kindness?" the queen asked, but she put it into the stream.

She thrust her feet back in the water and reclined on the bank. Suddenly she noticed an egg near her on the grass. Because she was still so hungry, she picked it up, thinking to crack it open and eat it. To her surprise the egg spoke. "Put me back in the nest," the egg said, "and if I can ever do you a kindness, I will."

"How can an egg do me a kindness?" the queen asked, but she saw the nest on a branch above her and placed the egg inside.

That night she had a dream. In the dream she saw her

daughter sleeping in a glass box at the bottom of a lake on top of a mountain. But the mountain was too high to climb and the lake was too deep to swim. The queen woke up weeping.

(Lizzie didn't know why the queen was so certain the dream was true. She hurried on before Jenny could ask about this, in case she, too, found it odd.)

In the nest above the queen's head was a bird. "Take my wings," it said, and as soon as it spoke she felt wings growing from her shoulders. She flew to the top of the mountain and stood at the edge of the lake.

In the lake was the silver fish. "Take my tail," it said, and as soon as it spoke she felt her wings turn to fins and her legs fuse to a tail. She dove into the lake and swam to the very deepest, darkest part and picked her sleeping baby up.

In that instant, she was transported to her own castle, dry, wingless, and tailless. When the ogre child saw her with the baby, it climbed from the cradle and ran into the night and was never heard of again.

"There now, dear," said the king. "I told you it would all come right in the end."

There probably should have been one more animal. Things in fairy tales always came in threes, but Lizzie hadn't been able to think of another. She'd cobbled this story together from bits and pieces of other stories she remembered, but it wasn't a bad effort for all that. She was rather pleased with herself. She'd mastered her intractable imagination and turned it to good use. No dead girls in this story. No dancing, no yellow dresses. Lizzie was having none of those thoughts!

In fact, Lizzie was feeling better about Malina Paillet.

When the headache receded, it took some of her suspicions with it. Maybe her father had attended a party or two, but he wouldn't kill a girl for not liking him. What kind of a daughter would think he might? Yes, he'd had a terrible temper, but he was a good man. A good-hearted man. The only thing Lizzie couldn't quite set aside was the fact that Mrs. Bell had told her about Malina. It was so indiscreet, it seemed the sort of thing that must have a motive.

Maud had awakened. She came and lay next to Jenny, taking her hand. "What happened to the ogre child?" Jenny asked.

Jenny didn't like to be touched. Lizzie remembered that from when she'd fetched her at the House of Mystery; now she saw it with Maud. When Maud took her hand, Jenny jumped as if she'd been pinched. "I don't know," said Lizzie. "I guess she needs a mother, too, doesn't she? She needs an ogre mother."

"But not *that* ogre mother," Jenny said.

Lizzie stood and looked down at the two girls, the blond head and the dark. She felt a sudden lump in her throat over the mother she'd created, the mother who walked so far and risked so much. It occurred to her that the story wasn't really over. The child would grow up and leave. The mother would spend her life remembering the one brief hour when she could fly like a bird, swim like a fish.

FIVE

On the subject of Viola Bell, Lizzie was utterly ashamed. What excuse could she make? She decided simply to give Viola the fifty dollars next time Jenny had a piano lesson, as recompense for her own appalling behavior. She couldn't believe she'd hired a young girl to snoop for her; Lizzie wasn't the sort to do such a thing.

About Jenny her thoughts were more tentative. If only Jenny seemed contented at the Ark, things could be left as they were. Above all, Lizzie must not pick her up only to set her down again. Viola had that quite right. Lizzie needed to be sure she could see it through before she even began.

And there was still the mother to consider. What if Lizzie adopted Jenny, grew to love her like a sister, and then her mother appeared and took her back? What if her mother was colored? How could Jenny go from white to colored with no preparation? Lizzie remembered the story Mrs. Wright had told—how Mrs. Pleasant had passed a tray at a party to which she'd been invited, pretending to be a servant so that no one would feel awkward about her being there. Jenny was already such a proud little girl. She wouldn't know to do this, and Lizzie didn't want her learning.

Lizzie meant to look in next on Mrs. Wright, but before she could do so, Minna Graham appeared in the doorway, clapping her hands. "Sam is here, Miss Hayes!" she said. "He wants to say hello to you!"

Sam had become a great favorite with the girls in the kitchen. He delivered Mrs. Pleasant's baskets with elegance, sweeping his top hat from his head and holding it at his heart. He had a gift for making orphans feel like princesses. It was kinder even than the food he brought. Lizzie excused herself to go see him.

Three of the older girls were still washing up from lunch. An obstinate landscape of creamed potatoes crusted the pots and pans, and the burnt-hair smell of cooked cabbage hung heavily. The kitchen steamed like a greenhouse. Sam stood amidst the dirty dishes, making a pyramid of strawberries. "This here's for you," he told the girls in turn, whenever he came upon a perfect one, passing it over. "This one's a jewel." On the counter, packed in ice, were five large silver fish with popping eyes.

"How are your headaches, Miss Hayes?" he asked, and sympathized over the recent siege. "I'll tell Mrs. Pleasant. She's smart with leaves and pastes. Maybe she'll have something new to try."

"Mrs. Pleasant is so good to remember us." Lizzie said

the words around a duplicitous taste in her mouth. Such lovely fruit, such lovely fish. Just when Lizzie had thought to send a spy into the nest.

Sam said Mrs. Pleasant was right as right. Had one of her dizzy spells, her spasmodics as she called them, but bright as a penny now.

"And Mrs. Bell?"

Mrs. Bell was also fine. She didn't always sleep so good, and sometimes she woke the household, screaming they were all being murdered in their beds, but this hadn't happened for a couple of weeks and they were all enjoying the rest.

"And Miss Viola Bell?"

Sam flipped one of the sorrowful, pop-eyed fish over with a slap. He turned to Lizzie. "Now, there's trouble," he said. He shook his head slowly. "There's a heap of trouble."

Last night, he said, just last night, Miss Viola had been thrown from the house. She didn't get on with Mrs. Bell, and Mrs. Bell was always suspecting Miss Viola snuck around in passageways and spied on people in their bedrooms, as if you couldn't hear her coming a mile with that heavy foot of hers. But last night it was Mrs. Pleasant found her, snooping around in some papers where she'd no business being. The one thing Mrs. Pleasant couldn't forgive was snooping.

Scarce an hour later Miss Viola was packed and gone, living at the home of the Boones now, colored friends of Mrs. Pleasant, since Mrs. Pleasant was not the sort to turn a girl out to the street no matter how angry she was. The servants had all been called together and everyone told she was never to be let back in and her name wasn't Viola Bell anymore, but was Viola Smith, which it always had been, Mrs. Bell said, only they'd all been too nice about it.

Sam was sorrier than he could say, but there were those made better by suffering and those made worse. Miss Viola Bell, Miss Smith, that was, had always been the second, but maybe now she'd be the first. The Boones were nice folks and would be good to her.

In all the horrors of the past few days, this was the worst yet. It demanded an immediate price; Lizzie didn't have to be a Methodist to see her duty, clear and terrible and unavoidable. She must go to the House of Mystery, where she'd sworn never to go again, and take the blame for Viola's disgrace. She must do this at once. She could not allow Mrs. Pleasant to throw Viola out over something Lizzie had put her up to. She could not let Viola suffer through one more night in a strange bed.

She blamed her headache, for she wasn't the sort to snoop and certainly wasn't the sort to pay someone else to snoop when she was in her right mind. Maybe Mrs. Pleasant, who knew about her headaches, would understand. Maybe she wouldn't forgive Lizzie, but would forgive Viola, which was all that mattered. Viola had never needed a mother more than she needed one now with Mr. Finney courting her, repenting day and night.

But Lizzie saw her duty more quickly than she did it. She sat in the parlor while working herself up, and by the time she'd finished, Sam was gone. She got her gloves and hat, and took the same walk she'd once made in the dark with little Jenny. She was glad it wasn't dark. The sun was out, pale as a pearl. The air was damp, and the smell of eucalyptus leaves intense. Lizzie passed beneath, opened the gate, climbed the steps, and knocked with the roaring-lion knocker. She remembered how frightened she'd been the first time she'd done this. Her mind had been a jumble of voodoo curses and headless dolls. She was much more frightened now.

No one came in response to the first knock. She knocked again, with her hand this time. And again. She took off her glove and knocked again.

The door was finally opened, by a blind man in a green butler's uniform. His hair was wild with gray curls, his nose a drunkard's blue. His eyes, pale and filmy, remained fixed on a spot just above Lizzie's right shoulder. No warmth came out through the opened doorway.

"Miss Hayes to see Mrs. Pleasant." The dark entryway yawned before her. There in the corner was the grandfather clock, ticking loudly, and there in the back, on the newel post at the base of the spiral stairs, the black statue of the naked woman. You couldn't see that she was naked from this distance, of course. You had to know the family.

"Not in. Are you a reporter?" His words slid up against one another; his accent was Scottish. His "you" was halfway to "ye."

"No. Of course not. I know Mrs. Pleasant. I've been a guest here. And I must speak to her urgently."

"Not in," the butler repeated. "And not often in to uninvited callers even when she is in." He began to close the door.

"Might I see Mrs. Bell?" she asked.

"Not in."

"Sam, then. Might I speak with Sam?"

"Not in," the butler said, shutting the door.

Maybe Mrs. Pleasant and Sam *were* out. But Mrs. Bell

was always in. When Lizzie made up her mind to something, it was made up.

She went down the steps. She looked back to check that the butler wasn't watching—instinct only; a moment later she remembered he was blind—and took the path that led around the enormous house to the back.

A white girl came in answer to her knock on the kitchen door. "I'm looking for Sam," Lizzie said.

"He's not here."

"Or Mrs. Pleasant or Mrs. Bell. Mightn't I speak with Mrs. Bell?"

The girl was uncertain. She stared at Lizzie, biting her lip. "I'm Miss Hayes," Lizzie said encouragingly. "I've called here before. Mrs. Bell knows me. Just go ask her."

"Try the front door."

"No one answers."

"Wait here," the girl said finally.

She let Lizzie into the kitchen. Two men and a woman sat at the table. The men were colored, the woman was white. Someone had been smoking recently. Lizzie could smell it. The stove was out; the room was cold. No one looked at her. They leaned toward one another across the table, murmured a conversation she couldn't hear. The woman laughed. The counters around the dry-sink were covered with dirty dishes, some so crusted Lizzie didn't see how they could ever be scrubbed clean. Over the sink was a line hung with dishrags.

Disorder was meant to be a private thing. Lizzie pretended not to see it. She'd forced herself in here. There was no reason she should be made welcome.

The girl returned. "She's in the drawing room. I'm to take you."

The house was as dim as always, and as quiet. Muted sunlight came through the glass dome and landed on the coiling snake of a staircase; everything around it was dark. As they passed the library, Lizzie caught a glimpse of the blind butler sitting in a chair, helping himself to Mrs. Bell's raspberry wine.

They reached the white-and-gold drawing room. "Miss Hayes," the girl said, and then withdrew.

The curtains were pulled and one lamp lit. "Come, sit with me," Mrs. Bell said, and Lizzie did so.

Mrs. Bell was in blue, her brown hair pinned into curls in the back, her skin dull with powder. She had an embroidery hoop in her lap, with a violet half-stitched into the cloth. Lizzie had seen and heard enough to know there was no point in pleading here on Viola's behalf. Those apologies would have to wait for Mrs. Pleasant.

But she could ask about Malina Paillet—ask why Mrs. Bell had chosen to tell her that story; she could pin down the date as much as possible. Then she could go home and check her father's business ledger. He didn't enter personal information, but there might be something. More important, there might be nothing. This would help Lizzie set Malina completely aside as a sad story, but nothing to do with her. Lizzie turned her head so she wouldn't see the stone statues of the begging women.

None of this went as she'd planned. Mrs. Bell opened with one of her startling conversational gambits; there was no recovery. "There are those wish to kill me," she said, but calmly. "Those who've already tried. No one is to get through the door when Mrs. Pleasant is out. Yet in you waltz."

"Your butler did attempt to stop me," Lizzie confessed. "I was persistent."

"Billy?" Mrs. Bell sighed impatiently. "I said it to Mrs. Pleasant, so now we've a blind man guarding the door. You think a killer won't be persistent? A reporter? My mother? A woman come here once, claimed our Muriel had been kicked in the head by a horse. Near to dying. Slid upstairs, smooth as honey while we were all wringing our hands and carrying on. She was going through my desk when Muriel walked in, fit as ever could be."

"How awful."

"Reporters are lower than lice. I can't offer you coffee. I can ring and ring, without anyone coming. When Mrs. P is out, the servants do as they please. Won't even protect me."

"Do you know when Mrs. Pleasant will be back? I really must talk with her."

Mrs. Bell smiled slyly. The tips of her perfect teeth rested on her full bottom lip. "You better not. You better go before she comes. She don't want surprises."

"It's too important."

As always, Mrs. Bell picked up Lizzie's hands. The room was cold and Mrs. Bell's hands colder. Lizzie's eyes were beginning to adjust to the dark. On the wall was a picture of two cherubs eating sponge cake. It was sweet and sentimental, something Lizzie's mother would have liked. Here, it didn't go with the statuary.

"All Mrs. Pleasant's business is important," Mrs. Bell said. "She's out on important business now. The city would fall without her."

"Do you remember telling me about one of her parties?" Lizzie began, but Mrs. Bell was still talking and didn't
stop to listen.

"I used to have such queer fancies as a child," she said.
"Voices in the wind and water. When I was three months
old my mother undressed me and put me on a windowsill
in an ice storm. She was a tiger-heart. Might still be looking for me, for all I know. She killed my two brothers."

"I have a dead brother, too," Lizzie offered. "He died
when he was a baby."

Mrs. Bell dismissed this. She released Lizzie's hands,
lifted the embroidery hoop, and began to pick at it with the
needle. She worked a purple thread loose, which grew
longer and longer while the half-formed violet disappeared.
"If your mother didn't kill him, then you don't know what
I'm saying."

"But I used to have queer fancies about him," Lizzie
insisted. Used to, as if she didn't still, nearly every day.
Who was she to think Mrs. Bell odd? She meant to be con-
genial, but Mrs. Bell didn't like it.

"Do you ever think you're not real?" Now it was a
competition.

"Sometimes. Sometimes I'm reading a book and when
it ends I believe in the characters more than myself. It
doesn't last very long, but I know the sensation."

Mrs. Bell shook her head. "You don't know anything.
What I'm saying is, maybe I was supposed to die when I was
three months old. That's why I've made no mark. The servants don't notice me. I've nothing that's my own."

"You have a husband and children," Lizzie said. "I
wish I had so much as you."

"All I have is six hundred acres in upper New York."

A feeling had been growing over Lizzie during this exchange. It rose from the unvarying at-homes of Mrs. Putnam, the endless circling of Mrs. Wright's memories, but it was strongest with Mrs. Bell in the House of Mystery. These were women under glass. Time had stopped.

Lizzie remembered again, but claustrophobically, her father's story of Dr. Toland's dead wife in her glass-topped coffin. What a good idea, in case you weren't quite dead yet, to leave a window through which you could get someone's attention. "We don't have to be the same person our whole lives," Lizzie said desperately, and then the clock in the hallway struck and the spell was broken.

Mrs. Bell seemed to come to herself, set the embroidery down, patted her hair. "You can probably catch Mrs. Pleasant at the mission," she suggested politely. "She's got another charity case out that way, some family she's feeding. But she likes the mission, she'll probably stop in after. That woman does love a graveyard. She has one of her own, you know. You can imagine how convenient that's been over the years."

They heard the front door open, boots stamping, the voice of a young man calling out. "Mother! Mother!"

Mrs. Bell was on her feet, moving more quickly than Lizzie had thought her capable, and speaking more loudly. "You don't be coming here, Fred! Billy! Billy! Fred's trying to get in!"

Clearly, Lizzie's interview with her had come to an end.

SIX

According to some, Mr. Bell and Mrs. Pleasant were very much in love. They built the House of Mystery to live in together after her husband (and daughter) had died of diseases caused by excessive drink. They mixed assets freely and, after his marriage to Teresa, deeded properties over to her as well. The Bell and Pleasant finances were a Gordian knot no lawyer was ever able to loosen, though for more than thirty years countless numbers of them tried.

In this version of the household, Thomas Bell's marriage to Teresa was something he was tricked into while drunk, "bibulous" being the adjective most frequently assigned him. During the various estate cases, servants testified that the Octavia Street house was a divided one, quite literally. Mrs. Bell was not to enter Mr. Bell's half. He would not enter hers. Nor would he ever speak to her. Any communication was to go through Mrs. Pleasant. Mrs. Pleasant and Mrs. Bell, however, were conceded to be very fond of each other.

Yet there were those eight children (two of them dead). Not a one of them hers, Teresa said. Mr. Bell had paid her fifty thousand dollars a child, so Mrs. Pleasant had produced one whenever the women were short of cash.

Thomas Bell died in 1892. Suffering from a flu, he rose in the night, lost his way, and fell into the well of the spiral staircase. "Where am I?" the servants said they heard him cry out.

Mrs. Bell was in Glen Ellen at the time, on the Beltane ranch owned by Mrs. Pleasant. Teresa recorded the death in her diary: "Oct. 16 telegraph from S.F. 10:30 about Mr. Bell. Took two Gal Red Wine to Officer for [word indecipherable] Mrs. Bell [a nephew's wife] and Mrs. Gordon go to town. Telegraph to Mammy 25ck [name indecipherable] 1 gal wine J Bergman 1 gal wine 2 o'clock Mr. Bell died."

On the day after his death, Mrs. Bell shipped two barrels of apples and one package of cheesecloth, paid some bills, and had some horses shod.

The will was contested by Fred, the oldest boy. He claimed that his mother, the executrix, was incompetent, because she was under the sway of her housekeeper. The court eventually agreed. Judge Coffey ruled that Mrs. Bell and Mrs. Pleasant's relationship was an inappropriate one for a white woman and a colored woman to have. Mrs. Pleasant's influence in the Bell household was unnatural, and illegal as well.

Ironically, the friendship had worsened by this time.

In 1902, after a noisy row during which the police were called, Mrs. Bell had Mrs. Pleasant evicted. "She passed out the door after her two trunks snarling like a mad dog," Mrs. Bell wrote in her diary. While Mrs. Pleasant said, "I am glad, very glad to go."

That same year, Mrs. Pleasant published the first chapter of her memoirs. Included was an analysis of her palm—the palmist H. Jerome Fosselli said she showed a "marvelous ability to read motives"—and also the startling assertion that she had never been a slave. She was born in 1814 in Philadelphia. Her father was an importer of silks, a native Kanaka named Louis Alexander Williams. Her mother was a free "full blooded Louisiana negress."

A dispute with the editor prevented the promised second installment. Mrs. Pleasant died in 1903.

Teresa Bell died in 1923, leaving an estate whose estimated value was $938,000. Before her death, she'd accused Mary Ellen Pleasant of having murdered an employee named Sam Whittington many years before, and also of killing Thomas Bell by pushing him over the stairs, possibly with Fred Bell's help. She'd accused Fred of murdering two wives. She'd accused Marie Bell's husband, Arthur Holman, of murdering Marie. She'd accused her mother of murdering her brothers. Her estate, which left nothing to either Clingans or Bells, was immediately contested by both families on grounds of insanity.

None of the large San Francisco estates seems to have passed without objection from one generation to the next, but the Bell estate is the standard by which all others are measured. Every case from 1897 to 1926 was as bad as the Bell business or it wasn't. John Bell, Thomas Bell's supposed nephew, made a claim, as did Viola Smith, as did the Clingan sisters. Decisions were made, appealed, reversed. The case went to the state supreme court.

In May of 1926, litigation ended in a compromise. Of the total, $370,000 went to the surviving Bell children, after they had pledged $100,000 to charity and made a settlement to Viola Smith of close to the same.

Maybe:

Fred Bell was the son of May Thompson and a gambler named Bill Thompson.

Marie was the daughter of May Thompson and Dr. Monser, the abortionist who died in San Quentin.

Robina was the child of Sarah Althea Hill and Reuben Lloyd, a prominent city attorney.

Reginald or possibly Muriel was William Sharon's child by Bertha Barnson (or maybe Bonstell), a maid at the Palace.

Eustace was born to "one of the Harris girls."

Or:

They were all, as they themselves claimed, the children of Thomas and Teresa Bell.

Reginald Bell gave the following statement to the *San Francisco Examiner:* "We always called her [Teresa Bell] mother and she was a good mother to us. Mammy Pleasant was a wonderful woman, but there was nothing mysterious about her and there was really no reason why the home should have been called the House of Mystery."

Viola. I just got it in my head that my father killed Malina Paillet. I couldn't stop thinking about it. I felt I had to know."

"Who's Malina Paillet?"

Lizzie told herself there was no way to offend Mrs. Pleasant more than she'd already done. No way back, in any case, only forward. "Mrs. Bell told me about Malina. The beautiful young girl in a yellow silk dress. Killed by a white man at one of your parties. Her throat cut."

"There's a Victoria Paillet has a place around the corner from us. Malina, I never heard of."

"But Mrs. Bell said."

Mrs. Pleasant turned. Her face was every bit as angry as Lizzie expected, deserved. The southern vowels hardened and shortened in her mouth. "Mrs. Bell says that she can fly. She floats over the bay to the Oakland estuary. The wind tells her stories. I love her dearly, but I don't credit everything she says."

"Oh," said Lizzie.

"Are you much of a reader, Miss Hayes?"

"Yes."

"I thought so. Now, I've left books alone and studied people. You don't have time for both. A woman like you will always go with the person who tells a story. You should watch out for that."

This was so obviously true. "I'll be more careful," Lizzie said, more and more ashamed. And still she couldn't stop. "Where is Jenny Ijub's mother?"

"Buried in the sea. You society women. You always think everything's about you. You think everyone else is only here to cook your meals or sew your clothes or be grateful for your charity or forgive you."

SEVEN

*B*ack in April 1890, Lizzie waited at the mission. Sunlight came dimly through the yellow glass of the small windows, so the room was lit with a golden daytime dusk, but there was little heat. The sky was a ceiling striped with Indian dyes. The ground was worn tile. At the far end of the adobe room the altar glittered. This place never seemed to change. The city grew in all directions, but here was its eternal, damp, still-beating Spanish Catholic heart.

To Lizzie's New World Episcopalian sensibilities, the room had a thrilling aura of overexcitement. Saint Ann clasped her hands together pleadingly. The Archangel Michael was dressed like a Spanish *grande*. Publicly, Lizzie disapproved of a religion that covered itself in thin gold leaf. It recalled the gorgeous medieval excesses of popery.

Privately, if there'd been no one to see her, she would have fallen to her knees.

She sat on the hard pews in the cold cave of the church, wondering how long she would wait. On the wall to her right was a painting of the Last Supper. This suited Lizzie, whose mind was very much on betrayal. The waiting seemed a lenient penance. And better to find Mrs. Pleasant here than have to return again to the still, clogged air of the House of Mystery.

Mrs. Pleasant entered an hour or so later. She did not seem surprised to see Lizzie, though, to Lizzie's chagrin, she did seem pleased. "I didn't know you were Catholic," she said. She crossed herself quickly and gestured for Lizzie to come outside. She wore a purple bonnet with a wide brim, and was wrapped in a purple shawl.

They went to the little graveyard, a garden of blackberries, brambles, and slabs. Mrs. Pleasant stooped over a marker. J Sparrow, whose epitaph was caught in a cage of twisted wrought iron. "There are three vigilante graves around here," Mrs. Pleasant said. "James Sullivan, Charles Cora, and James Casey. Only I can't remember right where. And any number of Indians. No stones for the hundreds of them."

Mrs. Pleasant sighed. "When you get to my age you'll find things that happened forty years ago are more clear than yesterday's doings. Part of my mind is always in those splendid, dreadful years." She shook her head, then straightened, brightened, and began to walk again. "Isn't this a lovely spot, though? Nothing like the company of the dead when you need a bit of peace and quiet."

This had never been Lizzie's experie[...] rier, then, to intrude on your peaceful tin[...]

"Have you ever given thought to your [...]

"No."

"No," repeated Mrs. Pleasant. "Of course [...] too young. I've picked out mine. Known it for y[...]

"What will it be?" Lizzie was genuinely curio[...] could such a long and tumultuous history be encaps[...] on a single stone? "'She was a friend to John Brow[...] Mrs. Pleasant said. "That's what I'd like."

"I have something very difficult to say to you," Lizzi[...] told her.

They'd reached the obelisk of Don Luis Antonio Arguello. Mrs. Pleasant paused to admire it. "Then just open your mouth and let it come," she suggested.

Lizzie took a breath. Sunlight dappled the leaves, twirled warningly in the wind. Something was corking her throat. She spoke anyway. "It's my fault that Miss Viola was snooping last night. I put her up to it. Please don't hold her responsible, since it's all my fault. I'm more sorry than I can say."

There was a silence. The shards of light, spinning like tops. Lizzie's breath coming through her mouth, thin as thread.

Then, "You astonish me," Mrs. Pleasant said. Her face was shadowed. Lizzie was glad not to see her eyes. *He was frightened of those eyes,* she'd once said, although Lizzie couldn't remember about whom. "I thought you a lady and a friend."

"I meant no harm to you. I certainly meant no harm to

Lizzie's father had once said that very thing to Lizzie's mother. "You think the poor are only here to provide you with a reason to be charitable," he'd said. "So why *are* the poor here?" her mother had answered.

Had Lizzie's moral position not been so compromised, she might have argued. If it's not all about me, she might have said, why does everyone watch everything I do? Lucky she didn't. Who would complain of this to Mrs. Pleasant, about whom the whispers never hushed? Mary E. Pleasant, who had only to touch a thing to turn it notorious. Mary E. Pleasant, Queen of the Galloping Tongues.

Lizzie tried to believe that Jenny's mother was buried at sea. She owed Mrs. Pleasant at least this much, so she tried her best. Unlikely as it was.

"It does tire me sometimes," Mrs. Pleasant finished, and Lizzie could see why: Lizzie was tired of Lizzie, too.

"I'm going to be different," Lizzie offered, and she meant it; she was determined to be so, but Mrs. Pleasant walked away while she was speaking. Lizzie trailed behind, though there were no more gestures inviting her to do so.

"I have never been given to explaining away lies," Mrs. Pleasant said. "And you can't explain away the truth."

Her voice was tight with hurt. Even so, Lizzie couldn't escape the brief suspicion that everything she'd ever done had been entirely as Mrs. Pleasant wished. Hadn't she produced all those signs out of her very own hallway, forced a magical juncture on Lizzie merely by asserting that she faced one?

An invisible bird sang in the blackberries, a fluttering, descending whistle, which stopped as they approached. They arrived at a large stone. Mrs. Pleasant pointed to the name—James Sullivan. And a prayer with an odd mixture of sentiments:

> *Remember not, O Lord, our offenses, nor those of our parents.*
> *Neither take thou vengeance of our sins—*
> *Thou shalt bring my soul out of Tribulation, and in thy mercy thou*
> *shall destroy mine enemies.*

Lizzie read the epitaph aloud. "'Who died by the hands of the Vigilance Committee.'"

"That was never proved," Mrs. Pleasant said.

The strings of her purple bonnet had come loose. She retied them briskly. Her fingers were long and thin, her creased face set. She did not look saddened or surprised or angry or vengeful. She did not look hurt so much as she looked like a person who could be hurt. She looked old.

"Now our acquaintance is at an end," she said. "Be so good as to leave me here with my friends."

EIGHT

On the seventh of April, Maud Curry's mother attended one of Mrs. Woodworth's revival meetings and was instantly cured of her tuberculosis. She came at once to the Brown Ark for Maud, who left in a daze of happiness, hardly able to believe she'd been collected at last.

April 14 approached. Without crediting the prophecy, without mentioning it, possibly without even thinking about it, the Putnams joined a number of residents about the bay who had decided to spend Easter week taking the waters in Napa or Middletown or Calistoga. Some went to confession. Some wrote letters that apologized for old faults, revealed secret loves, and otherwise settled accounts.

Most paid no attention to the Doom Sealers. The press, long bored with it all, gave the story less space than the Sharon trial had routinely taken.

Lizzie dressed in her corset and her apricot silk and went to see her solicitor, Mr. Griswold. It was raining just slightly. Wherever the ground was unpaved it had softened, but not all the way to mud. The air had a lovely laundered smell. Lizzie shook her umbrella off and left it with the doorman.

"I need some money," she told Mr. Griswold. "I was thinking maybe fifty dollars, but I'm not really sure what would be right. I have to pay off a blackmailer." This wasn't quite true, but avoided a longer explanation.

"How that takes me back!" Mr. Griswold said. "How often your father came to me with those very words!"

Mr. Griswold agreed that fifty was a standard payoff. Low for a man, but very standard for a woman. He thought he could advance Lizzie that much so long as it didn't become a habit. He supposed she'd require cash.

She was planning to give the money to Viola at Jenny's next piano lesson, assuming Viola was still Jenny's piano teacher. Otherwise, Sam would have to tell her where and how to find the Boones. It didn't make up for the trouble Lizzie had caused, of course; she wouldn't pretend that it did.

By the time Lizzie had finished her business, she'd taken up Mr. Griswold's lunchtime. The downtown streets were filled with women at this hour, the men all working in their offices, except for those in the bars. There was a matinee of *Rip Van Winkle* at the Tivoli. Lizzie saw groups of women going inside with their children, their skirts brushing together, the children's voices high and piping like birds'. Edward Bryan would be singing the lead, and his smoldering overacting was very much to Lizzie's taste. What a treat this would be for the wards. Lizzie determined to suggest it to Mrs. Lake.

A hack stopped beside her and Mr. Finney looked down from it. "May I offer you a lift?" he asked. "Nasty weather to be walking in."

It was nothing of the sort, a softer rain couldn't be imagined. "I like it." Lizzie went on without stopping.

He jumped down, tied the horses. When Lizzie looked back, he was running after her. He walked a moment by her side, catching his breath, a little water dripping from the brim of his hat. "I hope you've forgiven the messenger, Miss Hayes," he said finally. "I'd be sorry to think I'd lost you as a friend."

"Your interest in me was never social."

"Your interest in *me* was never social," he replied. "You know nothing about my interest in you."

"So you're not here to ask for money? I've quite mistaken things?"

Mr. Finney gave an awkward laugh, made an awkward gesture with his hand. Of course he wished there was nothing financial between them, that they were only a couple of old friends out for a stroll. He hoped someday that would be the case. Nothing would please him more. As to now, he only wanted what was fair. He entirely understood Miss Hayes's reluctance to pay anything before his information had been confirmed. She was a lady with delicate feelings. The things he'd told her were, no doubt, shocking to hear.

But now he had it on good authority that she knew

them to be true. Now was the time to determine a fair price for a secret delivered and a secret kept.

Lizzie hauled up her skirts to cross the street. There was a carriage coming, black with glass windows. The driver wore full purple livery except for a large white cowboy hat. Only in San Francisco, her father would have remarked, had he been there to see it. Heaven must be wonderful indeed to make up for all the things you missed by being dead. "You can say whatever you like about my father." Lizzie stepped up onto the far curb. "My father was a good man, and when he was alive he wouldn't have spared a thought for a sharper like you. I don't imagine he cares more now."

Mr. Finney tipped his hat and clucked his tongue in admiration. "I do admire the way you speak your mind. I never met a society lady like you. No pretense, what you think is what you say."

"Only to you." Lizzie was surprised to realize this was true. It made her suddenly, unexpectedly fond of Mr. Finney, in spite of his being such a loathsome man. Hadn't she always stood her ground with him? You couldn't say Lizzie was nobody's fool, but she wasn't Mr. Finney's.

She turned, stopping, and raised her umbrella so that he could slip beneath it, too. He took off his glasses to wipe them dry, and his eyes were that mottled, pebbled blue.

"What about the child?" he said. "There are details, things once said that can't be unsaid." But Lizzie had already reached into her pocket and drawn out the money, and this had nothing at all to do with Jenny. Lizzie was trusting her instincts. She put the fifty dollars into Mr. Finney's hand.

"Here's what I'm buying," she was already saying. "It occurs to me that Miss Viola Bell held an interest for you that Miss Viola Smith might not. For fifty dollars, you look into your heart. If you'll be a good husband to her, then marry her. If you won't be a good husband, then let her alone. The decision is yours. You've come to a magical juncture here, Mr. Finney, but you're a man who takes the long view. I trust you absolutely to do what's right."

He was staring at her, his face close to hers under the single umbrella, the light, intimate tune of the rain hitting the taut cloth and the stone street. The passing horses were polished and the air fragrant. It was a perfect day, one she would often remember. She'd just cursed Mr. Finney with his very own magical juncture. "The person I'm saving here is you," she said.

Then he went forward into his magical juncture and she went backward into hers. She returned to Mr. Griswold for another fifty dollars. He was far less agreeable this time. What an amateur she was at this! If she went on letting just anyone on the street blackmail her this way, her father's estate would be gone before she knew it.

When the morning of the fourteenth arrived, it came wrapped in a blue sky and a bright sun. Lizzie woke early and drove to the Brown Ark. "Isn't this a beautiful day?" people asked her as they passed on the street. All over the city people were saying the same thing to one another. "Beautiful day, isn't it? Did you ever see such a beautiful day?"

It was the day after the end of everything. Lizzie had chosen it deliberately as the day on which she would become someone new. She was a notorious woman now; there was no point in continuing to pretend otherwise.

She sent a letter of resignation to Mrs. Hallis. Included in it was her Atlantis-coin necklace and her written decision to remove the offending child from the Brown Ark. On April 14 she took custody of Jenny Ijub.

And then, because she still wasn't sure she liked Jenny all that much, she sweetened the deal by taking Ti Wong, too. Jenny was an obligation of blood, but she and God had a covenant for Ti Wong.

She'd met many times with Mr. Griswold, to discuss her finances. Luckily she had her experience as Ark treasurer to draw on. She knew more about money than some women of her class. Lizzie was going to court to challenge her father's will. It was a frighteningly public thing to do. A lady appears in the papers only twice—on the day she weds and the day she dies, Mrs. Putnam reminded her. The Putnams were, of course, most disapproving. She is *not* your sister, they insisted with some cause, and Lizzie couldn't make them understand that this had simply ceased to matter.

Lizzie hoped for a quick and quiet decision in her favor. She was not, after all, getting married, as her father had absolutely forbidden her to do. If she now had a family to support, there was no one to blame for this but him. She was prepared to say so in open court if it should come to that. She only hoped there'd be no further claimants on the estate, no additional children she knew nothing about.

In any case, it would all take time. Meanwhile she'd packed Baby Edward's picture into a trunk along with many other mementos and removed him to the attic. He protested this. She was burying him all over again. But it was nothing personal, just part of her plan to let her home to a quiet family of four and move with Jenny and Ti Wong down to the Big Trees house for the summer. This was an economy, but would, she hoped, also be a pleasure. Lizzie had every expectation Baby Edward would find a way to come along.

Lizzie arrived at the Ark with her things in a rented wagon. Neither Jenny nor Ti Wong had anything of consequence to add to it. They stood in the sandy lot saying good-bye to everyone. Mrs. Lake was in tears, as was, to Lizzie's surprise, Nell. "You come back and see us," Nell told Jenny, over and over. Her round shoulders shook. She held Ti Wong. "First Maudie and now you!"

Ti Wong hopped from foot to foot, so excited was he not to be drowned this morning. He knew about Lizzie's financial worries and discussed them as he lifted Jenny into the wagon. They could start a detective agency, he suggested. People would pay them to solve cases. "I'm not much good at sneaking around," Lizzie told him, although the ridiculous idea did appeal to her for a moment, she couldn't deny it. Her own detective agency!

Ti Wong argued that he *was* good at sneaking. All he had to do to go unnoticed, he said, was pretend to be Chinese.

His plans were interrupted by Mrs. Wright. She had not spoken a word during Lizzie's good-bye. She'd sat, her eyes stonily turned to the curtained windows as if Lizzie weren't in the room. Then, after Lizzie left, Mrs. Wright had gathered her clothes into her grip and made her way down the stairs alone. "I've decided to join you," she said, "so there will be no need to worry about money. I'll inform Mr. McCallum at my bank."

Lizzie saw her careful budgets disintegrating. She added the grip to the wagon. Then she knelt and hugged the dog so tightly she came away with fleas. Well, why not? she thought, lost for a moment in the heady smell of dog. They could all be different people. Ti Wong could be a detective. Mrs. Wright could be rich. Lizzie would learn to be a mother if she had to grow wings and a tail. She felt an optimism best explained by inexperience and a serious failure of imagination.

"What would you like to be?" she asked Jenny.

"Going," Jenny answered.

Lizzie helped Mrs. Wright climb aboard and scrambled to her own seat. "We're off to see some ducks, then," she said gaily, giving the reins to Ti Wong. He was now the man in the family, so he drove.

The next day all the newspapers were talking about the Doom Sealers. People as far away as Sacramento had scrambled into the capital dome for safety. Believers in Santa Rosa had climbed Taylor Mountain. Noted daredevil Sarah Pike had made a balloon ascension; the morning of April 14 found her aloft over Ocean Beach at just that time, the local papers observed, when the real daredevils were on the ground.

"Mrs. Woodworth All Wet!" the headlines read.

A colored evangelist named Mrs. Simmons had also predicted destruction. The date she'd chosen was 1898, and the method earthquake. Who cared? San Francisco would stand forever. The beautiful weather was compared with the Great Disappointment of '44, when Christ failed once again to appear to the Millerites.